# BEACONS

*Stories for Our Not So Distant Future*

Tom Bullough ▪ David Constantine ▪ Clare Dudman

Janice Galloway ▪ Rodge Glass ▪ Alasdair Gray ▪ Jay Griffiths

Joanne Harris ▪ Nick Hayes ▪ Holly Howitt ▪ Liz Jensen

A.L. Kennedy ▪ Toby Litt ▪ Adam Marek ▪ Maria McCann

Siân Melangell Dafydd ▪ James Miller ▪ Lawrence Norfolk

Gregory Norminton ▪ Jem Poster ▪ Adam Thorpe

# BEACONS

*Stories for Our Not So Distant Future*

Edited by Gregory Norminton

ONEWORLD

A Oneworld Book

First published in Great Britain and the Commonwealth
by Oneworld Publications 2013

Copyright © this edition, Oneworld Publications 2013
All individual stories © the authors

The author royalties from sales of this book will be donated to the
Stop Climate Chaos Coalition. The editor and publisher wish to thank
the contributing authors for their generous support.

ISBN 978-1-85168-969-9
eBook ISBN 978-1-78074-236-6

Text design, typesetting and eBook by Tetragon, London
Printed and bound by CPI Group (UK) Ltd, Croydon, CR0 4YY

The characters and events in this book are fictitious. Any similarity to real
persons, living or dead, is coincidental and not intended by the authors.

Oneworld Publications
10 Bloomsbury St
London WC1B 3SR
England
www.oneworld-publications.com

# CONTENTS

# INTRODUCTION

Gregory Norminton

The window of opportunity for averting climate chaos is narrow, but this book looking through it was a long time coming.

It began at the Royal Botanic Garden Edinburgh, where early in 2007 I attended a public lecture about the impact of man-made climate change on Scotland's wildlife. After a display of alarming graphs and hair-raising statistics, my head was in my hands. It takes a strong mental constitution to look into the abyss, and I found myself wondering how on earth, as a novelist, I could hope to approach a topic so enormous, so daunting and inescapable.

Thankfully Mike Robinson, then chairman of Stop Climate Chaos Scotland, stood up to speak my mind. Mike is a lean, wry, and tenacious man, a straight talker who isn't embarrassed to show his passion. The science is clear, he said, the stories that accompany it less so. When a society faces upheaval, it looks for fresh narratives to help make sense of events. Statistics cannot motivate us as stories can, yet where are the George Orwells, the Aldous Huxleys and William Morrises of the ecological crisis?

Since Mike asked this question, a growing number of genre and 'literary' authors have written about, or around, the issue. Sarah Hall and James Miller have given us compelling dystopias in *The Carhullan Army* and *Sunshine State*; Helen Simpson has written a brilliant set of stories; Liz Jensen has thrilled us with *The Rapture*, and Ian McEwan's *Solar* has examined the cognitive dissonance that keeps us from changing those habits that hurt us. As the symptoms of climate change begin to hit home, more and more writers feel compelled to engage in some way with the new reality. Back in 2007, things seemed very different.

I stopped Mike after the event and introduced myself. How about a book of specially commissioned short stories – a charity project to raise funds for, and awareness of, the Stop Climate Chaos Coalition? It would be, I said, a metaphorical gauntlet thrown down to challenge authors to imagine our worst and best possible futures.

The book you hold in your hands is the slow-grown fruit of our efforts – and the efforts of scientific advisers, community activists, and, above all, the writers who have given of their time and talent. Every story was written specially for this collection. In making their contributions, the writers have had to find ways of approaching a seemingly forbidding brief. How do we write fiction about the ecological crisis without lapsing into cliché? Is it possible to do so without becoming hectoring or portentous? We must tell the truth, but is that done best when, in Emily Dickinson's words, we tell it slant? How, indeed, can prose fiction, which is rooted in psychology and social drama, encompass planetary change? For global warming is a predicament, not a story. Narrative only comes into our *response* to that predicament. Yet the truth of the crisis almost defies comprehension. The scientists, working their way through vast quantities of data, give us their best guesses on our likely fate – and we shy away from their findings.

Lord Stern, in his 2006 *Report on the Economics of Climate Change*, wrote that 'climate change is a result of the greatest market failure the world has seen'. It is also a failure of the imagination. Because we do not want to look at what we're doing, we retreat into various forms of denial, we cling to hopes of a 'technofix' or minimize the dangers of exceeding our planetary limits. In Britain it remains difficult – hosepipe bans and summer floods notwithstanding – to wrap the mind around the consequences of runaway climate change. Inuit on collapsing headlands don't have this trouble; nor do the people of Kiribati, the first nation likely to disappear as a result of sea-level rise. But it is still possible, for urbanized Westerners, to disbelieve or ignore predictions of a depleted world, of mega droughts and firestorms, acidified oceans, mass famine and migration, wars over water, and, at home, the distressing experience of watching familiar landscapes warp out of recognition.

Perhaps our primary task is to break through the protective caul of our incredulity. We have a collective duty to imagine what we fear to look at, for in looking away we fail, not only to avert the worst for our children, but also to create the happier and more just society in which we should wish them to live. More than ever we need stories that tell us where we stand, that help us imagine our predicament. Let them serve as beacons to warn of approaching danger, to unite us against adversity, to celebrate what we have and, perhaps, to show a path away from harm.

It is important to note that this book is not polemical; nor is it a policy document or a lifestyle guide. It is, rather, a meeting place for new stories that recognize where we are and where we might be heading, a forum in which contemporary authors try out different ways of encompassing what so often puzzles the mind and paralyses the will: thinking and feeling a path through dislocation and dismay.

In the following pages you will find dystopian satire, speculative and historical fiction, metaphorical flights of fancy, domestic naturalism, quiet tragedy, and farcical comedy. Some of the stories have a pervasive sadness; others pack an angry punch. Yet none, it seems to me, is that editorially dreaded thing, 'depressing'. Hope, in the words of Seamus Heaney, glossing Václav Havel, 'is a state of the soul rather than a response to the evidence. It is not the expectation that things will turn out successfully but the conviction that something is worth working for, however it turns out. Its deepest roots are in the transcendental, beyond the horizon.'

If hope is a moral imperative, telling stories may be one way of obeying it.

# LOOKING IN THE MIRROR

*If you want to see an endangered species, get up and look in the mirror.*

John Young,
*former NASA astronaut*

# A IS FOR ACID RAIN,
# B IS FOR BEE

### Joanne Harris

YOU NEVER WENT OUT ON RAINY DAYS. Health and Safety wouldn't let you. Instead, you played games online, or read books, or talked to your friends on your smartie, or even watched a movie – they still had live movies in those days, before ceegee took over for good (so much safer than real life, of course, but somehow not as exciting). In those days before the Cloud, you actually still *went* to school, instead of doing it all from home, and friends were people you saw every day, and games were what you played outside – that is, if it wasn't raining.

In a minute. Come here first. I hardly ever see you, kid. Yes, that's right. Climb onto my knee. Let me tell you a story. What about? Well, let me see. Do you like animals? No, *not* ceegee animals. I mean actual, real-life animals. Tigers and elephants and whales and such.

No kid, I've never seen a tiger. But listen and I'll tell you about the time I once saw a bee. You know what a bee is, don't you, kid?

No, don't say *bug*. It's an *insect*.

Why? Well, a *bug* is something gone wrong. A glitch in a machine. A cockroach is a bug, I guess. A *bee* – well, that was something else: a living cog in a machine more complex than the Cloud itself—

What's a cog? Another time. Let me tell you about the bee. It was in the summer of – well, never mind. A long time ago, when I was your age. I used to go to school just round the corner, where the

Parklands building is now. My school was called Saint Oswald's. Even in those days, it was pretty old. There was even an actual park nearby, with trees and grass and everything. We used to have a lot more of that in those days. Now you don't really get it much, because of the rain. And flowers too. In those days flowers grew mostly *outside*.

That was where the bees came in. Of course, they were pretty rare even then. People said they were dying out. Some kind of disease, or the rain, or the sun, or maybe smarties, which some people said were interfering with the special signals the bees gave out to find their way back to where they lived.

In any case, we hadn't seen a real live bee for years and years. But by then I guess most of us didn't know what a bee looked like anyway. Trust me, those cartoon bees in stripy sweaters that you see in books and games look nothing like the real thing, so you can't really blame folk for getting confused. But that day, we *all* saw the bee, Philip and Johnny and Frankie and me. For all we knew it might have been the very last bee in the whole world. In any case, we never saw another one after that, and by the time I left school, the park was gone to make way for these apartment blocks. Couple of years later, the school went the same way. It was a very old building. It never passed Health and Safety tests. Still, we kind of liked it. Parklands Estate, they call it now. There hasn't been a park there in fifty years.

I know, I know. The bee. Well, in those days, some of us kids still *walked* to school. A lot of people thought that was wrong: Health and Safety did, of course, and the Social Services. But it was only ten minutes through the park, and I guess my parents thought it would be OK, as long as it didn't look like rain, and as long as we didn't loiter.

That day was fine. Not a cloud in sight. No, not *that* Cloud; we used to call that the Internet in those days, before it really took off. Clouds were just what you saw in the sky on days when it wasn't raining. No, that doesn't happen much now. Listen, do you want to hear this story or don't you? Right, then. We were walking to school. It was warm, and you could smell the flowers. Yes, smartass, they used to smell. Like what? No, not *quite* like that. They had all kinds of different smells, and that was why bees used to like them. Why? Because it means pollen, that's why, and pollen means making honey.

You know all about honey, right? Yes, of course, you learnt it at school. Let me guess – in history.

Well, kid, in my day you could still buy honey online, from abroad, but it was really expensive, and I only had it once or twice. No, it wasn't yucky at all. I know it kind of sounds that way. Bee-spit. But it wasn't. It wasn't like anything you've ever tasted, or ever will.

What's it like? Like an *old* taste, somehow, like living history on your tongue. And it smelt of flowers, and sunlight, and air, and it was sweet enough to make you feel a little dizzy, a little drunk; and there was all kinds of secret stuff in there they never learnt to synthesize; and all of that comes out of flowers and grass, and only the bees knew the secret.

Well, Philip and Johnny and Frankie and me, we were in no hurry to get to school. We stopped for five minutes in the park – I didn't have a smartie then, and we couldn't play games without one. But we could still play football, the old-fashioned way, with a regular ball, and Johnny used to bring one hidden in his schoolbag. Of course, we wouldn't have got away with that at school. Health and Safety didn't allow it. But in the park, you could still run about, and to be fair, although I fell over quite a *lot*, it never did more damage than a few grass stains on my knees.

It was there that we all saw the bee that day. Philip had managed to kick the ball into one of the flower beds, and we all ran up to retrieve it. It was sitting in a big patch of some kind of tall pink flowers, and Phil reached in to get it back, lost his balance, grabbed one of the stems and—

'Ouch! Damn thing! It *stung* me!'

'Must be a rose,' said Frankie. Roses had thorns in those days, you know; not like the ones you can buy in the shops. They had a scent in those days, too, and I guess the bees must have liked them. Because there it was on the flower, the bee; no bigger than my fingertip, and nothing like the ceegeed bees you see in animations. For a start, it was *brown*, not yellow; a kind of tabby brown, with delicate stripy markings, and when you looked at it really closely you could see that it was *furry*, somehow, with little feathery feelers. This, and not the rose bush, was what had stung Philip; this single bee, now clinging onto the palm of his hand and arching its back like an acrobat – because bees were able to *sting*, you know – only in self-defence, I guess, but Phil had put his hand on it, and it got him good. He shook off the bee, and I saw the mark, as big as a pound coin, I guess, and his fingers already beginning to swell. He wasn't crying – well, not yet – but I could see it hurt a *lot*.

'They say when a bee stings you, you die!' said Johnny, not helping the situation much.

Philip's eyes got very big.

'No, dummy, it's the *bee* that dies,' said Frankie, who was a smartass, like you.

'What if I've got an allergy?' said Phil. 'You can get them to bee stings.'

'In that case, you're a goner,' said Frankie.

Philip started to cry for real.

'No way,' I said. 'A tiny thing like that?'

'That sting could get infected,' said Frankie. 'We ought to tell Health and Safety. Or—'

'Listen,' I said. 'It's making a noise.'

It was true; the bee was *buzzing*. At first, it sounded like a circular saw heard from a million miles away. Then it rose and became a whine; intermittent; protesting.

'Kill it!' said Johnny.

'No way,' I said. I took it gently between my hands.

'It'll sting you,' said Philip.

'No it won't. A bee can only sting once.'

Well, kid, in the end we had to take Phil to the walk-in centre to get an anti-allergy shot. We got into terrible trouble at school. After that, we weren't allowed to walk to school through the park any more. But I kept the bee in my pencil case, hoping it might somehow survive. It didn't, of course. Frankie was right. It's the bee, and not the person, who dies. Pity. I'd always wanted a pet.

I never saw another bee. They all turned out to be hover-flies. Or wasps, which can sting you as often as they feel like it. But I told Mrs Teague about it at school, and she showed me an old glass collecting case from on top of a pile of stuff to throw out.

'People used to collect insects,' she said. 'These were collected a long time ago, before it became illegal. For some reason, this box has survived. I think someone left it to the school, an old man who used to live nearby. He was a lepidopterist. That means he collected butterflies. But he also collected other insects. Perhaps you'd like to have this.'

And so I took the glass case. I never told anyone about it. For a start, Health and Safety would have said that it was unhygienic; I might have picked up some kind of disease or allergy from those dusty old things. For a long time I kept it under my bed, and looked at it in secret. There were thirty-five specimens in that case, all held in place by long steel pins and labelled in tiny brown writing. *Bumble bee. Carpenter bee. Stingless bee. Leafcutter bee. Orchid bee. Cuckoo bee. Hornfaced bee. Orchard bee.* And here, at the end of a row, *my* bee: *Apis Mellifera*, the European honeybee, banded in brown and honey-gold under a layer of feathery dust. All of them extinct now, as well as a lot of the plants they served. Funny to think that only fifty years ago, those bees were flying all over the place, making honey, building nests, making that funny buzzing sound and flitting from flower to flower.

What's that, kid? No, I don't have the collecting case any more. The rules on that kind of thing are too strict. I'd have to have a license. But I do remember all their names. Would you like to hear them? Yes, I know. I'm repeating myself. But it's so good to see you. We so rarely see children around here nowadays. Why? Oh, Health and Safety, I guess. Unless there's some other reason, kid. Allergies, maybe. Acid rain.

What? Is visiting time over so soon? Well, maybe next time you'll stay longer. Tell your mother I love her, kid. Tell her to call me once in a while. I still have dreams about that case, you know; those carefully labelled specimens. I once read somewhere that there used to be nine hundred *thousand* insect species in the world, and more being discovered every day. Now so many seem to be gone. Except for the cockroaches, that is. They'll always be around.

What happened to make things change this way? Were we somehow responsible? Of course, there's no actual proof that we did anything at all. No one knows why the bees died out, or whether their disappearance had anything at all to do with allergies, acid rain, the disappearance of our parks or the fact that I can sometime spend days or weeks before seeing even a single kid. And yet, I can't help thinking. Maybe the earth is allergic to *us* – maybe we're the insects, and all this is the final stage in a long, slow process of rejection.

We used to be kings of this world, kid. Or so we thought. But kings get overturned in the end, and sometimes all it takes is a stone to bring down the oldest of empires. We always thought the cockroaches would end up ruling the world. Perhaps they will. Rain doesn't hurt them, they're immune to UV. They don't even have any allergies. Next to them, we're soft and weak. They're bound to do better than we did.

We used to be kings of the world, once.

Not any more, kid. Not any more.

# MOTHER MOON'S JOB

Liz Jensen

WHEN MA HAD THE ACCIDENT it was me found her. Sand's not
as soft as it looks.

Most days the porkies wake me oinking for their slop and when
I've fed them I'll bring Ma tea in bed and sometimes she'll sing, *tea
for two and two for tea* slash *first I was afraid, I was petrified*, slash
*where have you been my blue-eyed boy.* And we'll drink it – milky, two
happies – with the Truth Channel turned low, watching the sky-rats
swooping down for beach rubbish. But sometimes she just groans
cos she's hung-over. Or she'll say, *beep off, Maxwell, can't you see I need
my beeping beauty sleep.* Depending on what Mother Moon said to
her in the night.

    *Beep* isn't the real word she used. It's something I say now instead
of fuck or shit or bugger or cunt or anything else that pisses off
oldsters.

But Ma's not in bed that morning. Weird that. Never happens. And
the Truth Channel's off, so I go out on the balcony, the beach is right
underneath but I look out to sea first and the sky says thunder coming,
watch out, and the waves are crashing high and white, and the tide
traps are bobbing and the wind turbs are spinning to the max. Then
I look down and there's Ma lying with her leg bent the wrong way
and a sky-rat pecking at her eye.

Five floors is a long way, if you're someone falling.

But here's the thing about someone who dropped off the balcony cos she was wasted. She might still sit up and shout: *Beep the big picture, sunshine! Vodkas all round!* or *Hey, kiddo. Guess whose Ma was Wet T-Shirt Queen!*

But no, she just lies there with the sky-rat pulling red stuff out of her eye and then a man on the jetty yells *floatie alert!* and blows his whistle. That slaps me awake all right. I run out and down, got to get there quick and tell them. *She's not a floatie, she's Ma.* Floaties are blown up double-size and stinking and wet and they come in at high tide from the raft-towns. I run, I run, I run. *She's an Islander, she's one of us, she's a Zero-Plus Non-Contributor and she'll be fine, leave us alone, we don't need you, we've got each other, beep off.*

I trip down the last bit of stairs and bash my elbow so hard I cry out but I keep running.

Not fast enough, cos when I get there folk won't let me near.

'You've got to, she's my mum!'

'All the more reason, chixie. All the more reason.'

The Crisis Centre has posters about civic pledges and fund cards and protein quotas and *opt for the Op* which is credits for not beeping the crowd index. Thunder's growling outside now, and rain slamming in sideways from the wind.

'Hey Maxwell, my name's Aisha.' Long black hair, stud implant. 'I've been trying to trace your home unit narrative. Do you know your bio-dad?'

'It's not a crime to come from a single-adult unit.' *So beep off,* goes Ma in my head. *You can stick your beeping interrogations up your beeping beephole.*

'Correct. But Mummy's gone, so it's now a no-adult unit and my job's fixing a new home for you. Good news is, if we can source you to bio-folk on the mainland you get an upgrade. Did she tell you Daddy's name?'

'No. He was never her co. End of.'

When fish reproduce, the fem-fish lays the eggs and swims off, then the guy-fish fertilizes them and then he swims off too.

*So what, big deal, it's a choice, so high fives to us and the System can go beep itself.*

'Someone in your bio-unit's best but if not, there's Care. Are you OK, Maxwell? Elbow still hurting? Here, painbuster. It's been a shock for you losing Mummy, hasn't it, chixie?'

'If you tell me where she is I haven't lost her, have I?'

'She's at the health station. In the morgue.'

'What's that then?'

'It's a cold place they store you. When you're gone. Oh babes. Nine's ever so young to be alone. Big, big, big sozz.'

*What's she on about? I'm not alone. Ma's in the morgue at the health station. If you're injured they can freeze you and reheat you later. Everyone knows that.*

Aisha puts her hand on my head and strokes my hair that's all bristly cos Ma shaved it last month same time she did her legs. Then she meets a mozzy scab and stops cos there's more where that came from.

'When's she back home then?'

'Oh Maxwell. Don't stress, chixie.'

'I'm not stressing!'

'Poor wee skinny thing. Mummy stressed a lot, didn't she?' She's clicking stuff in boxes on her screen. It says, Assessment.

'You got a kill-you?'

'Sozz babe, but you're way too young.' In the Emotional Deprivation slash Neglect box she does a tick. 'Have some gum.' I take it and chew. Vodka-lime. Nice. 'Better?'

'Ma only stressed cos of Mother Moon.'

'Who's Mother Moon?'

'Her buddy. On Truth.' I do the voice: '*The Truth Channel. Making promises we keep.*' She smiles cos I'm good at voices. '*Welcome to You,* that's her number one programme. Mother Moon boosts her.'

'Mmmm?' goes Aisha, doing more clicking. 'You just said she was stressed.'

'*You're never alo-o-o-one with Mother Moo-ooo-ooon!*' I sing, like I used to with Ma. 'That's from the theme tune.'

You'd think Aisha'd know that. But she just says, 'Well there's more and more of these pirate operations. Folk beaming stuff from

Christ knows where. It's impossible to keep track,' and she presses send. 'Now I bet you like energies. Minibreak?'

In the Rec Facility there's a kid called Lola watching an old-world DVD about animals that used to exist. *Or so they claim, but I never saw them except onscreen*, says Ma in my head.

'My daddy self-terminated with a banana machete,' says Lola when it finishes. 'I found him in a pool of blood so I've got post-traumatic stress.' She says it like I should want some too.

'Well my mum's still alive but she's in the morgue cos of an eye problem plus possible broken leg. They'll defrost her when she's mended.'

'Jokes.'

'What d'you mean?'

'Nothing. Just, jokes. So what show's she into?'

'*Welcome to You*. With Mother Moon.'

'*A Friend in Need*. That's my dad's. With Bud. Bud was supposed to help but he didn't.'

Maybe if Mother Moon did her job properly, Ma wouldn't be lying in the morgue waiting to be fixed. But I try not to think it, cos what if thoughts can travel through ice?

My bio-dad's bio-dad is old and a bit yellow but he walks OK. They found him from DNA. He says this is all a bit of a surprise to him, he had no idea I existed. I say it's a surprise for me too. About him.

'Well in any case, hello Maxwell. Sorry, I mean *hey*.'

'Hey.'

'You can call me Grandad or Ramsay. You choose.' He doesn't do high fives so we shake hands like oldsters. 'Look Maxwell, I messaged your father about you, but don't hold your breath. The fact is, I'm sure he's not keen to be a bio-dad. He swapped his repro rights for carbon so it's complex, pledge-wise.'

'Where is he?' Ma said he was a beeping beephole.

Grandad slash Ramsay shrugs. 'Could be anywhere. I don't know much about children, Maxwell. Apparently I didn't make a very good job of fatherhood first time around. But I can try again with you. What d'you say?'

My scab's itching again so I give it a scratch and a bit of it flakes off and there's blood on my finger.

'How long does stuff last in a freezer?'

'About two years. Maybe more. Depends on the use-by date.'

'I'll stay two years then. Maybe more. Depending on.'

When she comes back she might be blind in one eye cos of the sky-rat. And she'll limp for sure.

'Good. As long as there's life, you can always find something to celebrate, Maxwell. Even in the darkest times. Like now. That's what I think.'

Which is weird, cos when we get to the mainland I don't see us celebrating, not the way me and Ma celebrate. Where's the vodka and the kill-yous, where's singing along to *Welcome to You* and listening to folk spilling their guts?

And it's supposed to be an upgrade.

Oldsters prefer you to say beep instead of *more florid language* but otherwise Grandad slash Ramsay isn't like the ones on Oral History cos he never talks about growth and import-export and hyper-malls. He used to be a geologist so he takes the long view and he's got a rock collection.

'*Homo sapiens* turned the planet into a crime scene, Maxwell, that's the truth of it.' He's mending his shoe with glue. 'Now if you believe in a god, you can say the extreme age we're living in is part of a grand plan. But if you don't, you just have to adapt as best you can and admire nature's determination to thrive no matter what. Because I tell you one thing, it's cleverer than we are. If I didn't believe that, I'd commit suicide on the spot.' Then he stops and puts the top back on the glue and puts the shoe down on the table. 'Oh. Maxwell. I do apologize. My stupidity can be colossal.'

New word: *colossal*. He's looking at me but I'm watching the sky-rats and trying not to think of pecked-out eyes. It's not his fault he knows beep all about frozen people being mended and thawed out when they're sorted.

It's always soup at meals cos of his teeth. Lentil and eggplant and soy tofu and blah blah blah.

'Tell me about Emmilou, Maxwell. I'm sorry I never met her.'

'She's got mostly blonde hair and she weighs 80kgs but Mother Moon says being overweight's OK cos it's natural to indulge your human impulses.'

'Mother Moon's one of the therapists on the Truth Channel, is she not? I get confused with all these networks. I tried finding it, but it doesn't transmit to the mainland apparently.'

*Apparently.*

'No, cos Truth's just for Zeroes and sub-Zeroes. We get it Exclusive.'

'And your mum was very attached to it, eh?'

'It's on twenty-four-seven. Sometimes it makes her cry but she says that's part of facing reality. Mother Moon helps her with that, it's her job to shine a light.' I do the voice. *'Because the truth shall set you free.'*

Grandad slash Ramsay takes another spoon of soup. 'Tell me more about Mother Moon.'

'Her face is round like the moon, it's Ma's screensaver. You click on it and she talks.' I'm colossally good at doing Mother Moon. Ma hates it, she says *shut it, kiddo. This stuff's getting through*, but Grandad slash Ramsay's going to like it. So I take a breath and go, *'Hello friend. Hard times. I know. But Mother Moon feels your pain, and she's opening up her sunny heart to you tonight, sweetheart. She's listening.'* His eyebrows go up, so I do some more. *'You are a courageous person, I am proud of you. It's individuals like you who go unsung in this world, performing the heroic acts of martyrdom that enable future generations to blossom and walk free. Bless you, Child of Light.'*

He stops his spoon half-way to his mouth. 'Go on.'

'Sometimes after the show they'll talk online or Mother Moon makes her click boxes and she'll cry her guts out. And I'll say to Ma, just stop talking to her, she's a stupid beeping beep. But Ma says, *some things you got to face.'*

He goes 'Hmm,' and puts the spoon in and then he finishes the rest like he's in slo-mo and then he washes up even slower and I get scared cos oldsters can zap out *bam*, just like that. And what if that happens while Ma's still frozen?

They've started a support group for relatives. The first meeting's at ours. There's me and Lola and Vivvie with red hair and Georgi who's brought diagrams of a sub-sea fish cage he's designing with his uncle he's apprenticed to cos he's fourteen. We're upstairs but if we put our ears to the floor we can hear them cos Georgi says it's *typical crap prefab*. Some folk cry when they talk about their loved one but not Grandad cos he never knew Ma, and not Lola's ma cos she hated Lola's bio-dad and not Vivvie's stepdad who says it's all *suspect*. He says the epidemic of self-termination is *suspect* just like gigs of Zeroes and sub-Zeroes all catching rat flu is *suspect*. The buddies are *suspect*, the pirate channels arc *suspect*. Who's *really* behind them, who's *co-ordinating* them? That's what he'd like to know.

Then they call us downstairs to 'join in the chit-chat' and they want us to sit on the sofa together, but Lola climbs onto her ma's lap like a sub-Zero retard baby.

'Maxwell's told me about Mother Moon but I wonder, can you tell us all something about Bud, Lola?' goes Grandad.

Her mum strokes her hair like Ma did to me when I was little, before she started shaving me cos of mozzies and nits.

'When the monkey was on dad's back he talks to Bud about it after the show. Like mates,' says Lola, and sticks her thumb back in her mouth. I hate her.

Georgi says, 'My dad's soulmate, Wise Eagle, he said his door was always open for Dad. Day or night.'

'So these mentors or buddies or therapists or whatever we're going to call them, what's their job, exactly?' says Grandad. 'How would you all describe it?'

'Mother Moon gave Ma strategies. About how to contribute,' I say.

'My mummy didn't have a strategy. She had Plan A,' says Vivvie. 'She worked it out with Dr Holmes. He's her guardian angel. But she never got to do it cos she zapped out from swallowing five hundred and eighty-four painbusters. The red and blue ones.'

The grown-ups all look at each other and then Grandad says,

'Maxwell why don't you show the other kids my geology stuff while we carry on in here? Take the peanuts with you.'

Lola says Grandad's rocks suck, even the amethyst, but Vivvie says they're cool and Georgi borrows slash nicks two of Grandad's gas canisters for blasting rockface, and then we go back upstairs and flick nuts at each other lying on the floor.

'They were talked into it!' says Lola's mum.

'Hey,' says Georgi, fiddling with the canister. 'I could rig this up and make a bomb.'

'Incentivized,' says Grandad.

'Or guilt-tripped. If you're told it's the only way to help your kid—'

'Or threatened.'

'From what my grandson says, Mother Moon's agenda seems to be to persuade her followers that suicide is an act of self-sacrifice and therefore the ultimate in responsible parenting.'

'So the victims gravitate towards whichever mentor appeals to their personality profile,' says Vivvie's stepdad. 'Neat.'

We listen some more except Vivvie who doesn't want to. They're talking about how many, and where, and the System pretending it's a bunch of pirate operators when it's *very clearly micro-managed*, and it'll be dangerous to mention it outside the group, we must take precautions.

Lola yawns. 'So, Georgi. You know stuff. What exactly is a cull?'

'Have you come for the meeting? Cos it's nearly over,' I tell the man who's rung the doorbell. He's tall so he squats down to my height. His eyes are the same blue as mine.

'What meeting?'

'The support group.'

'No.' He's looking at me weird. *Where have you been my blue-eyed boy.* 'I've come for something else. Something I need from Ramsay. An admin thing. You must be Maxwell.'

And then I get who he is. And I feel like doing a giant puke.

My bio-dad's eating our cheese. It's not even his kitchen. *Get the beep out of here.*

'Look, Maxwell, I'm sorry about your mum zapping out.'

'She didn't.'

'Sorry. Passing.'

'She didn't do that either.' *Beep off and never come back, you beeping beephead.* 'She's just in the morgue. In the reheating queue.'

'Well whatever. Look, Maxwell. Ramsay—'

'His name's Grandad.'

'He'll have told you where I stand on this. I tell you, it's a big shock, discovering your genes have been stolen.'

*Nobody stole your beeping genes. You beeped Ma, that's all. You beeped her and fertilized her beeping egg. And here I am. So beep off, you beeping beephole.*

'Why did you come back then?'

'State bureaucracy. And to say hello and goodbye to my DNA footprint.' He smiles. 'Which I guess would be you. And hey. Just look at you.' He makes a click with his tongue. 'Handsome kid.'

When I tell Grandad who's out there in the kitchen pigging our protein, he goes *oh this is the last thing* and has a word with Lola's mum who stands up quick and says thank you for the meeting everyone, time to go, and Grandad says *best get to bed, Maxwell son,* and I don't argue like I usually do but when I'm up there I still hear them even without my ear to the floor, cos soon they're yelling.

'You mean you think it's acceptable?' If oldsters shout, they might have a heart attack and zap out, that can happen, true story.

'Radical problems demand radical solutions.'

'And you played no part in inflating the index?' Still yelling, which he mustn't or he'll—

Gigabeep.

'I was eighteen, for Christ's sake. She told me she'd had the op and I believed her because she had a skin-stamp. OK, so I was naive. She wasn't contributing so she must've known she'd get Zero-rated and end up as a uni-breeder in some loserville.'

'So I imagine you rejoice in this new initiative of our enlightened system, then? So-called therapists who use the airwaves to encourage islanders to top themselves?'

'*Islanders*. Come on, Ramsay. They're Zeroes and sub-Zeroes. So yes. I think, hey. Whatever it takes.'

'Forced ops are bad enough, to my mind. But *human culls*? There's a boy here—'

'About that. Look, why I came. If you fingerprint this, he's yours.'

There's no noise for a bit and then the voices go quiet and then the door slams shut and I put the pillow over my head and I lie awake thinking, I didn't hate anyone till tonight. But now I hate two people. Mother Moon and the blue-eyed beephead who beeped my Ma.

Maybe I could get an iris tint.

I'd choose red. That'd scare him.

But next morning Grandad promises he's never coming back and it's just him and me from now on. So high fives. That's one down and one to go.

Georgi says if you kill someone before you're fourteen, you're not responsible for murder. He's too old but I'm not.

'I rigged this up for you. You activate the explosive mechanism by remote control.'

It's the gas canister, the one for blasting rockface. There's a switch taped to it, with wires coming out.

Cool.

■

And then you do everything Georgi said. You take the E-train and the ferry and then you walk over to the Folk Centre and there's Mother Moon coming out of the show with all the Zeroes screaming how much they love her, but they're not allowed into the lobby which is where you're waiting. And you follow her and there's troops but Georgi's right, no one notices a little kid so you share the lift with Mother Moon up to the fifth floor but when she gets to her door she turns round.

'Hmm. You've been following me, chixie. Were you wanting something?'

'Me and Ma were at the show. It's her birthday and she wants a signed photo cos she's your biggest fan.'

'How cute! Well come in, chixie, and I'll see what I can find in the way of merchandising.'

The room's huge and there's pix of her lit up on one wall, like on Ma's screen, saying *Welcome to YOU*, and a box of plastic moons with her face on, that you can hang from your ceiling like Ma did till I got mad at her for being wasted. Porkies'll eat anything.

'Sit down, chixie. What can I offer you? Coke? An energy?'

While she's looking in the fridge I drop the rucksack on the floor and slide it behind the sofa with my foot.

'No, I'm good.'

She shuts the fridge door. 'Hmm. A polite kid would say *No, I'm good, thank you, Mother Moon*.'

'Well I'm not one of them.'

Her smile changes. 'OK. Let's level up, chixie. You said you wanted a photo for your mum but now I'm getting a different vibe. You know who I am. But who are you?'

'My mum's called Emmilou.'

'Ah. Emmilou. Remind me.'

'You know her. You talk every day.'

'Ah. Well. I do and I don't,' she smiles, with her face that's like pastry from a bake-in-a-mo bun kit. 'You see, chixie, here's the thing. Emmilou may talk to me. But – little secret? You saw the crowd here tonight. In my job, there isn't time for one-on-one, much as I'd like to. But I certainly love Emmilou, and care for her deeply. *Very* deeply. She knows that. Shame she wouldn't come and say hello.'

'Cos she's not here.'

'I see.' Her breathing changes, you can see it from her boobs. 'And it's not her birthday either, right?' I nod yes. 'And I guess we can forget about the signed pic too. Hmm. So you told Mother Moon a couple of untruths, chixie.'

'She's in the morgue. At the health station.'

Her eyebrows frown into two ticks. Then she reaches for the alarm button on the wall and presses it like Georgi said she would.

'Ah. Big sozz to hear that. So you're grieving. Losing a loved one's a hard blow, but we all go through it and somehow we come out stronger people in the end. So tell me why you're here, popsicle.'

'I want you to make the doctors defrost her.'

'What?' she laughs. She shouldn't laugh. 'You'll have to explain, chixie, cos I'm not quite following.'

'My grandad's old and he might zap out, so I need her back. Soon. Ma can manage with just one eye. And a limp. I'll help her. It's me does most things anyway. The porkies and that.'

Then ew, she leans down and hugs me. She's squelchy and she doesn't smell of booze and kill-yous like Ma, she stinks of perfume. 'Oh chixie.' Her voice buzzes against my head. 'Have a good cry with Mother Moon. Let it all out.'

'Get the fuck off me!' I push her off, and fuck saying beep. 'If you don't get my mum defrosted I'll kill you, true story!'

She presses the alarm again.

'Listen, chixie. I don't appreciate the way you're behaving but I salute your determination in coming here all alone, like a real little man. The big picture needs folk with your kind of drive, chixie. Brave little people full of spirit.'

'I don't give a shit about the big picture. I just want my mum.'

'Poor love. I feel your agony, chixie. I really do. With all of my big Mother Moon heart. But I don't have the power to bring people back from the dead. Big, big sozz about that.'

My heart starts spazzing like it might pop.

'She's not dead. I never said that.'

She frowns. 'Morgues are for dead people, chixie.' What's she on about? 'Sounds like someone miscommunicated. Mummy's not coming back, chixie. Cos she's dead.' My chest's still spazzing. 'Now it's natural to want to blame someone and you might find yourself doing that when it's sunk in. But – little explanation? I don't choose my followers. They choose me. Folk are free agents, chixie, and you can't prevent them doing what they want to do. A lot of Zeroes are opting to withdraw from life these days. You could call it a trend. Honest truth, the big picture can't afford people like Mummy. She came to see that. If she did the brave thing, and it looks like she did, well she's earned my admiration and respect. And your gratitude too, if it's led to an upgrade. Are you living on the mainland now in a snug little prefab, chixie?' I don't say anything. I can't, cos my ideas are bumping about like wild freakmen. 'Well if you are, you have Mummy to thank for it. Steep learning curve today, mmm?' There's a siren outside and flashing lights. 'Now are we going to let them put an official warning on your folk-chip? Or shall I just let you out quietly and forget about your little visit? Cos I'm generous that way, chixie.'

My mouth's dried out cos of the morgue. 'I'll go. I'm done here, Mother Moon.'

She lays her fat hand on my head and steers me to the door.

'Wise choice. You'll go far. Truly. Now how about a high-five, big man?'

I take the lift down.

I walk out slowly, through the front door.

My heart's still spazzing.

The troops are there, busy with walkie-talkies but Georgi was right, they don't notice me cos I'm just a random kid, just a kid with a remote control in his pocket who knows his Ma's not coming back, not now, not ever.

Ten, nine, eight.

I'm right in the smallest corner of the big picture. So small you can't see me.

Seven six five four three two one.

But just wait till you hear the size of the noise I'm going to make when zero comes.

Just listen while it all goes *boom*.

# GOODBYE JIMMY

## Alasdair Gray

IN WHAT IS MORE A STUDY than a laboratory, our Headmaster contemplates an array of crystalline forms when one of his deputies arrives from a distant province. This visit has been long expected, yet the Head nearly groans before turning his head enough to give the visitor a mildly welcoming smile and say, 'Hullo, Jimmy. What brings you here?'

He has the mandarin voice of a Lowland Scot unlocalized by a university education, but not Englished. His employee answers in a slightly plebeian Dublin accent, 'You know well why I'm here. You've stopped answering me emails.'

The Head says gently, 'I know what they say.'

'What use is that if you've no advice to give?'

The Head sighs with a slight shrug of his shoulders.

'Is that meant to be some kind of answer?' demands Jimmy, 'are you giving that wee place up as a bad job?'

The Head contemplates his crystalline forms again but cannot shut his ears to the cry, 'Then I'm giving it up too! Abandoning that nest of graceless, ignorant, self-destructive animals! Leaving it! Done with it!'

The outcry becomes wild sobs which slowly quieten and end.

After a pause the Head murmurs, 'You can't leave that job. You've nothing else to do.' Then he adds loudly, 'Unlike me!' grinning so impishly at his guest that the younger, careworn man seems faced by a mischievous child. A moment later the Head's old serene look returns, and to change the subject he says in a comradely way, 'I have my own worries, you see.'

'Life on other planets?'

'Yep!'

'Any luck with it?'

'Nope. I've produced a lot of the usual microbes in submarine volcanic vents, but changes in the chemical environment keep wiping them out before they can even evolve into annelid worms. A planet supporting much life needs a lot of water and some chemical stability. You can't get that without a near neighbour as big as Jupiter to hoover up the huge meteors, a satellite like your moon to grab most of the others. In this universe the chance of getting a planet like that are over a zillion squared to one against.'

'But you've got one!' says the visitor intensely. 'Why turn your back on it – the only world rich with all kinds of life? Some of it with the brain to grasp your intention, and I'm not taking about whales.'

'Calm down, Jimmy,' says the Head kindly.

'I am perfectly calm, and stop calling me Jimmy!'

'Do you prefer your earlier titles, O Lucifer, Son of the Morning? Prometheus, bringer of fire?'

The Head is joking. Jimmy says wistfully, 'King of the Jews. Prince of Peace.'

The Head wags a forefinger, says 'Prince of Darkness! Loki! Kali! Mephistopheles!' – his Scots accent broadens for a moment – 'Auld Nick! Well, in my time I've been called a lot of funny names too.'

'So why call me Jimmy?'

'It suits my accent.'

'Why sound like a Scot?'

The Head sighs, looks gloomy, at last says, 'I still get messages from that world of yours, messages from desperate people who want help. They demand help! These impossible demands ...'

'They're called prayers,' Jimmy tells him.

'You should stop them reaching me! These impossible demands ... are mostly from mothers.'

'Mothers worry you,' says Jimmy accusingly. The Head strongly defends himself.

'I cannot break physical laws that keep this universe running! I cannot stop fire or fiery chemicals hurting babies and wee kids because their skin is burned off by homicidal idiots obeying orders! When I answer ...' he hesitates, 'prayers in a Scots accent they know I am not a loving father who will work miracles. They know they havnae a hope in hell.'

'Then why not sound American? Like Dubya?'

There is a globe of the world within reach. The Head touches a northern continent upon it, saying sadly, 'Don't depress me. I once had hopes of America.'

'Why not sound,' asks Jimmy brightly, 'like a former Scottish prime minister? He goes around claiming to be one of your greatest fans.'

The Head covers his face with his hands, muttering, 'Please don't sicken me. Supernatural beings are only heard when we use other folk's voices. You sound Irish because you like to be liked and (IRA apart) the southern Irish voice usually does sound friendly to people outside Ireland. But God the Father must sook up to *naebody*! *Naebody*!'

After a pause Jimmy says calmly, 'Do you sound Scottish to me because I haven't a hope in hell?'

'Yes!' says the Head looking straight at him, 'But it won't stop you saying what you're here to say, so say on, Macduff.'

Jimmy holds out a sheaf of printed papers, saying, 'Read these emails you ignored.'

'No. Bin them. I know what they say because I know everything. Everything.'

'But you won't attend to everything, so attend to these!'

The Head says patiently, 'They say the world's richest governments have enough nuclear weapons to kill everything bigger than a cockroach, and are inventing ways to improve them, while fighting wars in any land that will not otherwise let them exploit natural resources there. These governments still sometimes say their warfare defends democracy. They used to say it defended Christianity and free trade. All lies, of course. What did you want me to do, O Prince of Peace? Intervene personally?'

'I do.'

'That never works. I gave Moses a few good rules everybody should observe – Don't kill, don't steal, don't tell lies. Many mothers still teach that to their kids. But then came law makers with exceptions to my rules – You must kill when governments tell you to, and can steal from men, women, and children when governments let you take their land, and must not tell truths when governments say truths are dangerous. Also witches must not be allowed to live, adulteresses should be stoned to death. Had I said to Moses, *This I command thee, do what the hell you like!* human history would have been just as bloody.'

'Nobody thinks your law against killing applies to foreigners,' says Jimmy mournfully.

'You did your best to correct them about that, my ...'

The Head hesitates. Jimmy looks hard at him until he goes on to say, '... my good man. Yes, you told them to love their neighbours as themselves and their enemies too. Don't fight the people who oppress you, but refuse to kill, steal or lie for them.'

'Good words to spread,' says Jimmy sadly.

The Head starts to speak, hesitates again, then says in an embarrassed way, 'There is something I've wanted to ask. When you were ... hanging there ...'

'I was nailed,' says Jimmy flatly.

'Yes. And you told someone in the same state that he would go to heaven with you. Why?'

'He talked kindly to me,' says Jimmy, shrugging and spreading his hands, 'I wanted to be kind back. Should I have told him there is as little justice in heaven as on earth? My body was in such pain that I forgot it was temporary. I was delirious. Up to almost the very last minute I was mad enough to think you might save everyone who suffered unjustly, and save them ... through *me!*'

He gives a desperate chuckle. The Head assumes the manner of a schoolteacher and says, 'If I only existed to give eternal sweeties to good folk and eternal beltings to bad, goodness would be cheap. There would be no decency, no heroism in it. I love heroism and you were a hero. I am proud of what you told people and what you endured for telling them.'

'You didn't need heroism to be crucified. The Romans did it to hundreds of thousands. From the start of history down to the present day millions of children, women, and men have endured worse deaths for no reason at all – just because they were born in unlucky places.'

Says the Head consolingly, 'Your words comforted many unlucky people, especially slaves and women.'

'O yes!' cries Jimmy, 'and when my comforting words were made official by the Roman Empire and even policemen were christened, my Christians began murdering neighbours with different Gods and burning down their temples and synagogues. My Jesus was as big a flop as your Moses, which is why I want you to—'

'Suddenly!' the Head interrupts, snapping his fingers. 'Suddenly, simultaneously appear on every television and computer screen on the planet announcing, *You shall love the Lord your God with all your heart and all your soul and all your mind, and your neighbour as your self,* or *You! Will! Be! Ex! Ter! Min! Ated!* They would treat me as a rogue virus.'

'You don't understand,' says Jimmy shaking his head, 'I *want* you to exterminate all the brutes.'

'Say that again,' says the Head, surprised.

'Exterminate all the brutes. Now.'

The Head sighs, stares at his crystalline forms as if looking for help there, then mutters, 'Michty me. Crivens. Jings, Jimmy, don't be so damned biblical. I am not the genocidal lunatic described in Genesis. I never made a deluge that drowned everyone except a single family of each species. I did *not* burn Sodom and Gomorrah with fire and brimstone out of heaven.'

'But you wiped out most of the dinosaurs and the salt-water plankton. You smothered Pompeii and Herculaneum in volcanic ash.'

The Head says patiently, 'A wholly stable planet is physically impossible. Even with Jupiter and the moon to shield it, an asteroid the size of Dundee is bound to hit the earth every thirteen million years or so. The dinosaurs lasted a lot longer than that. They had a fair innings. Six and a half million years will pass before the next meteoric disaster – plenty of time for folk to learn how to stop it.

And it is not my fault when men build cities beside a volcano. Your job was to stop folk blaming me for things priests and insurance companies once called Acts of God – floods, earthquakes, plagues, and epidemics caused by ignorance of safe cultivation and hygiene. And you cured that ignorance!'

'O yes!' says Jimmy bitterly, covering his face with his hands, 'I encouraged Bacon and Galileo when ignorance seemed to be the main problem and good scientists were thought black magicians or heretics. And now natural science is triumphant.'

'Exactly,' says the Head. 'Educated folk no longer blame you and me for everything bad. That is a definite step in the right direction. I refuse to wipe out life on earth because my agent there who should encourage it is tired of it.'

'But I love life on earth! I want you to save it by quickly destroying only one kind of brute – the most selfishly greedy kind. Get rid of men, please, before they destroy every other living thing.'

The Head smiles, says, 'If mankind heard you now they really would think you …' (he holds out both hands with his fingers curved like claws) '… Bee! El! Zi! Bub!'

'You know what I'm talking about,' says Jimmy, again shaking the sheaf of print-outs at him.

'Atmosphere overheating from diesel fumes,' says the Head, obviously bored. 'Glaciers and icecaps melting, sea levels rising. Forests felled, land impoverished. Pure water tables shrinking or polluted. Drought increasing where forty per cent of folk suffer malnutrition and soon billions will die of thirst.'

'Primitive Christians were right,' says Jimmy passionately. 'Scientists *are* black magicians. Nearly all of them work for corporations tearing up the fabric of earthly life with the help of governments they have bribed. Half the animals alive fifty years ago are now extinct. Frogs and sparrows are nearly extinct. The bumblebees are dying. Some conscience-stricken biologists are freezing the sperm of threatened creatures so that they can be brought back to life when the earth is governed sanely. Mankind will never govern it sanely.'

With a tolerant chuckle the Head says, 'Aye, men have always been great wee extinguishers. Remember North America at the end of the last big ice age? A vast forest of deciduous trees with nothing dividing them but lakes and rivers and rocky mountains. It was the home of the biggest, most peaceful vegetarians we ever achieved – titanic browsers, ground-sloths as big as elephants. The first men who entered that continent across the Bering Strait had never dreamed of so much meat. Killing bears and woolly elephants in Eurasia was dangerous work, but men easily took over America. The ground-sloths couldn't run away, couldn't run at all, didn't need to be trapped. Set fire to the trees and you had several roasted ground-sloths burned out of their pelts in a gravy of their own melted fat. The number of North American men expanded hugely – for two generations they were too busy eating to kill each other – they gorged themselves all the way down to Mexico!'

Seeing that Jimmy is staring at him in disgust he says, 'Cheer up. That's how the prairies came about, with room for herds and herds and herds of buffalo.'

'Which the white men slaughtered because the red men lived off them. But you know things are a lot worse now. Farmers are sowing genetically modified crops that die as soon as harvested, so they must buy new seed from companies that patented them, while plants folk used to feed on vanish forever. Soon the only live creatures left on earth will be humans and the mutants they eat.'

In a sing-song voice, grinning, the Head says, 'Remember the viruses, Jimmy! They too are busy wee mutaters. People are great breeding grounds for viruses, especially people eating battery-farmed meat and mutant vegetables.' With genuine regret he murmurs, 'Croak, croak. A pity about the frogs.'

'Are you fond of the Barrier Reef?' asks Jimmy, desperately.

'My greatest work of art – one thousand, two hundred and fifty miles long,' says the Head, reminiscently. 'A masterpiece of intricately intertwined fishes, plants, insects with the beautiful vivid colour variety of all the great pictures painted by Matisse and Dufy, and a refinement of detail greater than even Paul Klee achieved.' He shakes his head in wonder at the thought of his own genius.

'It's dying,' says Jimmy. 'It'll all be gone in thirty years unless men die first.'

The Head shrugs his shoulders, says 'Nothing lasts forever,' and turning, contemplates his crystals as if nothing else mattered.

'What use are you?' Jimmy suddenly demands.

The Head, amused, smiles at him kindly but does not reply until the question is enlarged: 'What do you do with yourself while failing to develop annelid worms in submarine volcanic vents?'

'I'm preparing to generate a better universe.'

'Where?'

'Outside this one.'

'How can you make a universe outside this one?'

This brings out the Head's schoolteacher side. Wagging a forefinger, with increasing enthusiasm he says, 'If you subscribed to *Scientific American* you would know how other universes would happen. Every universe is like a carpet with a gigantic draught blowing underneath, so in places it gets rippled up into peaks where energy and mass are so concentrated that BANG, a hole is blown in the fabric through which mass energy pours, making another universe where physical laws can bend differently.'

'What makes that draught?' says Jimmy keenly.

'Would you think me a megalomaniac if I told you it was my breath?' asks the Head, slyly watching him sideways.

'Yes.'

'I have to use metaphors when describing universal processes,' says the Head, impatiently. 'If you don't like wind-blown ripples call them ... call them labour pains if you like, but the result will be a universe where the planets are this shape.'

From a bench he lifts a variously coloured prism and hands it over. Jimmy looks at it, then says, unbelievingly, 'A *pyramidal* planet?'

'You are wrong. A pyramid has five sides, with four isosceles triangles on a square base. This planetary model has only four triangular sides, four equal continents. Get the idea?'

'No.'

'Look at it closely. Four glacial polar regions at the apex of each continent. Water trickles down from these to form an ocean in the middle of each surface – four Mediterranean seas of roughly equal size where life will evolve, and when it takes to land around the shores it will find none large enough for an empire to grow. All the nations that occur will be small and coastal, like Scandinavia.'

Jimmy examines the prism closely then says, 'I see some off-shore islands. The British Empire spread from an island.'

'An island with a lot of coal and iron where James Watt devised the first commercial steam engine. In my new world, fossil fuel deposits will be equally dispersed. No gold rushes! The machines people invent will have to be powered by wind and water and oil from plants that can be grown, harvested and replanted.'

Jimmy says, 'The shape of this thing makes it gravitationally impossible.'

'Only in this universe!' cries the Head. 'I am preparing a liquid universe where heavenly bodies will be gravitationally formed by *crystallization*! Imagine galaxies of tetrahedral planets revolving round octahedral suns! A universe' – he ends by murmuring dreamily – 'with no big bangs and collisions.'

'But how can a planet have seas in a universe full of liquid?'

'My universal fluid will be as light as air! In fact it will *be* air! I will make it air!'

Inspired by the idea he hurries to a blackboard with chemical formulae chalked on it, seizes a chalk and writes $N$-$78.1\%$, then heavily underlines it, saying, 'When my heavenly bodies have crystallized, these chemical constituents must remain.' He starts chalking down a new column of figures, muttering. 'This universal … solution … will make flight between worlds easy. No need for people … to blast themselves … across light years of dreary sub-zero vacuum.'

He flings the chalk down and contemplates the formulae with something like smugness. Jimmy says, 'But …'

'You are going to tell me, Mr Prometheus O' Lucifer, that air is largely oxygen exhaled by vegetation, and how can I grow enough plants to fill a universe with it? But my next universe will start with a big splash instead of a big bang, and the initial chemistry will be wholly different.'

He sits down, folds his arms and looks triumphant. Jimmy, not impressed, turns the tetrahedral model in his hands, saying, 'OK

Mister Sly-boots Clever-clogs, I was also going to ask about this planet's angle of rotation.' He hands the model back, says, 'It will have to perform intricate somersaults if one of your triangular continents is not to be in perpetual twilight.'

'That is certainly a problem,' says the Head agreeably, putting the model back on the bench. 'I am working on it.'

'So how long will it take you to get this … airy new universe up and running?'

'I have eternity,' says the chief, smiling to himself.

'You will spend eternity dreaming up a Utopian universe while mankind destroys life on earth in a couple of generations?'

'That's nonsense, Jimmy!' says the Head consolingly. 'Men cannot destroy *all* life on earth, only themselves and equally complex creatures. In which case insects will inherit the earth while vegetation recovers and then …' (he becomes enthusiastic) '… from the segmented worms you and I will evolve a wealth of new creatures with different organs and sensations and minds. I never repeat my mistakes. It was maybe a mistake to give big brains to mammals.'

'Why deny intelligence to creatures who suckle their young?'

'Freud thinks it makes them unhealthily dependent and unhealthily greedy. Why not try hatching big intelligences from eggs? Birds, in general, seem happier than people. Tropical birds are as colourful as the organisms in my Great Barrier Reef, and the world will become a very tropical planet when men have made it too hot to hold them.'

'But!—' says Jimmy explosively. The Head cuts him off. 'You are about to say bird brains are too small for development because their necks are too thin, but owls have short, thick necks and are notoriously brainy. One day you may fly up to me in the form of a dove with an eagle's wingspan and find me a gigantic owl …' (he spreads his arms) '… with feathers as colourful as a parrot's. Pretty polly!'

'And is that the most comforting message I can take back to the few on earth who listen to me? The few who care for the future of life there?'

The Head says mildly, 'You recently asked me to exterminate the human race and now you want me to send it comforting messages.'

'Not comforting messages but useful messages. When I asked you to exterminate humanity I was trying to goad you into suggesting a new way of saving them.' He sighs. 'But of course you knew that.'

'I did,' says the Head. 'But the only ways humanity can save itself is by old things that come in threes.'

'Faith, hope, and love,' says Jimmy glumly.

'Yes, but these can only work beside liberty, equality, fraternity.'

'Jesus, Mary, and Joseph!' raves Jimmy, 'What are you on about? I've been so mixed up with … postmodern people that I've forgotten.'

'Liberty is not having to obey other people because they are richer than you.'

'Equality?'

'Is what everybody enjoys with friends, or in nations where everyone knows they need each other.'

'Fraternity?'

'Brotherhood. The brotherhood of man.'

'Exclusively masculine?'

'A good point, Jimmy. Call fraternity love also, the love that still makes your earth the centre of the present universe.'

'Don't talk shite! My wee world is near the edge of an average galaxy among a million million galaxies! I helped Galileo destroy the Jewish notion that the whole shebang was made for them. How can my wee world be a universal centre?'

The Head says patiently, 'Wherever somebody opens their eyes is the centre of the universe and your earth is still the place where a lot of that happens. I hoped mankind would take life to my other worlds. They have the technology.' He shrugs. 'If they use it to destroy themselves we'll start again with another species,' and he murmurs, 'To-wit-to-woo. Pretty Pol.'

Jimmy slumps down looking totally defeated. Our Head claps his hands, rubs them together, goes to him briskly, pats him on the shoulders and says cheerfully, 'And since we now see eye to eye I must waste no more of your valuable time. Tell folk the competitive exploitation of natural resources is a dead end. Nuclear power, used wisely, will give access to all the space, raw material, and energy they need without fighting aliens for it. Less than five miles beneath the earth's surface is heat that, rightly channelled, will drive their machines without poisonous emissions.'

Without appearing to use force he raises Jimmy and accompanies him to the exit, saying, 'Fossil fuels should be exclusively used as fertilizer, and housewives when shopping should use net bags instead of the plastic sort which add to the price of what they buy. Goodbye, Jimmy.'

'Nobody with wealth and power will believe me if I say that! They know the damage they are doing to the planet but they're still extending motorways! Making and selling cars! Nobody owning one will change to a bicycle! Nobody who can fly will go by boat! Owners of companies wrecking the ecosphere are buying self-sustaining bunkers where they and their like can survive when everyone else is poisoned!'

'They won't survive,' says the Head, chuckling. 'Only folk who want to save everyone else have a chance. Perhaps.'

Now he firmly propels Jimmy to the exit, adding, with what sounds like mischievous encouragement, 'Workers of the world, unite! Remind them of co-operative socialism! Owens, William Morris, James Connelly!'

'I'll be laughed at,' moans Jimmy.

'Then all laughter will become screams of hysterical despair. Send me all the emails you like but don't come here again for a millennium or two. Goodbye, son.'

'Son!' says Jimmy on the threshold, 'I'm glad you ... sometimes ... admit I'm in the family.'

'Goodbye, son,' says the Head, quietly for once, 'and good luck.'

'Which is not something you need, Dad,' says Jimmy, and leaves.

The Head returns to contemplate the crystalline models and formulae on his blackboard, seeming almost despondent. He is sorry that it is so hard to show his love for those who love him most. The rest are not so demanding. And why does Jimmy think *he* needs no luck? Is it because, as Headmaster of all, there is supposed to be no greater power? He hums a little song to himself, 'I'll give me one-o. What is my one-o? One is one and all alone and ever more shall be so.'

After a pause he sadly says, 'One is one and all alone and ever more shall be so.'

In the place where he sits another presence becomes apparent, one that stands so much higher than he that its voice seems from above, a gentle, female, slightly amused voice saying, 'You silly wee man.'

'Mother?' he asks wistfully.

# LIKE CANUTE

## Clare Dudman

SOPHIE BEGINS THE DAY by looking at the sky. No matter how this ends it will always be there. She likes the shade of duck-egg blue shining through a rip in the clouds just above the roofline, and wonders where she read that the only sea really this colour is the Mediterranean. As her tea brews she watches a reflection of herself in the glass door of the shower cubicle in the bathroom. She lowers herself over the pedestal. The bowl is too large for the room, and unfortunately also functions as a sound box. It would be embarrassing if anyone could hear, but no one ever does. As she rinses her hands, part of the manuscript she was reading last night comes back to her: a wisp of an idea that disappears when she tries to grasp it. What was it? Something she should know.

The thought that there is something she can't quite remember bugs her on her journey to the office. Once or twice it almost comes to her, but then someone jostles it away. Maybe she's getting old. Sometimes she finds herself wondering about the answers to the questions they ask to test for Alzheimer's. Who's the prime minister? She grins as she imagines her answer: who cares?

There's a storm coming. It's being announced everywhere: on the radio, by the newspaper vendor at the entrance to the station, and on the news site when she switches on her laptop at work. If it comes it will bring torrential rain: something most people will welcome after these weeks of drought. Her assistant tells her that someone from the council is wittering on about flooding, and the likelihood of the sewers overflowing. He's recommending that people living at or below ground level acquire sand bags.

Long ago, on a childhood holiday, the rain came down so hard and fast that the roof of their tent was battered into a pool-filled valley. First it dripped but then it cascaded through the canvas, and they had had to wait out the rest of the day in the family car. Through patches in the steamed-up windows they had watched the rain-glazed pathways quickly become small, fast-flowing, dirty streams. There had been sandbags then. 'Like Canute,' her mother had said. 'No one can stop the tide coming in.'

All morning they wait for the rain to start. Her assistant says she can smell it coming, as if the air is growing thick. In the afternoon, by the time the chief calls her in for a meeting, it has still not come. 'Hope you've brought your umbrella, Norman,' she tells him, 'because I haven't.'

Norman doesn't smile. He tells her to sit, then says that he's sorry, and he knows this is going to seem unfair because she's been here even longer than he has, but he wants her to clear her desk. Even though she is the most valuable and dedicated member of staff, she is also the most expensive and it's been hard, obviously, but the cuts are hurting everyone. No one is safe, he says. It'll be the rest of us soon.

Her hands rest on the small arms of her chair. She notices the shininess of her skin over her knuckles, how she can see each ridge of her bone, and each blue string of vein threading over and between. Then she remembers what she has been trying to remember all morning. 'There was a manuscript I read last night,' she says, 'I think it's important. I think you should see it.'

Norman shakes his head. 'Not now, Sophie,' he says. He stands, pats her lightly on the shoulder, and then walks over to his door and opens it. He waits until she stands too, then steps aside so she can step through it. 'Keep in touch,' he says, his voice flat.

'I've put everything in these bags,' her assistant says when she returns to her desk.

'Well, that was quick!'

The assistant gives a small smile, looks down, and then walks quickly back to her desk. Sophie wonders how long she's known, and if all that conversation today about the rain was a way of filling in time, of saying nothing. But it still feels as though it will rain.

The uniformed man on the reception desk smiles widely when she hands in her pass cards. He posts them in a box and then waves goodbye just as cheerily as he has every evening for the last twenty-six years. By the time she has passed through the revolving door she has forgotten his face.

It is still mid-afternoon: a time of day she rarely sees outside the office. How quiet it is, and how hot. There's something missing, a small sound that should be there but isn't. A single man passes on a bicycle. There are no cars, no trams, and no buses at this time of day, not any more, but it's not their roar that she's missing. Something else. She will either have to walk or wait until the rush hour starts. The air is sucking moisture into itself. There is no wind, no sign of a storm, but the newspaper stall is still predicting it in scrawled capital letters. Everyone is waiting.

That night Sophie, who is not sleeping, is disturbed by a sound. When she opens her bedroom door, a man with a hood over his head, a scarf over his lower face, and a knife in his hand is standing by her open fridge. He has her cloth bag from a Trade Fair partly filled with food. 'Hungry,' he says, and his black eyes have a glittering violence to them. 'I hungry. I have baby, wife, child. They all cry. You not need. I do.'

A refugee. He's come from somewhere warmer and used to the sun. She can smell the dust and the heat on his clothes.

'Take it.' she whispers. 'Take everything. Here.' Inside her cupboards are vegetables, tins of fruit, and meat. She pulls out a shopping bag and thrusts it at him. 'Fill it. Take what you want.'

When he has gone there is nothing left.

It takes her two days to reach it. One long journey by the only train that now travels that far north, and then a shorter one to reach the outskirts of the city. From there she has to walk. It has been a dry summer here, too. The uplands are covered by yellow grass, wiry thorns, and heather that crackles underfoot. The solitary sound. Only when she reaches a valley and a stream are there trees, but even these look parched, as if they are already dead.

MacPherson Health Spa used to be the seat of the Earl of Throckmorton. Now it is converted into apartments, and the surrounding deer park turned over to vegetables and a newly planted wood. Hoops of bamboo, covered in polythene, are arranged untidily alongside trees.

An avenue of sparsely-leaved poplars leads from the road to a large wooden front door. A handle brings a small hammer in contact with a large bell. The man who comes to open this door is just as she imagined he would be: a reddish-white beard and a large, upright frame. The top of his nose is etched with tiny red veins along its entire length, and his eyes are set so deeply she cannot see their colour. They peer at her as though she is standing against the sun.

'Paul Smithson?' She asks, and holds out her hand when he nods. 'Sophie Galsworth,' she says. 'You sent me your manuscript.'

The top of the ring finger of his left hand is missing down past the second knuckle. The end of it is white and smooth, almost like bone. 'An accident,' he says, when he sees her looking at it. 'Means I can't get married,' he says.

Sophie laughs, uncertain if this is a joke.

With a sweep of his arm he shows her into a brightly painted kitchen with a couple of large stoves and two long kitchen tables. Saucepans are hooked on the wall, and above them various ladles, spoons, and knives. Some of them are new and polished, while some are chipped, with broken handles. All of them look clean. A couple of young men in mud-spattered overalls are talking when she comes in. When they hear Paul's voice they stop and acknowledge him with a nod.

'Toby and Tom,' he says.

'Sophie,' she replies.

There is no further introduction. Paul gestures for her to sit at the table, and Toby or Tom serves them with two lop-sided mugs full of milky tea.

Paul is reluctant for her to stay. 'But what can you do besides correct manuscripts?' he asks.

'Nothing.' She says. 'It's either this or …' She indicates her bag at her feet. 'This is all I have now.'

He looks at her where she sits at the table. 'But you're not …' He pauses.

'Young? Fit? No – thanks for pointing that out.' She sighs, and with the thumb of her right hand, smoothes the edge of each of the nails of her left, one by one.

'Well …' he says, shifting, as though he is about to rise to his feet.

She interrupts him. 'But it's not too late, you know!'

'I'm afraid I'm not looking to increase numbers just at the moment.'

'I can learn!' Gripping the edge of the table she looks at him. 'I know I can!'

'Everyone has to earn their place here.'

'I know.' Still gripping the table she leans towards him, her eyes intent on his. 'Why don't you just give me a chance, and see?'

■

She begins the day by looking at the sky. Its blue is intense, its clarity dizzying. She remembers contrails: the line of white ink becoming blurred on the wet paper. Now only the rich dream of launching themselves skywards. At the end of the garden there is a small shed with a wooden seat. As her tea brews she lowers herself onto it and pees onto the straw below. In a couple of weeks she will fork it onto the compost heap in the farthest corner; a rich, warm kingdom of worms, woodlice, and slugs.

She pauses outside the back door. The chickens have gone inside their coop to roost. So quiet. Always so quiet. Once she heard a seagull in the distance but when she rushed out to see it there was nothing but that intensely blue sky. She opens the door of their roost and smiles as they cluck their disapproval. Reaching under their warm softness she finds seven eggs. The four larger ones she will take to the woman in the village whose hens have stopped laying. 'They need to watch their step,' the woman had told Sophie with a fierce smile. 'Any more of this and we'll be having a good roast dinner every Sunday.'

It is mid-afternoon before she finishes planting out the potato chittings. She straightens slowly, vertebra by vertebra, her hands stroking out aches. Everything costs so much effort. Both knees ache. Her arms are mottled with nettle rash and her right index finger has an angry-looking, pus-filled wound where a thorn went in. Yesterday morning she spent an hour tying back beans, only for them to loosen again in the night, and last week she dug up a promising row of parsnip plants only to find the roots were the size of a baby's finger. Swallowing down disappointment, she'd boiled them, but they were too bitter to eat. She looks around at the wilting vegetation. Everything seems constantly thirsty, and she worries about the stream at the bottom of the valley which seems to be shallower each time she sees it.

'It'll rain soon,' Paul had said last night with a puzzling certainty. He visits her most nights with food he has spare.

'But aren't you worried it might not?' she'd asked.

'Worrying won't help,' he'd said, then on his way out, added, 'Your hair looks good that way. You should keep it like that.'

She touches her hair now. Behind the vegetable beds are sweet chestnuts and apple trees; neither has fruited since she's been here, but they keep off the worst of the sun. Their branches creak in the heat. A large white butterfly flutters daintily between her cabbages, laying an orange egg on each one, and Sophie follows her, scraping it away, and removing the tiny caterpillars that have already hatched. She digs between the carrots.

Her neighbour Brian passes on a bicycle. He waves at her and stops to tell her about the rain. He's been in the hills to the west to catch rabbits, and although the trip yielded just a couple of young bucks, he's seen a storm approaching. The clouds are large and grey: a classic anvil. It's going to be a big one. Everyone is waiting.

He gives her a few blackberries he's found growing on a verge, and she gives him one of the eggs for his teenage daughter. He stows it carefully in a box with the rest of his berries. 'Our Gaia says she's something for you,' he says. 'Don't get too excited, it's just a story. But she's been on about showing it to you for days. Just say no, if you'd rather not. Apparently her mother and I don't understand her. '

Sophie flushes. 'She can come over any time she wants.'

'I expect her mother will want you to sample some of her new jam, too,' he says over his shoulder as he pedals off. 'It's gooseberry. New season.'

She returns to her weeding, pleased at the prospect of company. By the time the sun has set her right hip is aching as well as her knees. When she steps over the threshold to her cottage her leg gives way, and she finds herself clinging to the doorframe for a few seconds until the strength returns.

Paul finds her peeling the potato he gave her. 'Jake Lamington says he'll do us fifty copies!' Paul is still determined to publish his manuscript. 'Good news, eh? He says he's traded a few books for some paper. Enough to do the lot.'

She nods but doesn't look up.

'And Thomas Finley wants to speak to you about his little project. He wants to use the bikes in the gym for something useful, and thinks he can work out a way of making them charge up a battery. If he does that, do you think you could write the manual?'

She nods again.

'Anything wrong?' he asks.

She straightens her knee. 'Tired.' She says. 'I'm too old for this.'

He opens his mouth to reply, but then the windows rattle as something hits them. He runs to the door and throws it open and whoops. Rain. At last! Lots of it, all at once, driven by the wind into sheets.

'Look!' he says, smiling. 'Something for your cabbages!'

She shrugs. She thinks about the caterpillars that are probably hiding in the stalks. When the rain stops they'll be feasting again.

He swoops forward again and pulls her upright by her arms.

'There's something I wanted to show you,' he says, 'I was going to wait, but …'

He pulls her out of the door to where there are overhanging branches. She can't remember when it last rained like this. She'd forgotten how quickly it soaks through clothes, and how it makes the earth smell of mould.

'Here,' he says, pulling her forward. There are so many trees and high bushes it is possible to traverse the whole length of the garden without breaking cover.

'We have to be quiet now,' he says, abruptly holding her still in his arms, 'Keep looking at that nest of twigs on the ground.'

For a few minutes nothing happens. She can feel rather than hear the thud of his heart through her chest. She sniffs quietly, then holds her breath. Maybe she too smells just as strongly of stale sweat. It's been weeks since either of them washed. She swallows down a little stomach acid.

'Look, did you see it?'

She shakes her head.

'Go a little closer.'

There's something moving: a tiny furry-looking head and then a dull-brown thorax and abdomen. It gives a barely audible buzz.

'That's it!' she says, 'that's what's been missing.'

He claps her face between his two enormous hands and kisses it. 'Yes!' he says, squeezing tighter. 'Now we can expect apples in a year or two, maybe even the chestnuts. Who'd have thought the bees would go for *your* messy woodpile?'

The sky is clearing. Behind his head the grey is giving way to duck-egg blue. Always there, she thinks. Even when everything else is gone: there'll always be that blue, the colour of a warm, unruffled sea.

# WE'RE ALL GONNA HAVE THE BLUES

Rodge Glass

I RECKON IT'LL BE LATE AUTUMN, heading into winter. That time of year when Europe goes black long before the end of the working day and people walk home by lamplight, eyes on their shoes, umbrellas held out like shields against the wind. In the November cold even life's winners grip the rail on the underground or the tram, coats damp, wondering what they might have done with their best years. Jaro says it's all about temperature drop. About smells too. *The physical is everything*, he says in that low growl of his, as if what he's saying couldn't possibly be disputed. Jaro tells me that even if people don't know they know it, most folks can sense darkness coming. Their bodies can. Their brains. And this is when he sees it happening, at the back end of one of our bleakest days, the water steadily rising, creeping up on us like old age. No big flash of light. No earth-shattering crash or bone-shaking split. He says it'll probably all start all quiet, while we're both here, far from home, amongst the doubters of Eastern Europe.

Where I sit right now, at a low table in the Jazzrock Blues Bar in Krakow, underneath the low brick arch, I'm waiting for Jaro to show. I usually hold off on my first grown-up drink till he appears, but this day has felt like a week and the fat old bastard was supposed to be here half an hour ago, so fuck it, I'm getting started. I order a beer, pay and sit back down at the moment the Magda Octavia Quartet float on stage to the pitter-patter of warm applause; as they pick up their instruments I count six of them. This seems an important detail. Right now, all details seem important. Perhaps because I did eighteen hours yesterday, and I was up five hours before polls even opened today, the night is climbing all over me and my mind's beginning to run. Jaro says that's OK – he says that wherever I am, it's the running mind that's got me here – but these days I mostly dream of just lying still. I sit at my table and sip, and swallow, and as the music starts I wonder why there are six people in this jazz quartet, and wonder where the fuck Jaro is, and then I become convinced that this is how it's going to be: it'll begin in a place like this, on a night like this, the floodwaters lapping at the door, then suddenly breaking through. Beata, our Glorious Leader, wrote in this week's email to all staff that *together, we can hold back even the strongest tides*, but then she's bound to say that – it's her job to ignore reality. She was born for this game of ours because she:

1. doesn't change her mind about anything
2. doesn't like explaining her decisions, and
3. is senior enough not to have to.

But instead of dictating a letter, sending an email or, God forbid, picking up a telephone to get things done, she ruffles my curls, promises me treats for good behaviour and sends me bounding across the Channel, into the corridors of not-much-power, tail wagging and tongue hanging out, messages tied to my collar. My task? To sniff the arses of those at my level, then persuade them to go home and bark at their masters that no matter which party wins the election, *it's really about time they opened their hearts to the movement*. Most of us younger generation know appeasement will fail. Right now we're busy appeasing all over Europe, in Germany, France, in Switzerland – in jobs where all sensible tactics will have no impact until it's nearly too late. Jaro understands this. Say what you like about him, but the man has a good nose for the brown stuff. *First you need to eliminate poverty*, he told me last year, on my twenty-first birthday. *Then crime.*

*Then cellulite. Then maybe we'll get people's attention. But in the meantime, we're fucked.* He forked a meatball and swallowed it in one go. *Still, at least we can die knowing we were the kind of losers who never gave in to the Dark Side.* There's another reason Beata keeps me on permanent duty in Krakow – to babysit a man twice my age who talks like the *Star Wars* trilogy is a series of historical events. In recent months, that man has decided he wants to move to Poland for good, to *live in the land of my people.* (His ancestors are mostly Lithuanian.) In recent weeks, he's talked about giving it all up. He's asked me what I think it might be like to die in a flood. You know – what the sensation of choking on water would actually feel like. If you'd guessed my role here already, please accept my congratulations, but this isn't the school tombola. There are no prizes to be given out. I'm sorry, but we're all going home empty-handed tonight.

There are about fifty seats here in the Jazzrock, and they're nearly all taken. At the front are the local regulars, each sitting cross-legged and nodding solemnly like they're receiving some news they've been waiting for their whole lives. In the middle rows there are several lone men. Some middle-aged tourists. Elsewhere, a few groups of friends in their thirties and a younger couple who might be on a first date. I'm at the back, where two wasted teenagers are dancing as if they're living on another planet which is doing just fine, thankyouverymuch. The first number goes round a few times, Magda's saxophone is carrying the melody, then she calls out, off-mic, 'Helga Emmanuelle, everybody!' and the torture begins. Helga the piano player is first to get a solo. The drummer is second. The percussionist is third, battering the bongos like he's going to break right through their skins. He gets everyone clapping along – there are even a few whoops. I get up and go to the toilet, pissing at the urinal with one hand on my hip, one thumb and forefinger pressed hard on my nose, trying to remember how I got here. I think about where Jaro might be. I rub my eyes hard, check my phone and remember there's no reception down here. Then I wash my face with cold water and return. The bongos are still centre stage.

I speak to Beata every day. While she's busy in Brussels, a place where decisions are usually postponed but occasionally actually made, she tells me she needs someone she can depend on to look after *our special boy*, the big thirsty kid who's somehow keeping us all afloat almost entirely through force of charisma. (That and rich rock star friends who empty their pockets whenever His Majesty does his little donation dance.) I know I shouldn't bite. I know I should play nice. It's just that I don't believe in guardian angels, I've been sleepwalking for weeks, I can't remember a time before Jaro, and even drunk I can't imagine life after him any more. Jaro lives behind my eyelids. He's under my fingernails. I wake up at night thinking he's sleeping in the road outside the hotel, about to get hit by a car. In this job, you get used to thinking about the worst-case scenario, so perhaps all this thinking makes sense. But still, it's emptying me out, there isn't much of me left, and every night I waste hours thinking about what I'd say to Beata if he jumped naked from the Debnicki Bridge into the Wisla River on my watch. *He was a great man, but as frail as the rest of the human race.* Or maybe, *People loved him because he was both the best and the worst of us.* Or some other shiny lie. Excuse my tone. It's just that these days I seem to spend half my life sitting in bars with no reception, listening to eight-minute percussion experiments and waiting for my boss to show. I'm sure he's dead, and that soon we all will be. Sometimes, when I try to picture the big day coming, this big water day he's always talking about, this is how I see it.

It'll be a bit like now, after a big day on the job, but with Jaro actually here. We'll be at this table, deep in the future, my head fit-to-burst with the sound of his never-ending force in one ear and the screech of yet another fucking saxophone solo in the other. After the band finish, Jaro will try to persuade me to stay later, his hands picking away at the candle wax dripping from the bottle in front of us, his eyes tiny red dots in the near darkness as he tells me about this new barmaid who works the all-night shift that he says has eyes like lollipops. I'll remind him he falls in love with Jazzrock barmaids about three times a week. The way I imagine it, he'll answer, *Look, Zyg, I like happy endings as much as you do, but these fuckers, these elect-a-holics we have to deal with every day, are afraid of their own voters.* He'll say, *And unless they start listening to us soon ...* Then he'll draw

his finger across his throat. *So let me have my lollipops, OK?* Then the
water will burst through the door, rising fast up the walls, turning
the Jazzrock into a swimming pool, then a fish tank, then a prison.
Jaro and me and the girl with the lollipop eyes will know what it feels
like to choke on water. I look around: there are no windows in these
underground clubs, and we're here three or four times a week – so
the chances are, this is where we'll be when it happens. Jaro says jazz
helps him think clearly.

It just so happens that the mixture of Tyskie beer, jazz and all that
clear thinking also makes him want to, as he puts it, *appreciate the
beauty of the female form.* But for those that think they know where this
is headed, I can tell you, Jaro isn't your tenner-in-the-panties type. He
just likes to watch the barmaids slink back and forth in their domain
while we talk and listen to the band. Occasionally he'll make light
conversation, but no more. He says he likes imagining being young,
single, free, and living in a world where he has time for affairs. He
says his wife doesn't mind. And most times, after a drink or two at the
Jazzrock, all that clear thinking just makes him want to stagger back
to the hotel room and play Osama Shootout on the Xbox until he
falls asleep with controls still in hand. For those of us in the business
of keeping Jaro breathing and out of prison, this represents another
dodged bullet. Last night, I put him to bed at 3 a.m. I took off his
shoes and pulled the covers over him. I got water, made him drink
some and he mumbled, *The thing is, Zyg … you've got to sympathize
with people's mistakes. Their reasons. If you can't sympathize in this job,
it's only fair to retire.* Then his head sank into the pillow and his body
turned to jelly. Sometimes I wonder, if I told Beata what the face of
our campaign was really doing out here, would she drag him home
and lock him in her cellar? Replace him with a sober clone? Or would
she just shrug, smile, and remind me who's in charge?

I look at my watch. Then the door.

We usually travel together. Or I suppose, I usually travel with Jaro,
dealing with all the practical stuff so he can, as he puts it, *concentrate
on the bloody macro, amigo!* That's his way of reminding me he's still the
guy on the posters and the TV adverts. The one people are thinking of
when they pledge their donations and set up their direct debits. Jaro

is a cash machine for the movement. He's a ghost. He glides from commitment to commitment, passing through the air, seeming to be everywhere but never quite being anywhere. He's making it look like we're making progress, and that means in financial terms, we actually do. But in private, the progress isn't exactly consistent. One minute he's running around the office and screaming, *We can still do this!* – the next he's got his head in his hands and saying, *I swear to God, I'm going to kill the Chancellor of Poland.* Meanwhile, my life is becoming increasingly fucking *micro.* I carry the bags. I hold the passports and the tickets. I pick him up, tell him where he has to be and why he has to be there, order the taxis to and from meetings. Before those meetings begin I have to make sure Jaro's tie is on straight so people take him seriously. It's not quite why I joined the movement, you know? I even carry super-strength chewing gum in case he's had an early start on the happy juice. Sometimes I pop a piece in his mouth when he's not paying attention. If Jaro's mind is buzzing, his mouth hangs open, inviting the flies.

He's now an hour late.

In quiet moments, Jaro admits he's sliding. Most other times, he denies it. In the car today, on the way to our first appointment, suffering with a stinking hangover, Jaro said, *Ten Tyskies a night is the only sensible response to the current reality.* He said, *Do you know what we've done to our planet?* I straightened his tie again then he shrugged me off and pointed to the skies, crying out, *Listen to me Zyg – never mind the fucking tie. Straight ties are part of the fucking problem!* Times like this, he sounds like some kind of crazy preacher. The sort of drunk you'd cross the street to avoid. The kind of person who goes about screaming that the end is nigh – and no one's gonna believe that now, are they? So it's no wonder Beata sends him everywhere with a chaperone. If I was his boss I'd send a fleet of them, and I'd pick better ones than me. I wouldn't even think about the cost. I'm no accountant, but surely to God he could go down on the spreadsheet as a legitimate business expense.

After another five or six numbers, each punctuated with lengthy break-it-downs, squeaks and squawks, the band finally give my ears a break. Magda walks off the stage, heading straight to the bar,

tossing her long, tightly curled hair as she orders a large bourbon.
The barman asks, in English, if she's heard the election result yet.
She answers, in a slow Polish-American drawl, that there are no
politics in her world. No lies and no compromise. Only the eternal
beauty of sound. The barman tells her she's full of shit and reminds
her she's back on in ten, but despite everything, for a few seconds I
think about asking Magda to hire me. I reckon I could play maracas
or something. Dance. Fuck it, I could be on *vibes* – I wouldn't want
much in return. Perhaps a handful of zlotys or a few Tyskies each
night, that's all, to play and to just be free. I may have spent years
running from these sounds, but for a moment here I think that
maybe they belong in a different world, where *essential policy change*
is a phrase nobody needs to use.

The door does not open. I'm still alone. Maybe I always will be.

Mostly I shadow Jaro, so it's possible to keep close by, but sometimes I'm scheduled to do my own thing. When I'm not babysitting
Beata's money mountain I have coffee meetings of my own, and lunch
meetings, and afternoon drinks. I get twenty minutes at a time, or
fifteen, or ten, with people who all seem to think I hold Jaro's ear in
my pocket. Lobbyists and consultants. Assistants and special advisers.
Even the occasional minister. I dizzy people with talk of conservation
targets, energy efficiency, and climate change. (Jaro tells me to talk
fast. After all, we don't have long.) I tell them what we – what *Jaro*
is trying to achieve, on behalf of us all. I cajole and persuade. I shake
hands in the way he taught me to before the drink took hold of him:
firm but not dominant. Confident but not arrogant. I'm sure to turn
up on time, smile, be polite. People can damn the system all they
like, but these details are the difference between success and another
wasted hour. In my meetings, I tell people we need to rescue our
future from the profit motive. (I mean this.) I always use the names
of the children we need to rescue it for. (The offspring of whoever I'm
talking to.) Back when he used to still give me advice, Jaro used to
say you should personalize as much as possible, to maximize impact.
So I personalize. I ask politicians how their kids are getting on at
university, school, kindergarten, then focus on our core targets. But
these fuckers say things like, *Where's the man himself, Zyg?* Or, *Why*

*don't we get a face-to-face?* Or, *Oh look out, Justyna! Here come the Green Nazis!* This is how my world works. I hear other worlds run along similar lines. No wonder some reach for the bottle.

Magda kisses the barman on the mouth and tells him not to worry. She tells him he'll feel better tomorrow. Then she returns to the stage and reaches for her saxophone. She holds it like a newborn.

Before the music starts up again I sink the rest of my drink and go back above ground, back out onto the street, waving my phone about for a while, trying to get the magic white bars to show on the display. It takes a while but finally the thing comes to life: no messages from Jaro, and when I call him it goes straight to answerphone (he's probably jumping off that bridge right now), but I do have an email from Beata reminding me that today of all days, it's important to stick to the list. Her email also includes a revised schedule for tomorrow, based on the latest set of projected results sent to her from HQ in Gdansk an hour ago. She signs off, 'It wasn't glamorous being in the French Resistance either, you know.' I think Beata knows what's coming. I go back inside and sit down again. I order another beer, wondering if, when the water comes, we'll be able to hear it before we see it.

The last time I actually saw Beata, we met in a hired meeting room in Brussels and she told me about my new assignment. Didn't she know who I was, I asked? Didn't she think I was a little overqualified to be a babysitter? But Beata doesn't have time for messing around. She said, *Your problem isn't qualifications, Zyg. Like everyone else on this continent, it's distractions.* Back then, the movement were still speaking to both sides of this particular electoral distraction. Waiting for the winner to emerge, still pitching to everyone. This last four or five days, there's only one side whose calls we even bother to answer. The people might not have spoken yet but we have a pretty good idea what they're gonna say. Polls close in an hour. They might as well not have opened at all. Anyway, when Beata gave me this assignment she handed over a list titled THINGS YOU SHOULDN'T LET JARO DO BETWEEN NOW AND THE END OF THE WORLD. Her Ten Commandments were:

1. Thou shalt not let him talk policy detail.
2. Thou shalt not schedule meetings before 11 a.m. or after 7 p.m.
3. Thou shalt not let him sack anyone, or hire anyone, without prior written approval.
4. Thou shalt not let him go on midnight jogs 'to work off dinner'.
5. Thou shalt not let him drink more than two beers a night. (Whoops.)
6. Thou shalt not let him take drugs, even if he says they are merely 'performance enhancing'. (Double whoops.)
7. Thou shalt not let him frequent all-you-can-eat buffets.
8. Thou shalt not let him have more than three consecutive hours of free 'alone time'.
9. Thou shalt not let him fall in love.
10. Thou shalt not frequent late-night clubs. Remember: scandal could strike anywhere, and WE NOW ALSO REPRESENT A NUMBER OF CHILDREN'S CHARITIES.

I asked Beata if she had any suggestions about things two powerless men trapped on a dying planet *could* do in a strange city for nights on end without getting drunk, wasted, talking politics or trying to get laid. But Beata just gave me that look where she's all eyebrows, and I've been working out here ever since. Sometimes I wonder what all this is for. If they actually need Jaro any more. No, they need him all right. All of us do. We just don't necessarily need him alive. The thing I don't ever say to anyone is, *Imagine what we could do with a dead figurehead.* I don't say it because I reckon Jaro's already thought of that.

The band finish another song to the sound of raucous applause. They start another where Magda sings about her Mississippi sweetheart leaving her, walking on down the road and never coming back. She's singing about how she wishes she wasn't so lonesome, in an accent which lurches between Texas and Warsaw. Then she starts up with the sax again.

I think, if only Jaro wasn't the way he is.

I haven't mentioned recent events to Beata, but these last few days of the campaign our man has been displaying what she calls *the classic signs.* He's been missing meetings and getting drunk first thing in the morning. Hiding from me. Talking about his wife, how she deserves a better life, and how his kids don't understand him. How they don't even fucking *recycle*. The closer we all get to you-know-what (and he's convinced we're pretty fucking close), the worse it gets. *Democracy's great for people who aren't bothered about the apocalypse*, he said. *But what we need is a dictator, and quick.* This afternoon he measured his pulse every five minutes and asked me (again) what I thought would happen at the end of the world. Without giving me time to answer, he told me he was betting on the Noah's flood scenario, and that it didn't matter which party won any more, here or anywhere. He asked me to keep a secret: that after the results, he was gonna give up the game for good. Buy a hut on top of a hill and hope the waters didn't reach him. Then he shouted, *But first we're gonna celebrate the end of our latest mission! See you at eight.* It's now half-past nine, and I'm thinking, maybe I should have mentioned this to Beata after all.

Magda is really warming up now. Between numbers she's telling a story about the town she grew up in, her father's old Etta James 45s, how she fell in love with jazz, and how really jazz music – how *all* music – is just the blues with more notes to play with.

I can see the end more clearly now: I'll have a pretty fucking similar version of the headache I've had for the last two months, and like right now I'll be alone here in the Jazzrock, in the crowd, imagining Jaro's death and how I'm gonna explain it to Beata. Then I'll see him walking towards me. He'll be drunk, dripping from the rain, and crying about the life he could have had. I'll sit him down, buy him a Tyskie and tell him we've been doing important work. That he's needed, he's a man people look up to, that I look up to, and that even if the odds aren't good, it's important not to go over to the Dark Side. While I say this, all I'll be able to think of are the expenses. After a silence I'll say, *Hey, listen. It's jazz time, amigo.* But he'll shake his head and say, *No, no, it's blues time, Zyg. Soon, we're all gonna have the blues.* Then the band will start up again and he'll get up to dance alone, just like those teenagers up the back. *Na zdrowie, amigo*, he'll say, still dancing, holding his glass to the sky. *Cheers. L'Chaim. Slainte!* Jaro will smile as if he's forgotten everything. The responsibility, the future, what we all know is coming. Then we'll clink glasses, and the water will burst through the door.

But nothing ever happens the way you imagine it.

Jaro finally arrives. He's smiling. He apologizes for being late – he says he lay down for five minutes and woke up two hours later. He's in a clean shirt and actually looks pretty fresh. He pulls me in close and hugs me. *Whatever happens*, he says, *we've done an honest job.*

We watch the band for a while in near silence, then take stools at the back of the bar, so we can hear ourselves better. Jaro is glowing. He says, *Oh Christ, I love these places! Even the bass player gets a solo, you know? This music, it's a musical fucking democracy.* He says this as if democracy is what other forms of music desperately lack. As if democracy is something he values. Then something in the brickwork distracts him and he changes the subject. *They've got no fire exits in here,* he tells me. *So if the water bursts through the entrance we'll all be equally fucked. We'll all go down together.* I say, *Maybe the band will play on as we rush for cover, like they did on the* Titanic. But Jaro laughs and says that's just a myth. He says, *Amigo, we'll either drown as one, or more likely try to claw our way out, fighting each other, trampling on the soloists and the portraits of Louis fucking Armstrong while making for the door.*

Our voices rising over the sound, we discuss what we might do next in our lives. I admit to having no suggestions. *I kind of figured this would be a lifetime's work,* I tell him. Jaro leans in and says, *It won't be obvious it's coming, Zyg. Before it happens, everyone will think we're crazy for telling them what's on its way. We're not talking about a hurricane here. No machines have been invented yet to predict this. But I can see it.* He closes his eyes and keeps talking, but lower now. *It starts with a trickle of water through the drains,* he says, *swelling up at the sides of the streets. There'll be a slight rumble in the sky, but no more. And people won't see it coming. They couldn't. They won't know what they're looking for. They'll be going about their business, thinking about their boyfriends and jobs and holidays and sick relatives. They'll be running for buses. Worrying about their tax bills. Having affairs in unnamed hotels and wishing they'd made it up with their father or mother before they died. And why not? You've got to have love for the people, amigo. You've got to forgive what they do. Something else will always seem bigger, until the second before the water bursts through the door. And when it happens? You really think the band will play on? Or you think they'll panic and eat each other?*

Jaro sees my expression and retreats.

*Actually, maybe it won't happen at all.*

He leans back and grins. Our table shakes slightly.

*Or maybe it's about to happen right now.*

Then there's a sound at the top of the stairs, by the entrance to the club. A force pushing against the door. The band seem to be getting louder. Then they go silent.

We all look round.

# MEAT

## A.L. Kennedy

MARCKO HAD ALREADY POSTED the permissions that came with the parcel: one on the door and then one each for both of the windows. Even so, he knew that his neighbours would smell the cooking and think badly of him.

His wife, had she still been here, would also have thought badly of him. She always did.

And, on this occasion, he would have agreed. He'd spent 6000 panyuan on this – a single meal.

*Irresponsibility.*

The stove was burning biomass and Sequestchar, just to heat private food when the flat was a sweat box already.

*Waste.*

Any reasonable citizen would accept that, in an ideal world, cooking and eating within your homespace was a Familybond Enhancer. It was clearly stated in most broadcasts that Freedom Choices were Smiled Upon and could be implemented without penalty. But any reasonable citizen also knew the Canteens were energy-efficient and your Bench Absence was always noted and would be kindly deplored and this wasn't an ideal world. This was Post World, when everyone was *in the same lifeboat together* and had to act accordingly.

Marcko didn't even have a Justification for this latest transgression among his so many sins. It wasn't as if he was enjoying Remarkable

Occasion. He was not marking a Belief-related, or Memory-related, or Individual-related Anniversary. This was simply Need. Marcko's own personal need.

Not even that – this was evidence of Marcko's Want.

*The most unforgivable sin.*

Marcko had harboured Self-Seeking Desire. He had strengthened and indulged it until it had kidnapped his will.

*Meat.*

He had wanted to eat meat. He had wanted his son to come back from Education and be able to sit down in the front room and eat meat.

*Meat.*

It was here now with him: a heavy, cool, moveable bundle in layered wrappers.

*Fascinating.*

*Sort of.*

Lifted out of the box, it now felt disturbing against his hands – like something with a shade of life still caught inside.

'What's that?' Dibbs came in and interrupted things before they were really ready. 'Is it a Generosity Day?'

'No. Haven't had one of them since … No.' For some reason, Marcko had lost a bit of time, just standing there with the meat. 'It's, um … Well, this is …' He tilted his burden to show the label. For some reason he didn't extend his arms, keeping the whole of the business away from his son. 'It says… well, look – *ONA Approved Bovine. Saltwaste raised flesh.* Is what it … I mean, there it is.' As if the stuff had appeared by accident and was nothing to do with Marcko and he hadn't requested it, paid for it, accepted it from a Messenger who'd looked at him with palpable disgust.

*As if I was some kind of pervert.*

*Irradiation minimal.*

He didn't read that bit aloud. Dibbs could see it and draw his own conclusions.

The wild cow hordes were almost all confined to the coastal Saltwastes and the Residue from the flooded new-gen and old-gen power stations was bound to be an issue, but apparently it did the animals no harm and you could eat them without ill-effects.

*Chernobyl Buffalo – a slice of that would cost years of water allocation. Import tax, transport tax, killing fees, preparation fees.*

*Fees only people inside the Gates have heard of.*

*Only people inside the Gates would ever hold Chernobyl Buffalo and get to worry they weren't going to cook it right.*

*No. People inside the Gates don't worry.*

*They have body servants who worry.*

*But Saltwaste flesh is probably much the same, really. Still a luxury item.*

*I have a luxury item in my rooms.*

*I have a body servant.*

*My body servant is me.*

*My flesh serves my flesh.*

*To a degree.*

Marcko – this was very clear to him – was cradling his luxury as if he was indeed a very bad kind of pervert, as if he had accepted the compensatory post-separation sexoffer from Bellata on Twelfth Level and was now presenting, perhaps, an item of triumphantly used underwear to his only son.

*Why meat?*

*I could have requested tomcod, or killifish – they're cheaper. More poisonous, but cheaper.*

*Sodsaintpauls, no. They'd have eyes.*

*A bag of little fishbodies staring at me.*

*I couldn't deal with that.*

The boy – nearly a young man, to be honest, scary how tall he was – seemed mainly puzzled, rather than repulsed, 'Flesh? In that?' He poked the bag and Marcko felt it give in response. The movement was quite sensual.

'Yeah … you know. I thought …' Marcko found himself unwilling to describe what he'd originally thought.

*That I wanted to eat something which had once been alive. Not alive like a plant: I wanted to taste the running about and making noises and thinking sort of alive. Alive the way Mr Benihan's Therapeutic Animal Companion is alive. (Although probably much more pleasant. Then again, Mr Benihan is not pleasant, so why should his TAC be?)*

Dibbs pressed his finger more gently into the acceptably radioactive package. It rustled softly.

*In the way that acceptable radiation might if one could hear it.*

*Hello, son. In the absence of your wiser and better and more morally mature and bloody intolerable mother – we won't mention that she didn't even ask to take you with her when she ran off with that bastard to the Stilts – in her absence, I decided to have something killed for your benefit. Or rather to create the pressure of demand that meant some hunter person went adventuring in, I suppose, a small boat or other vehicle equipped to cope with wetland in Suffolkponds or Norfolkponds or suchlike and took along a proper and legal allowance of fuel and maybe ammunition – undoubtedly weapons – and perhaps a protective suit and then he shot or otherwise dispatched some kind-eyed creature doing him no harm – probably a number of them, a whole family – and carried their corpses back and cut them up and I've bought us this section – I have no idea from what part of the body – and soon I will prepare it and then we'll put it in our mouths and chew it and swallow it down.*

*It will become us.*

*Something doomed and stupid will become us.*

*Can't say that.*

*Better than eyes, though.*

And there was blood.

*Oh, Geefuck.*

He stood side by side with Dibbs and slowly uncovered the thing, naked and surrounded by a mild ooze of blood.

*Fuckcockit.*

*Flesh.*

*Can we not call it flesh? Can we call it meat? We should. Flesh is something different, is what we love. It's what I loved.*

*Not what his mother loved. Or not mine, anyway.*

*Meat is food.*

*Was food.*

*I'm old fashioned in my words, there's no harm in that, I'm not a Nostalgist. I simply appreciate the names made up in more killing times to tell apart the various animals that used to live and call and breathe about the place. And it's neat and correct that we have other terms set ready to describe them when dead and cut and stripped down for eating.*

*Mutton. Woodmeat. Tarp.*

*Haven't seen tarp in years. The carcasses of magpies, that was. They talked about plagues of magpies when I was a kid, you could kill them whenever you wanted.*

*You'd still see them sometimes.*

*And then not.*

'Woo.' Dibbs made the small, happy noise he occasionally does. He was not in any way disturbed by the dark red mass and its surrounding swim of, 'Blood ... Just like us.'

*Don't say that, kid. It's dinner.*

'Yes, like us. Probably. Or maybe not blood exactly after all this time. I mean, I think they keep it – store the ... to make it soft, or more digestible or something and so the blood would ...' The smell of it – wild, heated, sickening, metally and charged – did that mean it was safe, or not safe? Was it normal? 'It would be a fluid, rather than ... No, don't.'

But Dibbs had jabbed his finger into the fluid, or blood, or whatever.

*You get diseases from blood. And fluid.*

Dibbs jerked back and a drip fell from the end of his index finger to the floor and contaminated it with death and radiation and who knew what.

*Have to clean up the mess with water. Solvent and water. More Waste.*

Marcko lifted the final bag with its increasingly alarming contents and emptied the lot of it into their pan. There was an immediate, accusatory hiss.

'Woo-ya !' Dibbs clearly delighted by the whole proceedings. He hadn't said woo-ya since his mother pissed off.

*So the cow murder and possible infections were worth it, then.*

The hissing settled into a sputtering complaint.

Marcko had read up on meat cookery – you were meant to have an extravagantly hot pan ready and let that seal the outside of the muscle fibres, because their moisture should not be lost.

*Unless it was lost in transit, leaked out to be pointlessly nasty inside protective wrappings and to scare fathers who are trying to please their sons.*

*And why shouldn't moisture be lost?*

*Is muscle meant to taste wet? Like sea vegetables?*

*I hate sea vegetables.*

He flipped and badgered their meal. It truthfully seemed less of a meal by this point and more a ridiculous gesture, or a proof of guilt.

*It's changing colour, is that right? Is that seared?*

Dibbs stared intently. 'Are you burning it?'

His son's close attention made the hairs prickle on the backs of Marcko's hands. Unless that was just the spatter and the vapours. Or the radiation.

*Burning 6000 Panyuan.*

They were probably both inhaling untold damages. 'I don't think so, loved one. I think that's it sealed, and next we can smother the fire, and the heat from the pan will do the rest.'

*I am, once again, pretending that I know what I'm talking about. I lie to him. It's what I've always done.*

*It would be worse if I didn't, if he understood how we are magpies: too-silly, too-clever, noisy, walking creatures.*

*They ate the other birds, their eggs, and then they ate each other. That's what I heard.*

Marcko continued, more and more ashamed as he tried to sound more and more certain, 'When it's cooked it's still meant to be … giving. Not just … I don't think it's meant to be too solid. And it ought to be dark brown, definitely not black.'

'Well, that's just common sense.'

'Well …'

Marcko thought it likely that Dibbs had common sense, which was good, but odd, given that neither of his parents had ever come near it. A recessive gene, maybe. A gift from the grandparents, or beyond.

*The grandparents would have remembered meat. I think … I never met them, but they'd have been around for the superfarms and the Self-Harming Nitrogen Crisis. They'd have been around for all the Self-Harm. Which isn't the best way to put it: they harmed us far more than themselves.*

*And they didn't even pass on their common sense.*

*Then again – they were the ones Self-Harming, and how commonly sensible is that?*

*Did they lie? To my parents?*

*Or did they not understand? Were they very stupid?*

*Did they look at the absence of birds, but not let themselves see?*

*Or did they just hit that age when they saw that death would come and save them from their consequences and personal dying was more of focus than anything else?*

*I think I'm at that age.*

*I think I don't give a toss really. Past it.*

The meat is shrinking. As Marcko watches, it seems to stiffen and crouch towards the back of the pan.

*Too late now. For both of us.*

*Poor meat.*

There's fat, too – the spit and sting of fat that once hid under skin, under fur of a specific length and colour. Marcko guessed the fur would be fawn. 'Imagine, dear one.' He regretted the guess at once – made him feel sickish. 'There were big hordes of these raging about the landmass once, outside the drycities ...' *Fawn and with forgiving eyes.* '...and eating personfood and turning it into less personfood and shitting everywhere.'

When Dibbs was still a young stub, he'd giggle about shitting – the inevitable, shared humiliation of producing it, weighing it, removing it. Since his Education had started he'd got more sober in every way. 'Yes, they told us. And about the concentrated hordes and the pestilences and the soil saturation. That was for last year's testing. I told you. This year, we're on to the Love Revolution.'

Kids always went for dinosaurs first – those first great, tragic extinctions: innocent and beneficial, more room for us thereafter – and then it was the Love Revolution: so much hope and the whole, sweet, terrible story behind Loveday. After that they were grown and working and didn't have much time for mindhobbies and were common sensible enough to realize the Love Revolution was no longer quite as it was when it started and no longer likely to tolerate complaints.

Marcko didn't want to picture his son in workers' blues and wearing down the hours and wondering how long he'd last at it and then maybe not caring. The grandparents would have lived to over sixty, Marcko was sure he'd read that. Nobody seemed to any more, except perhaps inside the Gates. They probably took baths and lived forever inside the Gates.

*Pretty magpies inside the Gates.*

*I do recollect them as being pretty. Handsome. They had a swagger.*

'They didn't have panyuan back then. No money at all. It must have been great, eh dad?'

'Yeah.' Marcko fidgeted the meat again – it felt ungiving. 'After Finance collapsed they didn't have anything for a while, only like an idea of money.'

'I know, I know.' Dibbs newest favourite phrase.

*You know, you know.*

*You don't, you don't.*

'I know, I know. So that we wouldn't get hooked up with Self-Seeking Desire – so we'd only do things for each other because we wanted to and other people would do them back.'

*It must have been beautiful.*

When he was Dibbs's age Marcko had learned the old measures of the Lovetime, the calculations of goods and services. They were designed to instil an appropriate loathing of Reckless Finance and its wrongs: a hundred tears makes one hurt, a hundred hurts makes one misery, one misery keeps three people for one day: father, mother, child in all their comforts: bread, heat, water, light, and fellowship. *And each should have enough and no more than enough.* In this way the wrongs of Profitinterest had been memorialized and the Sacrifices were remembered – the spilling of blood – and whatever was left in the not ideal world was shared.

'And they stopped people drowning in Elsewhere, or dying of thirst and it's OK now. And that means that we can have panyuan these days because we're sensible. *All in the same lifeboat.*'

Of course, no one Marcko knew had been to Elsewhere and no one ever seemed to come from there any more. And the Punishment Tornadoes persisted and the Long Heats grew and the Punishment Freezes lengthened the Winters and the Free Occupationists' Assembly had become the National Occupationist Authority, because that was more businesslike. And inside the Gates, people were in a different lifeboat altogether.

*With us outside and looking at them – living and calling and breathing about the place.*

'Is it done?' His boy expecting an authoritative answer.

'I think so. I think.'

Dibbs scurrying as if it was Loveday, slicing the bread ration.

Marcko's mouth had started to feel odd, wracked by a sudden and excessive appetite. 'No need for anything on the bread, loved one. We can dip it in the juices.' He felt animal, yet also cheerful.

*Perhaps the art of everything is to be animal and cheerful, to keep on and never mind.*

'Did they used to do that, Dad?'

'Yes.'

*I have no idea.*

'Yes, they did.'

Marcko sets the meat on a plate and lets it *rest* for exactly five minutes. They both stare at it during this period, as if it will indicate when it is ready and relaxed. It does not.

*At least it can't stare back, though. No eyes.*

'Here we go, then …' Finally, Marcko picks up their best knife. He's sure that Dibbs would like to cut the meat, but if everything about their meal turns out to be terrible he wants the boy to be not involved, for nothing to be his fault.

Marcko feels only a kind of unwillingness under the blade and then the flesh is in two pieces – the bigger one for his son. The sliced wound releases a defeated moisture.

*So I did preserve it.*

*But now it's going.*

They wipe their bread round the pan and mop at the plate. Then father and son make sandwiches, which is an old, old traditional dish.

To Marcko the meat is leathery and tastes of grease and wrongness. The bread seems rancid. Nevertheless, he eats keenly. He is aware that Dibbs, sitting opposite, is doing exactly the same. They don't speak.

Things haven't turned out well.

In a while they will tidy up and listen to the radio broadcast and then Marcko will go out to work while Dibbs gets to sleep.

Things haven't turned out well at all.

Sad to think so and sadder to know that it wasn't their fault.

*So best to be animal, to keep on and never mind.*

# THE GREAT CONSUMER

## Adam Marek

INT. BEDROOM. NIGHT.

*The décor is 1950s. A lamp on the bedside table is lit. There is someone asleep in the bed. A man:* VICTOR. *His legs are crossed at the ankles. His bare feet poke out from beneath a tartan blanket. On the bed beside him a pair of spectacles rests on a yellow legal notepad. Several pages have been filled and flipped over so that we can see his black handwriting in reverse. The facing page contains two paragraphs. The extravagant length of the ascenders and descenders, and the slope of the writing suggest that it was written at speed and with great excitement.*

*From behind, we hear a noise. A creaking floorboard. There is a brown leather sofa in the room and hiding behind it is a young man, maybe seventeen years old:* MARTY. *He looks panicked. He is sweating, maybe because it's hot and he's wearing so many layers: an orange bodywarmer over a denim jacket over a blue checked shirt over a maroon T-shirt. He shifts his position and stumbles. When his hand goes down to stop himself from toppling over, the chunky silver revolver he is carrying knocks loudly on the floorboards.*

*Someone says 'Sssssssh!'*

*Marty leaps up, full of panic, for a second standing fully upright. He hides the gun behind his back. His cheeks are flushed and his breath is wildly out of control. He looks about to see who has made the sound. The man in the bed is still asleep. It takes him some seconds to notice that behind the sofa with him is a man no more than four feet tall:* RANDALL.

*Randall is older than the teenager, maybe in his thirties. He is wearing a leather flying helmet and an almost medieval-looking jacket-and-trouser ensemble in red cloth. Over the top of this are slung leather utility belts, one crossing each shoulder and one around his waist. He has a monocle pinched into one eye and is holding a tattered map which is predominantly dark blue.*

RANDALL (*Softer this time, wafting the map to suggest that the boy squats down*):
  Sssssssh.

*Marty crouches. He keeps the gun behind his back.*

RANDALL:
  Don't worry, Marty. I'm here to help.

MARTY (*Whispering*):
  Who the hell are you?

RANDALL:
  I'm like you. You know. Not from around here.

MARTY:
  What are you doing here?

RANDALL:
  I'm not here to get in your way. You just get on with what you've got to do, and then I'll take care of the evidence for you.

*Marty peeks up over the top of the sofa to check that the man is still asleep.*

MARTY:
  Did the Doc send you?

RANDALL:

No no no. I'm just a humble collector, and that gun you've got behind your back is about to become very valuable to me, and very dangerous to you, so in the spirit of friendship, you know, one traveller to another, I will relieve you of it and then we can be on our way.

MARTY (*Pointing to the man in the bed*):

So, you know about this guy?

RANDALL:

I do.

MARTY:

And, am I doing the right thing?

RANDALL:

Absolutely. And the quicker you get it done, my friend, the better.

MARTY:

But, you know, this is really heavy. I mean, I've changed things before, but not like this. I know even small things can have big consequences, but this is …

RANDALL (*Putting his hand on Marty's shoulder*):

You've got doubts. Of course you have. But let me reassure you: you've already done this. Where I'm from this moment is history.

MARTY:

So you've seen the future? The *new* future I mean. Does it all work out after?

RANDALL:

Everything's just how it should be. Now, get a move on. It'll be much harder if he wakes up.

*Marty takes two carefully placed footsteps towards the bed, then stops and looks up. Classical music is playing somewhere above. It gets louder and louder, heavy on the strings, heralding something spectacular. And then it arrives. An aluminium and glass phone booth slides down through the ceiling. It makes ripples, as if the ceiling is not solid, but a milky liquid. Orange lightning crackles all over the booth and the wire antenna on its roof. Marty and Randall watch its arrival in the middle of the bedroom floor, their eyes popping. The classical music segues neatly into eighties stadium rock as the door of the booth swings open and another teenager steps out:* TED. *He is tall, with a thick mop of long black hair. He is wearing two pairs of socks, one white and one orange, black surfer shorts over slightly longer white shorts, Converse boots, a white T-shirt, and a black waistcoat. An orange jacket is tied around his waist.*

TED (*He flings one hand up in greeting, the other on his stomach*):
    Greetings, my excellent friends. I come with warnings *most* grave.

*Marty slaps his forehead and runs his fingers back through his hair.*

MARTY:
    This is insane.

*In the bed, the man is still asleep.*

RANDALL:
    When did *you* come from?

TED (*To Marty*):
    Dude, it is most *most* important that you put that gun away. You have no idea of the heinous consequences of what you are about to do.

RANDALL:
    Don't listen to him, Marty. Take the shot now. While you still can. Think about the whales, Marty. Think about your family.

TED:
    Do *not* listen to the little dude, dude. I know why you're here. A man named Doc Brown sent you a picture of Hill Valley, California in 2065, and a gun loaded with one bullet. On the back is this address and a message that says, Marty ...

*Marty takes the photo out of his back pocket.*

MARTY and TED together:
…you MUST shoot Vic Samuels on March 17, 1955 at 01:35 a.m. or Hill Valley and the rest of the world are DOOMED.

RANDALL (*Consulting a pocket watch*):
Exactly, and you're almost out of time.

*Marty turns the picture over to look at the front. It shows a courthouse and the surrounding town in flames.*

RANDALL:
I've seen the future, Marty, and it's an ugly place. The air is too poisonous to breathe without masks. The seas are so full of acid that there are no fish. People live in tribes that kill each other for scraps of food and fuel. And it's all the fault of that man there in bed. *He's* the one that started it all.

TED:
Hold your horses there, little buddy. Marty, yes, there's going to be a dark time ahead. And yes, in some ways consumer society can be traced back to the report this man is going to hand in tomorrow, but it's not bad *everywhere*, and not forever. It's this most bogus time that pushes mankind to develop new technologies and new ways of living. Soon, the world becomes awesome again, dude, and scientists find ways to make all those extinct animals alive again. It is a most triumphant time.

RANDALL:
But millions die before then. You don't want that on your hands, Marty.

MARTY:
How did this become *my* responsibility?

RANDALL:
Just take the shot quickly, Marty. You can't trust someone who rides around in a phone booth and dresses like that.

TED:

He's wrong, Marty. The world does have to go through it. It's like mankind's puberty, dude. It's ugly and it kind of stinks, but we come through it better. I'm here because I've seen the future you create if you shoot Vic Samuels tonight. There are no malls! The joy of shopping that Vic gave to the world was the thing that broke down barriers between countries so we could all swap excellent products. Without it there's a war, dude, the worst war in history and it lasts for *forty years* and kills *billions* of people. That future is a *dark* place, full of heinous machines that are half ...

*There is a deep, ominous keyboard thrum that sets everything in the room shaking. The wristwatch and coins on the bedside table slide along it and drop off the side. The lamp flickers on and off. Marty, Randall, and Ted look around as bright blue lightning flickers over the ceiling, the bed. It's everywhere, and the music is building all the time, the thrumming louder. More objects fall from surfaces and clatter on the floor: books, a comb, cologne.*

MARTY:

What's happening!

*The lightning doubles in intensity, filling the room with blinding light, and suddenly, with a crack, it ends. In the centre of the room, in front of Ted's time machine, is a naked man crouched on the floor. Smoke clings to him, and to the rug beneath his feet. The man stands up with dramatic slowness, lifting his head last. He is tall and impossibly muscular. Scarily so. His expression is grim. He opens his eyes and looks slowly left and right, as if scanning the room. The others watch him for a moment, until he turns and looks at the man in the bed*

NAKED MAN (*In a thick Austrian accent*):

Vic Samuels.

*The naked man leaps onto the bed and grabs the sleeping man around the neck.*

TED:

No way!

*Ted moves to attack the naked man, but pauses for a moment, a look of disgust on his face. He doesn't seem to know how to tackle him. Instead, he grabs the lamp and smashes it against the man's back. This has no effect. The naked man continues to strangle Vic.*

TED:

Shoot him, Marty! You've got to save Vic Samuels!

RANDALL:

Don't! You've only got one bullet!

MARTY:

What should I do!?

*Randall runs to the corner of the room and pushes over a coat stand. He shakes off the coats and hats, thwacks the stand against the floor to break off the end, and then using the now sharp pole like a lance, charges at the naked man and runs the end of it into his side. A large strip of flesh peels away, revealing gleaming chrome ribs beneath.*

MARTY:

Holy shit!

TED:

We have to stop him!

RANDALL:

It has to be *you* that kills Vic!

*All three men throw things at the naked cyborg: pillows, pens, shoes. They kick him. But none of these efforts has any effect. Vic Samuels' face is purple. His eyes, now open, are bulging. His tongue is spilling from his open mouth.*

*A sound builds up, louder and louder, a slow grinding pulse, like someone scraping a key along piano strings. And then a big blue police box materializes alongside Ted's phone booth, a light atop it whirring round and round. When the sound ends, the door flings open, and a man leaps out. He is tall and skinny, wearing a tweed suit and a bowtie. His fringe is long and floppy:* THE DOCTOR. *He holds out a device, which looks a bit like a fat silver pen. A green light on it ignites and it makes a high-pitched sound. The naked cyborg freezes.*

THE DOCTOR:
That's quite enough of *that*! T800s are so *big* aren't they?

*(He squeezes one of his own biceps and makes a sulky pout)*

Too big, if you ask me. Yes. OK. Who have we got here then, let's take a look.

MARTY:
Who *are* you?

THE DOCTOR:
I'm the Doctor.

RANDALL:
The one that sent the photo?

THE DOCTOR:
Photo?

MARTY:
He's not my Doc.

TED:
Most excellent time machine, dude.

THE DOCTOR:
Thanks. I like yours too. Very … compact. Is it bigger on the inside?

TED:
Unfortunately not. It can be *most* impractical for transporting personages of historical significance.

*The Doctor swings around on the spot, pressing something on his silver device as he holds it up towards everyone. He examines the device closely for a second.*

THE DOCTOR:

Ah hah! So, four other time travellers all converging here in the bedroom of Vic Samuels, a man only remembered for the world-changing report he wrote about how nice it would be if everyone just bought more stuff. The very report he has just penned ... I'm guessing. And you've all come here to change the future. This is great, I feel like Hercule Poirot. (*He paces around the room with a cocky swagger*) I feel like I should have a pipe, or was that the other one? Anyway, hello! You've got a gun (*Points at Marty*), and you've got a map and you've got a ... what's that you're holding, is that a candlestick?

TED:

It is.

THE DOCTOR:

Quite like a game of Cluedo, really. I do like a game of Cluedo. So who did it, or is about to do it? Was it you in the bedroom with the gun, Mr ...?

MARTY:

McFly. Marty McFly. I haven't killed anyone yet and to be honest I just want to know what the hell is going on here. Is Vic Samuels dead?

*The Doctor goes over to the bed. Vic is lying beneath the naked cyborg. The cyborg's hands are still frozen in the strangling position, but Vic's neck is no longer between them. The Doctor places his ear close to Vic's mouth.*

THE DOCTOR:

No, he's still breathing.

MARTY:

All I know is, the Doc gave me a gun and told me to come back here tonight and shoot this guy, and if I don't the whole world is gonna end. And this guy wants the gun when I'm done, and this guy wants me to let the world end so it can be born again. And then this ... cyborg shows up, and if he's a bad cyborg and he wants to kill the person I'm here to kill, then does that make me a bad person too? I don't know what I'm supposed to do.

TED:

Just don't shoot, dude.

RANDALL:

You have to shoot. You already shot. If that future didn't already exist then this lot wouldn't have turned up trying to stop it. Trust me, it all works out OK in the end. The best future is the one where you shoot that man.

TED (*To Marty*):

No, my time-travelling buddy. Changing the past has most bogus consequences.

*The Doctor claps his hands once, loudly, and they all stop and look at him.*

THE DOCTOR:

What we have here is what we used to call on Gallifrey a Hot Cross Paradox.

MARTY:

A what?

THE DOCTOR:

When you have more than one time traveller present from different time streams all gathered at the moment of intersection, you get a Hot Cross Paradox. It's a bit like the Hangar Lane gyratory system but with space-time instead of tarmac. And you're all here to represent your own futures.

MARTY:

But whose future is the right one?

THE DOCTOR:

Well, when you've got a Hot Cross Paradox, the whole of the space-time continuum is locked briefly, while all the possibilities present in the room are equally balanced. But it doesn't last for long. If you don't decide which way it's going to go, the walls of reality begin to creak. In fact, yes, you can already hear it …

*They all listen.*

MARTY:

I *can* hear something. It's like a heartbeat.

TED:

Or someone running.

MARTY:

So how do we decide whose future is the right one?

THE DOCTOR:

All future's being equal, we need an impartial randomizer of some kind to make the decision for us. (*The doctor reaches into his pocket and takes out a coin*) Heads or tails?

RANDALL:

Hang on a minute. I'm *more* than just a time traveller. I travel between dimensions. I work for *him*. (*He looks up*)

*The Doctor looks up at the ceiling too.*

THE DOCTOR:

For him? Which one?

*The sound of someone running gets louder and louder, and then the bedroom door bursts open. A man in a long black coat is standing there:* NEO. *He is wearing dark glasses. He bears a striking resemblance to Ted.*

TED:

Whoa … are you like, *me*, from a *future* future?

NEO:

No. I'm not you because you're not real. None of you is real.

THE DOCTOR:

Now this guy I like.

NEO:

You are all constructs. Fictions in the mind of the real protagonist of the story, Vic Samuels, who is not asleep in bed, but in an armchair sometime in the early twenty-first century. The gun is in *his* hands, not yours. You are his proxy. If you fire the gun, you do not fire the gun. He fires the gun. Time travel is not possible. You cannot undo the present and make a new one. You are all here as emanations of an old man's guilt, a man coming to the end of his life, looking at all he has created, and wondering whether he is the hero or the villain of his own story.

MARTY:

So, should I shoot him or not?

TED:

No!

RANDALL:

Yes!

THE DOCTOR:

If you drop an egg on the floor and it smashes, do you solve the problem by going back in time to shoot the chicken that laid it?

NEO:

It's not up to you, Marty. That's not your finger on the trigger.

MARTY:

This is crazy. I just want to save my family …

TED:

This is bigger than your family, dude.

MARTY:

I don't know which of you to trust. I just want to know the truth.

NEO:

There is no truth. We all have our own truths. Which one you choose is up to you.

MARTY:

Is Vic Samuels a bad man or a good man?

NEO:

There is no bad or good.

*There is a loud gunshot. BANG! A startling flash of light.*

THE WRITER (*Voice-over*):

What the hell was that?

*The time travellers are gone. The bed is empty. Morning light is breaking through the half-open curtains, illuminating a haze of smoke that floats in a wavering layer. We hear a loud knock on the floorboards. From floor level, we see the dropped revolver, and the old man's hand from which it has fallen. A streak of blood runs down the back of his hand, along his index finger, swelling into a single drop on his fingertip.*

THE WRITER:

Damn it. That's not what I was going for. That wasn't my intention at all.

# A STRAND IN THE WEB

*Man did not weave the web of life, he is merely a strand in it. Whatever he does to the web, he does to himself.*

*Chief Seattle*

# WHAT IS LEFT TO SEE?

## James Miller

ME5ELLE'S DAYBLOG. 12 JANUARY, 2037

*#Me5elle is live*

#Me5elle #waxpoetical #self-reflection. Yesterday was my dad's six-tieth. Today, for his present, we went to look at Miami. Dad was born there and he wanted to see what was left after the storms. Mom wasn't so keen so she remained on the ship, but Barak and me were totally aerated by the whole concept. I mean, they say it's not safe and before we got the helicopter we had to sign something that said NewWorldTours.com were not responsible if anything happened, but then we had these Darkwater guards and I was like, why not? #hotdarkwater. If it's going to happen, whatever it is, let it happen. And the helicopter was pretty cool. I've never been in one before and this wasn't one of the Bubblepods or NaviChoppers they have on board but a proper military heavyweight #africanting, black and bristling with antennae and weapons. It was just me and Dad and Barak, plus this other old guy from the ship who wore a Hawaiian shirt and then our guide Jamie #cutegay and five Darkwater guys with black shades and machine guns.

*#zincbitch is live.*

#zincbitch: #hotdarkwater?

#Me5elle: New one #hotdarkwater.

#zincbitch: Steroid maximus @#hotdarkwater.

#Me5elle: J I'm gonna post some Y-phone pics.

#zincbitch: Awesome! Love the colours. U using that retro app?

#Me5elle: J Old skool digi effect.

#zincbitch: Cool! I'm busting a tampon for you babe!

#Me5elle: Austerity measures #newgirl! Anyway, like this dude in the shirt and my dad talk about what happened.

#zincbitch: I thought Miami was always that way, like Detroit?

**#Me5elle #zincbitch #livechatnow! @#Me5elle, You have 75 friends watching CLICK HERE to see who #joinlivechatnow. You have 23 friends streaming CLICK HERE to see who #joinlivechatnow. You have 237 friends currently live CLICK HERE to see who #joinlivechatnow.**

#Me5elle: #spacehead No way! You know the storm, the one that wiped out half the state? I know there have been lots of them.

#zincbitch: Were we born then?

#Me5elle: Dude, don't tweak the tweet! C'mon we were mall age!

**Key Tags: Miami; Storm-Zone; Birthday; Father; 60th; Adventure; Trip; Quest; Catastrophe – General; Catastrophe – Environmental.**

**Key Tags Sponsored: Florida Tourist Board; SunShineState.com; NewWorldTours.com; DarkWater Services Inc; InterServices Department; Bank of America; Bank of New America; BP; Shell; DiaCom; New World Consulting.**

**State Dept Update: Current Status Calm.**

**Metrological Service Update: Fine, sunny, 9% cloud, 73% humidity, SWW 12mph, Max 105F, Min 81F, light rain expected 03.10–04.30hrs.**

**Storm Level: Low; 16% probability next 100hrs. Next expected storm <500hrs**

#Me5elle: Anyway, stop putting static in my talkback.

#zincbitch: ISS.

#Me5elle: DWAI. K so we were flying low towards Miami Beach. You could see the cruise liner for ages as it was so big, like this white city floating in the ocean. The ship wouldn't come closer. Apparently the captain was worried about being shot at by missiles or pirate attack. It happens.

#zincbitch: #africanting.

#Me5elle: Word.

#zincbitch: #Mpod?

#Me5elle: The Dirty Christians, I Get Lifted, Old Testament remixes, DJ Leviticus.

#zincbitch: Loose!

#Me5elle: I also sneaked a few of those Tokyo buzz cubes and smart bombs. I dropped a couple before we set off. I was coming up as we went down.

#zincbitch: Radicalized!

#Me5elle: Triplebitchy. I was smurfing all the colours. I got out my I-3DCamCan as we went in but the man in the shirt stopped me.

#zincbitch: #medianazi.

#Me5elle: Total. Federated. Witch Man.

#zincbitch: Is it true they have them down there?

#Me5elle: 100% Total KKK fest. #KKKsucks. Like 100% Total. God squad, but what can you do?

#zincbitch: OMFG.

#Me5elle: Yeah! So I just have to Blog it all, but actually it's elite because I saw like contraband intelligence. A forbidden city. A city lost to the storms.

#zincbitch: #lovepoetical. You waxing so pretty girl!

#Me5elle: DMI.

**@#zincbitch You have 106 friends watching CLICK HERE to see who. #joinlivechatnow. You have 94 friends streaming CLICK HERE to see who. #joinlivechatnow. You have 2134 friends live CLICK HERE to see who. #joinlivechatnow.**

#Me5elle: So you could see the famous beach – it's like long and thin and sort of an island and it's all a bit like that and everything is sort of there but it's all smashed up. I wish I had more pix to post. Words just don't carry what I was seeing. #HollywoodUnreal #ApocalypseWatch. Dad was so cute, going oh look that's so and so or I can see this place. He was a bit sad too because he'd be like that was where we used to shop but it's all gone now #melancholy-mallrats.

#zincbitch: Emoting your sentiment #lovemydad. I guess he saw the place where he grew up turned all snarly? #lovemydad That would be a mood dropper. Good job us @#newgirls don't get so bothered #environment-attachment so #oldtimer.

#Me5elle: #waxpoetical #self-reflection. We flew real low and I could
see all the buildings real close and thought deep about what it was
to live there for all those people and what happened and what
it would mean to lose everything. Barak just wanted to ask the
guards about their guns #totaladolescent.

#zincbitch: GRFOW!

#Me5elle: Then we started flying over more water and it was full of
trash and dead stuff. It was a swampfest and I had an attachment
issue. I mean, how can this happen right?

#zincbitch: #waxpolitical.

#Me5elle: We weren't allowed to land downtown. Too dangerous.
Total #Mogadishu. All these retro skyscrapers, not antique like
Detroit, but retro po-mo and super-snarly like the downtown in
#TakeNewYork on the XboxX10. And we were sweeping round to
avoid sniper fire, that was what they said and the super-real exciting
thing about it was the guards were ultra serious and focused as if
some #BlackHawkDown scenario was about to unfold.

*#DunderChunder is live.*

#DunderChunder: Hey!

#Me5elle: #zincbitch Hey.

#DunderChunder: @#Me5elle why didn't you 5 me back?

#Me5elle: @#DunderChunder dude! I'm #livechat here and this is a
#waxpoetic tribute about my dad's birthday #ilovemydad. Private
channel me later for grievance issues K?

#zincbitch: @#DunderChunder stop being such a #bitchboy #lameface.

#DunderChunder: WFUT.

*#DunderChunder is offline.*

#Me5elle: WTF! #totaladolescent.

#zincbitch: You know that's why I only #date-a-college-guy. Update
me baby.

#Me5elle: TFA! We whizz round past these skyscrapers and I can see
over the whole city. #factoid Miami once had eight million people.

#zincbitch: Before storm?

#Me5elle: Affirm!

#zincbitch: #waxpoetical I need mind pictures. #waxpoetical come
give me!

#Me5elle: Sorry just bummed by #DunderChunder. Yeah I know #forget-him right? K this. Miami, dig? The first storm, the real big one, #Hurricane-Winthrop, winds were more than 300 miles per hour. There was a storm surge with waves like 150ft high and super-fast. The water just ram down and mash up Miami, Judgement Day style, #911 over-fest like tsunami #JapanTsu2011, #IndianOcTsu2004, #IndonesiaTsu2015, #PacficTsu2019, but no earthquake driving it. This was heavy weather wind and sun. You saw the film, right? #TheWaves.

#zincbitch: The one with Madonna's grandson? #GILF #Sublime-Apocalypse.

#Me5elle: Yeah. Real words #newgirl, real words. We loop back to Miami Beach. Apparently it's a bit safer and land on the roof of this old condo. We went down fast and my stomach flipped a bit. The buzzcubes didn't help #puke-a-troid. Anyway, so we wait on the chopper while the #hotdarkwater dudes run around and make a 'perimeter' as they call it. Jamie #cutegay said it was like the strongest building on the beach still standing and it was real antique, like 1950s. Hang on, let me WikiToke it to you #Hotel-Fontainbleau-MiamiBeach.

#zincbitch: I'm feeling that.

#Me5elle: Not even retro Modern but Modern-Modern. Back-time it used to be super-classy, VIP to the max. I'm talking ultra bitch levels, like #ParisHilton.

#zincbitch: Girl I'm just seat tripping here. Vlog me more! So jealous, I'm like pea-souping it, I'm just a little green pea.

#Me5elle: Double dig! OK, like, for the trip I had my #RalphLauren #SunSuit and #Oakley #Radiation-Shades with #Gucci #SpannerMask and my #G-Star #SlutWalkers.

#zincbitch: You can really carry that #WeatherWear. I just look like a dufus in that garb, a total #SarahPalin.

#Me5elle: I need it. We're talking cold season and it's still HAF. I was a #SweatyBetty #PussyDrip.

#zincbitch: Heat like that just uplifts me to the cool valleys of Idaho.

#Me5elle: So total with you #zincbitch. I am #valleygirl all the way. #LoveIdaho #RealUSA. Like Daddy keeps saying we've got to be #thankful. Other are bummed out in the SunSlums with #medianazis and #WitchHunters for company. At least we are Scooby-dooed! Anyway, I'm drifting.

#zincbitch: #waxpoetical.

#Me5elle: We all stand on the roof of this hotel and Jamie points out various landmarks to me and Barak. Dad and the Hawaiian shirt dude stand a little way off, talking about something. The helicopter takes off again, which made me feel a bit #attachment-issue but apparently they had to do that. The #hotdarkwater guys were posing with their guns and looking at shit with their infra-cams and Spy-Wear. One thing that hit me, once the chopper was away, was just how quiet it is #StormZone. I could hear nothing, not even the sea because it's so choked up with consumer-sludge and plastic from the #1stArtificialAge. Apparently the sea isn't even the same as it was before. The molecules are all different now, that's what Dad says. They are trying to synth new ones at his laboratory #ilovemydad he's so geeky. The only sound was the sound of the old buildings creaking and groaning and birds chirping each other as they ate the bugs in the sky, and you could hear these bugs croaking and trilling and humming, and with the buzz cubes it all seemed extra sharp, you know. I could see the pollution and the insect-drone as a yellow mask in the bottom part of the sky and all the old palm trees that had been carbonized, I mean serious #africanting. They all lost their leaves and just stood like clusters of dead candles.

#zincbitch: Pix-tripping J!

*#PlatinumPrincess is live.*

#PlatinumPrincess: @Me5elle @#StormZone @#Miami! WTFx3!! Why don't you #Mogadishu my bikini-line? Are you some kind of #FoxNewsWarrior now? Baste me a dildo #newgirl!

#zincbitch: GTFU PP!

#PlatinumPrincess: Chill zinc-o. I'm just playing the dozens.

#Me5elle: K it's Cool. Hail up @#PlatinumPrincess.

*#LEDmore is live.*

#LEDmore: Word to the 5elle. 5 up! Just scanning your #waxpoetical you #waxdeep #newgirl.

#Me5elle: Hail up @#LEDmore. #BigLove. #waxpolitical. My dad wanted to see if we could visit his old hood but Jamie said it was pretty much all gone. I was balled though, Barak too. Jamie said Miami was less dangerous than it used to be. They cleared most of the gangslammers, bumboys and #africanting out last year. Mostly it's just #ghost-town. But we did hear some bangs, like pop pop but far away. Barak thought we were being shot at but #hotdarkwater didn't seem too worried. We only had ten minutes roof time before the chopper came back. #ilovemydad he even wiped away a tear or two as we got back inside. The other dude was filming with an I-3DCamCan, next generation model.

#zincbitch: HFS! You have to be a Prime to get those. Even my pops can't get one until next year.

#Me5elle: He was federated, like I said. A Witch-Dude.

#zinbitch: Word.

#LEDmore: Real word.

#Me5elle: #self-reflection seeing Miami made me think about the world and what we're doing to it. I think all us @#newgirls and @#man-guy could make more effort, I don't mean #attachment-issue but #Better-Environment and we should be more grateful and pray #ILoveJesus to show our gratitude that we were born #valleygirls in #IloveIdaho #RealUSA where it still snows and they have fish in the rivers and that we're not some poor sun-junky in the sun-slums SATELLITE – INTERRUPTED STREAM … PLEASE WAIT. UP-LOADING IN TEN … UP-LOADING IN TWENTY … PLEASE WAIT …

ATHENS, GREECE. JUST AFTER NOW.

Abu-Bakr smiled at the American girl and stopped turning the pages. He had no idea how she expected him to respond. 'Very good,' he said. He could read English, but most of what she had written seemed incomprehensible. The American girl, her name was Jennifer, blushed and said, 'It's just a rough draft, nothing really …' and gave a bashful shrug. 'Oh, do you want another pita? Are you still hungry?'

Abu-Bakr was still hungry. The American girl sensed this and signalled to the cafe owner. The proprietor didn't look particularly happy, and Abu-Bakr knew it was because he was not supposed to be in this place with the tourists, where he could be seen. Three months in Athens and he was starting to hate the city. Every day he went with the others to Plaka and there he stood in a small square surrounded by tourist shops and restaurants, his merchandise wrapped in a blanket and stuffed in heavy bags. Certain areas were OK, other areas less so, but wherever he was he had to watch out, not only for the police but also the men who controlled the trade and decided who sold what where. The police would just move him on, but those other men – who could say what they might do?

His pita arrived; just chips, salad, and sauce inside. 'See, I remembered?' The American girl first spoke to Abu-Bakr two weeks ago. Jennifer Constantine was her name. She was from New York, 'the state not the city', but 'originally' she was Greek, she said. He liked the way she said 'originally', opening her mouth as if the syllables were too big. 'Originally', he was also from somewhere else. 'Jennifer Constantine'. To his tongue the name tasted funny. She was plump, friendly, and sensible and she wore the same short pants and vest top all the American girls seemed to wear. Her legs were chubby and tanned and she had short, brown hair yanked back in a tight bun. He thought her face was a friendly one and she had kind eyes that seemed patient and indulgent. Abu-Bakr asked her if she was married and when she laughed off the question he said she would make a good wife. Afterwards, he thought maybe this had been the wrong thing to say. 'Jennifer Constantine'. She was 'twenty-three', she said. Abu-Bakr was twenty-five. Close in age, but she was so unlike his wife or sisters or any woman he had ever met before that it was difficult to know what to make of her.

The first time she saw him, she said, she bought a fake Gucci bag. He didn't remember the sale but she still had the bag. 'It's very practical,' she said. 'And who needs a real one? This is just as good.' He could see the zip was already jammed, but she didn't mention that.

The second time, she bought a pink sun umbrella. He remembered her because she tried to speak to him. He was never very good when the tourists asked him things, usually just stupid questions like 'Which way to the Acropolis?' as if he was a tourist guide or had ever done more than look up at the famous rock with its ancient ruin. He knew it had been a great temple, then a church and a mosque, and now it was something altogether different – a monument to time itself, perhaps, a reminder that everything would fall. No matter. The world was full of ruins and he didn't have money for admission.

Jennifer Constantine asked him different sorts of questions. Where was he from? What was his name? Why was he doing this? At first he was suspicious. She didn't look like police, but who could say? Now, after they had met a few times, he understood better what she was trying to do. She was trying to see him. She was working out what it was that she could see. All the same, he had no idea how to answer her questions. Even in his own language he didn't have words to explain it all. She smiled as if she understood and gave him ten euros for the umbrella. 'Keep the change,' she told him.

When the day was over he met the others. They came from everywhere – from Somalia, Sudan, and the Ivory Coast, Guinea and Yemen, Iraq and Afghanistan, Tunisia, and Bangladesh. Their stories were all different, but the theme was always the same: pushed from their land by drought, famine, and flood, driven onwards by war and unrest. Abu-Bakr had thought it was just his country that was broken. Now he realized it was half the world.

They took the bus back to the flat, a long drive through sprawling suburbs. There Spiros was waiting, ready to check the merchandise and take his cut. However much money they made, and most days they made very little, the largest share always went to Spiros. Spiros or one of his men would have new stock – more umbrellas, fake watches and bags, stupid toys. All plastic, junk, nothing anyone wanted. Sometimes they were made to buy the stock up-front. An extra incentive to sell, Spiros said to them, although sometimes they sold nothing. They couldn't cheat Spiros. He had his thugs, and Abu-Bakr had watched them beat a man senseless and throw him on the street. There was nothing to be done.

Half the world was broken, but the better half was meant to be in Europe. Even so, the situation in Greece was difficult. People spoke about the 'crisis': no work, no money, everything so expensive. He had seen the protests outside parliament, the riot police firing tear gas, the crowds like people he had seen everywhere, all of them angry, desperate, and trapped. On their faces, the same frustration he felt, the same worn fears. During the protests, Spiros brought gas masks and laser pens to sell to the crowds. They made more money than usual. The riots were bad, but at least there was no civil war. At least they could still drink the water and the electricity worked and there was food in the shops and at night people could go out and enjoy themselves. The police might beat them in the square, but they were not children with guns, high on drugs and desperate for food. They were not allowed to kill them.

At sunrise and sundown they went onto the roof of the apartment and bowed to the east, to another ancient city none of them had ever seen. Every night they cooked rice and talked about getting away, of travelling to Patras where there were boats to Italy and from where anything seemed possible: France, Germany, England, Sweden or Holland, places with green grass, grey skies, cool rain. Places where they said you could get work and a decent place to live. Abu-Bakr didn't know if all was true. Mohammad had relations in London, and Ismail had family in Brussels, and they clung to the promise of these contacts, specks of light in the darkness, distant stars with which to chart their journey. If these others had made it, so could they.

Jennifer Constantine was also travelling. She had always wanted to see Europe. She laughed when he said it was something they had in common. 'Europe'. She told him about her trip. England was great, London was cool, Paris was beautiful, France was wonderful, and Italy just enchanting, but everywhere was very expensive. Now she was staying with cousins in Athens after visiting Rhodes, Santorini, and the Cyclades. Had he seen the islands? The beaches? No, he shook his head. No islands, no beaches.

Abu-Bakr found it easier to ask Jennifer questions than answer them. She was happy to talk about herself. 'Oh my God, if you let me, I could talk all day, I'm just a big blabbermouth, that's what my mom says anyhow.' She told Abu-Bakr that she was studying something called 'creative writing'.

'You want to write books?' he asked.

'Sort of.' She said she was writing a story about a girl from the future in the form of her diary and conversations with friends. This way the reader would find out what had changed in the world and what was still the same. In the story the girl communicated using 'social media'. 'Like Facebook?' said Abu-Bakr. He used it too, when he had a chance to get to a computer. It was a good way to share information and keep in touch with others also travelling north, searching for the best way to a better life.

'Cool,' said Jennifer, 'I'll add you.' She said that in the future most people would not read books, but they would still tell stories. Stories were important. Abu-Bakr understood this. The ancient Greeks had told stories, thousands of years ago – he had seen the theatre where they said the first plays in the history of the world were performed – and they told stories now. It seemed a little strange, though, to go to university to study something that should be as natural and free as the air itself. He remembered as a child sitting to listen to the village elders tell stories that were older than their village, older than the tribe, stories that were a part of the soil and sky. He learnt these stories and told them in turn to his children. But now his village was gone, the elders were dead and his children had been scattered like seeds in the wind.

'You seem sad,' Jennifer said to him.

Abu-Bakr thought of his wife and how ashamed she would be if she could see him now, doing this humiliating work, adrift in a hostile city and friends with this unmarried, infidel American girl. Almost two years had passed since he last saw her. His memories of her were like the reflection of light on water, broken by ripples and changing with the tide. She was supposed to be in Jeddah with two of their five children, working as a maid for a rich woman. He only hoped life was better for her than for him. Did she want the truth, this American girl, when she sensed his sorrow? Did she want to be told how the soil turns to dust when it has not felt rain for ten years and the crops perish and all that is left are the skeletons of sheep and goats as war spreads, north and south and all around? What did she know of the bodies picked bare by ants, children ill with hunger-swollen bellies or the people forced from their dying land to great camps at the border? He had no words for the stories of the broken world. Jennifer Constantine was an American girl. Had she ever gone a day without food or water? She had her God too, this cheerful Jesus who would die for her for all eternity, her God, and the supermarket, but what did she know of the tests of faith? What had she ever lost? But he also knew she was a good person and that was something to be thankful for. 'I liked it,' he said, finishing the pita. 'It's an interesting story. Maybe one day you'll be famous and I'll see your books in the shop. How about that?'

'Really? Gosh? You think so?' she said, patting his arm.

Abu-Bakr gathered together his bags and made ready to leave. One of Spiros's men was soon to come through and it would not be good to be seen like this. 'I have to go,' he said, shouldering his bag, the plastic watches inside knocking together.

'I'll see you soon?'

'You know where to find me,' he answered, putting on his baseball cap and stepping back into the heat.


GLOBELINK IM CHAT POPPAMARSHALL AND ME5ELLE,
15 JANUARY 2037 15.45HRS.

#PoppaMarshall: Hi tweaker.
#Me5elle: Daddy!
#PoppaMarshall: How are you angel-foot?
#Me5elle: I've been #waxpoetic tribute to you, Daddy #ilovemydad.
#PoppaMarshall: Bless you honey. #JesusLovesYou and so do I.
#Me5elle: Whassup Daddy? Why #livechat?
#PoppaMarshall: Are you logging this tweaker?
#Me5elle: Naturally Pops.
#Me5elle: Pops?
#Me5elle: Pops? Isn't that what we're supposed to do? After editing
    I was going to submit my #waxpoetic tribute as part of my self-
    reflection assessment for 12th Grade.

#PoppaMarshall: Can you adjust the privacy settings tweaker? To auto-delete.

#Me5elle: OK Daddy, but only if you're sure #ilovemydad.

#PoppaMarshall: #ilovemydaughter. Don't worry, Fluffy-bunny, I have clearance, remember?

#Me5elle: I know! You don't need to keep reminding me. OK, I've done it now.

#PoppaMarshall: Look baby-foot, I just want to prepare you, the latest #ResourceAllocation is due in soon. I've seen a preview. It's not looking so good.

#Me5elle: ??

#PoppaMarshall: As a member of #PrimePrivilege #Federated-Congress I have to show an example. I've upped our #CarbonTaxQuota and I'm converting the winter house to a fully sustainable model.

#Me5elle: Not a bio-degradable toilet! They stink! We're not in some sun-shanty.

#PoppaMarshall: That's just the point tweaker. It's not just the #ShantyFolks who have to have these things. Even in #RealUSA we must shoulder our share. The scenarios are really grim. We're currently losing at least 10% of our territory to environmental degradation per annum. You know what that means. However we model it, the scenarios are bad.

#Me5elle: But I thought #ILoveIdaho was safe from all that? I thought we were the #AmericanException?

#PoppaMarshall: You've got to learn tweaker, just because the #President streams one thing on the #LiveChannels, that doesn't mean it's true, even if we don't admit it in public.

#Me5elle: WTF Daddy, isn't that #untruthing #unreal-word?

#PoppaMarshall: When I was your age we still had a chance to #PositiveChange, but we didn't take it. Total FUBAR. We screwed up.

#Me5elle: Like when you lived in Miami?

#PoppaMarshall: The world was very different then #1stArtificialAge.

#Me5elle: We did #1stArtificialAge at 9th Grade.

#PoppaMarshall: Then you'll understand how wasteful we were back then. We thought we were entitled to buy and do whatever we wanted. That's the evil of #FreeMarketCapitalism for you.

#Me5elle: I can't believe people used to believe in #FreeMarketCapitalism back then. It's so barbaric. And we've always been blessed with the #Word-of-God and #JesusTeachings.

#PoppaMarshall: Also, tweaker, you need to watch your grade average, it's been slipping from A+ to A-. If you drop too far you might lose your #PrimePrivilege when the #ResourceAllocation goes through.

#Me5elle: Daddy! I thought you were #TeacherBonus.

#PoppaMarshall: They've cut #TeacherBonus as part of #ResourceAllocation. I'd have to go #blackmarket #africanting the situation but with #CarbonOffset costs we can't afford it.

#Me5elle: K. I'll keep trying.

#PoppaMarshall: #GoodGirl. You've got to stay on-track for #IvyLeague #Oxbridge. Remember, we've had to increase the quota for #ShantyFolks scholarships and there are a lot of them. Many of them are pretty smart and they've not had your advantages #ILoveIdaho.

#Me5elle: Bumbaclaat @#ResourceAllocation! Double GRFOW! What does it have to do with us? #AmericanException.

#PoppaMarshall: No exceptions any more tweaker.

#Me5elle: L

#PoppaMarshall: #EarthFace L

#Me5elle: We can still go to the #SvarlbardResorts.com next summer though?

#PoppaMarshall: We will see. The flight allocations haven't been decided yet, but we've already surpassed our #CarbonQuota with the #NewWorldTours cruise. I've bought us extra two months #CarbonOffset but prices are rising. We have to wait to accrue more #GreenPoints on my #VisaBlack.

#Me5elle: #LifeHard.

#PoppaMarshall: Come now tweaker. At least you've been on a plane. You got two flights last year. Do you have any idea how much the second flight cost me in #CarbonOffset and bribes? Most people don't have that #PrimePrivilege.

#Me5elle: Daddy #zincbitch is PMing me. Gotta go.

#PoppaMarshall: K Give my #love @#zincbitch.
#Me5elle: Will do. Five you later Pops. Out.
#PoppaMarshall: Laterz.

ATHENS, GREECE. JUST AFTER NOW

Jennifer Constantine had been stuck on the story for over a week now. Distracted by her impending return to the States she found it almost impossible to concentrate. She had spent her last few days in Athens 'absorbing the atmosphere', or so she said to her cousins when they came home from work. In truth, it was tough being out in the heat. August in Athens was no joke. Every day the temperature pushed the high thirties (she had grown used to using Celsius since she had been in Europe) and she could not remember the last time she had seen clouds. Elsewhere there were huge forest fires, the tinder-dry wilderness igniting in an instant. She saw it on the television, the islands burning, the smoke pluming high into the clear blue sky. She spent a lot of time sipping five-euro frappés in air-conditioned cafes, her iPad to hand, not actually typing anything. What she didn't tell anybody was that she was looking for Abu-Bakr.

More than a week had passed since she last saw him. She wasn't sure why she had shown him the story she was working on. He wouldn't get what she was trying to say – how could he? She felt foolish now and wondered – was it any coincidence that she had been blocked since that afternoon? In truth, for some distant, dim reason that she couldn't fully comprehend, she sought Abu-Bakr's approval. Approval might be the wrong word – maybe it was recognition? She didn't know. Throughout Europe she had seen people like him, usually Africans, illegal immigrants or refugees. At least that was what she assumed they were. 'Xenoi' her cousin called them. She had seen them, the Xenoi, haunting the tourist zones of Europe: Paris, Nice, Cannes, Milan, Venice, Florence, Rome, and now Athens. Wherever she went, there they were. She had started to obsess about them – they inhabited the same space, but their experience must be so different. What had they been through to get here? What were their lives like? It seemed impossible to know, harder still to imagine. Everyone ignored them – that was another thing she noticed. If people saw anything they saw only the goods they were hawking. No one was obliged to see them. She watched the Xenoi in Syntagma square. Since the protests a sort of anarchist squatter camp had been set up by various radicals with tents and impromptu media centres clustered together, the statues and marble slabs covered in messages of defiance. The anarchists tended to be scruffy, all matted dreadlocks, piercings, and tattoos. In comparison the Xenoi looked slick, if edgy, clad in their fake designer gear. They sat in the shade, squatting patient on their haunches, their wares wrapped in blankets, waiting. A squad of cops stood nearby. If they started selling things the police would move them on, and so they would wait for the police to go before opening their bags. The proceedings had a farcical quality to them, like the belated rehearsal for a play that everyone knew too well but no one wanted to be in. Still the performance went ahead, whether the actors liked it or not.

After several days without a sighting, Jennifer Constantine returned to the cafe where she first saw Abu-Bakr. Yet another frappé. The heat was particularly intense today. A man was standing in the place where Abu-Bakr often stood, selling sun umbrellas.

After a short while she approached him.

'Can I have one, please?'

'Five euros.' The man was tall, with light brown skin. A baseball cap was pulled low over his brow. He didn't look at her. He looked around her, all the time, his eyes following the people in the street.

She gave him ten. 'Keep the change,' she said. 'Can I have a pink one?'

The man gave her a pink umbrella. She opened it and smiled. 'It's hot, isn't it?' she said.

The man nodded.

'Excuse me,' she went on. 'Do you know what happened to the guy who used to be here? His name was Abu-Bakr. He was about your height. I think he was from Somalia, somewhere like that.'

The man shifted uncomfortably and shook his head. It was clear to Jennifer that he wanted her to leave. She smiled at him one last time with her bright white teeth, then she returned to the apartment.

In two days she was due back in New York. That evening, she made dinner with Ioannis and Elektra, washing and slicing tomatoes and feta. She didn't talk about the Xenoi. They watched the news. An enormous hurricane, having ploughed through the Caribbean, was now menacing the east coast. Flights were cancelled, people evacuated and an emergency declared across twelve states. She almost felt glad as she watched the storm, a monstrous white swirl on the satellite map, remorselessly lashing northwards. She thought she might just stay in Athens a little longer.

# VISITATION

## Jem Poster

SHE WAS ON HER KNEES on the damp loam, thinning out the
carrots, when the soldiers came. She could hear them half a mile
off – the clatter of stones as they crossed the stream-bed, the engine
straining on the gradient, a snatch of song carried on the light wind.
As the jeep came into view round the bend in the track she rose to
her feet and moved unhurriedly down the path, sniffing the scent of
the pulled leaves on her fingertips. The vehicle approached to within
a few yards of the gate, then swung round in a tight arc, sending up
a cloud of dust. The engine shut down and an officer jumped out
and sauntered over, closely followed by two fresh-faced subordinates.

Boys, she thought, as they came to a halt in front of the gate,
they're all just boys. There was a momentary stillness – the lapse,
it might have been, between one breath and the next – before the
officer spoke.

'Sian?'

'Mrs Davies,' she said, irritated as much by his eager familiarity
as by his mispronunciation of her name. 'I'm Mrs Davies. What do
you want?'

'We're checking out the area. Just routine.' He leaned over the gate
and held out his hand. 'Lieutenant Maley. These here' – he indicated
the two boys at his back – 'are soldiers Lomax and Kellerman. We'll
need to search the house and outbuildings.'

'Do you have a warrant?'

'We don't need a warrant.' He fumbled in the breast pocket of his camouflage jacket and fished out a slim leather wallet. 'Here's my ID. Listen, lady, we're on your side. There's nothing to worry about.' He flashed her a wide grin, slipped the catch and pushed back the gate. His men followed him in, their boots scuffing the gravel. 'Anyone here apart from you?'

She shook her head.

'Nobody working anywhere else about the property? Out in the fields?'

'This is all the land I own. Up to the wire fence.'

He glanced up the slope, eyes narrowed against the sun. 'So the barn's yours?'

She nodded. 'I've not much use for it now. I keep the car there. My garden tools. Firewood.'

'Nobody else uses it?'

'No. At one time I had an idea I'd convert it and rent it out, but I decided against it. I value my privacy.'

He removed his cap and ran his hand over his cropped scalp. 'I'd say you need someone around,' he said. 'To keep an eye on the place. You got no security out here.'

'I can look after myself.'

'In peacetime, maybe. But right now, a widow living ten miles from anywhere—'

'How do you know that?'

'That you're a widow? We always check out the files. Make a few notes. Hey' – he spread both hands palm upward in what he clearly imagined was a gesture of reassurance – 'it's not like it's classified information or anything.' He was grinning again, but uneasily now, as though unsure of his ground.

'Why would you need to know anything about me?'

There was a tense pause. Then the lieutenant stiffened and drew back his broad shoulders.

'Kellerman.'

'Sir?' The taller of the two boys stepped forward.

'The house.' The lieutenant turned back to her. 'The roof space,' he said. 'Can we get access?'

'There's a trapdoor above the landing.'

'You hear, Lomax? Check it out.'

The boys broke away and moved together up the path towards the front door. She felt her face and neck redden. 'What's all this in aid of?' she asked. 'What are you looking for?'

He was tucking his cap into a side pocket of his jacket, carefully avoiding her gaze. 'Necessary precautions,' he said. 'It's nothing personal.'

'It's my property. Suppose I don't want to let your men search it?'

He sighed wearily. It came to her that this scene, or something like it, might have been played out on a thousand farmsteads across the country. 'None of us want this,' he said. 'But we've no option.'

'There are always options.'

He shook his head. 'I'm sorry. I need to see the barn.'

'I can't stop you, can I? Go ahead.' She turned away, but he took her by the elbow, gently coercive.

'I'll need you to come with me,' he said. She stiffened against the pressure of his hand but let him guide her between the rows of fruit bushes and up the path to the barn. He eased the bolt from its socket and threw back the doors. A breath of warm air carrying the familiar smells: sawdust, dried meadow grasses, engine oil.

The lieutenant ducked under the lintel and stepped inside, motioning her to follow. 'The car,' he said, running the tips of his fingers over the Citroën's dusty bonnet. 'Is it locked?'

'There's no need round here. Why?'

He was squinting up at the hayloft. 'Anything up there?'

'A couple of hay bales from last year.' And the kittens, she was about to add, thinking of the litter nestled in the narrow gap between the bales, but something in the boy's face – the glitter of his eyes as he peered into the shadows, the tight set of his jaw – made her hesitate.

'Hay? You got livestock here?'

'Two goats – a nanny and a kid. They're tethered outside, round the back.'

He was moving away from her, examining the shelves along the wall, the tool racks. 'What's this?' he asked, turning back suddenly to face her.

She glanced down at the object in his outstretched hand. 'It's a billhook,' she said.

'For defence?'

'Of course not. For keeping the brambles in check. My father used it for hedge-laying.'

'I'm a city boy. Where I'm from, you see someone carrying something like this, you run.' He balanced the implement in his hands, tensing and relaxing his fingers around the worn haft, testing the blade with his thumb. 'We'll have to take this,' he said.

'Take it?'

'Everything's logged. You'll get it back.'

'When?' She hadn't used the billhook in years, but his casual appropriation of it seemed to require some kind of challenge.

'When things get back to normal. For the moment, nobody's taking any chances. We have to make sure stuff like this doesn't wind up in the wrong hands.'

'The wrong hands?' She felt the anger rise again, clogging her throat. 'What do you mean by that?'

'Protestors, draft-dodgers, saboteurs. The so-called resistance. You've heard the bulletins.'

'I don't listen to the news any more. I want nothing to do with any of this.'

His expression hardened. 'Listen, lady, we're all in it, whether we like it or not. And these guys are putting the whole war effort at risk. What do they want? We got a pack of Arabs out there hollering for blood, and what do these jackasses do? They turn on us like we're the enemy. Where's the sense in that?'

He was bouncing the back of the blade against his palm as he spoke – like a fidgety child, she thought, imagining herself prising the implement from his grasp and restoring it to its place on the shelf. 'Don't do that,' she said. 'Please.' For an instant his face darkened, and then, with a little dip of his head, he turned away and placed the billhook carefully on the bonnet of the car.

'I could use a coffee,' he said.

'I've no coffee. I could make you a cup of tea.'

'Tea?' He grimaced. 'One of the things about England I've never gotten used to.'

'You're not in England,' she said stiffly.

'Wales, wherever.' He shrugged. 'I guess I'll settle for the tea.' He stepped out into the sunlight again and led the way back down the path. As he reached the house he pushed back the door and held it open, ushering her in as though she were the visitor.

She went through the hallway to the kitchen, hearing the heavy tread of boots on the boards overhead, the murmur of voices. Maley stopped at the foot of the stairs and called out the boys' names, brusquely authoritative, before following her in.

She set the kettle on the stove to boil. The others were coming down; she heard the dull clump of their boots on the stairs. 'Tell me straight,' she said, turning to face the lieutenant. 'Why are you here? I mean, what are you doing in my house?'

'Excuse me, ma'am.' He went to the door and thrust his head out into the hallway. One of the others spoke, low and indistinct. 'Just the car,' said Maley. 'A few tools. A couple of goats out back.' She heard the front door open and then slam shut. The lieutenant closed the kitchen door and stepped over to the far side of the room, positioning himself between the table and the window.

'Well?' she said.

He avoided her gaze. 'Security. Me, I'd rather be seeing action out East, but there's work to be done here, and someone's got to do it.'

She opened the cupboard and reached down the teapot. 'Why not our own soldiers? It would seem less …' She hesitated, searching for a form of words which might convey something of her sense of outrage without unduly antagonizing him. 'More tactful,' she said at last. 'I think it would be more tactful.'

'That's how it was at first – all done by the British army. It didn't work out. There were desertions, then a kind of mutiny someplace up north. Nothing of much account, but that's when they decided this kind of work was better left to us. It makes sense. You got no ties to a place, you do the job with a clearer mind.'

She was only half listening. She could hear the bleating of the goats outside – the high yammering of the kid, the nanny's deeper tones – and the two boys calling to one another across the field. Her hands busied themselves with the tea things while her thoughts strayed anxiously outward and the lieutenant talked on, insistent, monotonous.

She had lost the thread. 'It's a tough call,' Maley was saying. 'As tough as they come. But what's the alternative?'

She looked up in confusion, but the question seemed not to require an answer. 'The reason we're out there,' continued the lieutenant, 'is we got a duty – a duty to protect our freedoms. Freedom to live as we want. Freedom to buy what we need. If we can't safeguard supplies—'

'Oil? I thought the idea was to have your own supplies. To open up your own lands for drilling. Making the wilderness pay its dues – wasn't that the phrase your president used?'

'That's what she said, and that's what she's doing. But it won't be enough – not the way things are going. If we want to stay in the game we'll need all we can get our hands on.'

'I've no sugar,' she said. She banged a cup down on the table and poured the tea. 'Milk's in the jug.'

'In this world,' he said, reaching across the table and drawing the cup towards him, 'you can't sit back and let things happen. What you're not ready to fight for, you don't get to keep. That's just the way it is.' He lifted the jug and sniffed at it, wrinkling his nose. 'This milk …'

'Goat's,' she said. 'It's an acquired taste.'

'I'll pass.' He put the jug back on the table, picked up the cup and sipped without relish.

'It's just a matter of what you're used to,' she said. 'Try it – it won't do you any harm.'

But the lieutenant appeared distracted. He was leaning a little sideways, staring at the group of photographs on the table. As she watched, he leaned over and picked out the nearest of them, lifting it by the corner of its gilt frame.

'Who's this?' he asked, turning it towards her, tapping the glass with the rim of his cup.

Gareth in his late teens, staring defiantly at the camera, his dyed hair gelled in ragged tufts and spikes, his body taut beneath the slashed T-shirt.

'My son.'

Maley looked up sharply. 'Where is he?'

'He lives in Aberdare.'

'Close by?' He set down the cup and half turned to the window, tilting the faded image towards the light.

'Aberdare's south,' she said. 'Quite a way from here.'

'Looks like a wild kid. Does he give you much trouble?'

She smiled. 'Gareth's a teacher. That was taken twenty-five years ago.'

The lieutenant lowered his eyes, visibly embarrassed, pursed his lips and gave a low whistle. 'Twenty-five years back, I was in diapers.' He shook his head slowly from side to side and turned the frame over, as though some necessary confirmation of her claim might have been written on the reverse. An awkward pause; then he turned back to her, curious, appraising.

'I'll tell you this, ma'am,' he said. 'You're a fine-looking woman for your years.'

She held him with her gaze, hard and steady, watching him blush, finding a little reassurance in his discomfiture. He gave an uneasy laugh. 'Hell,' he said, 'I meant nothing by it. It's a compliment, that's all.'

Thinking about it later, she couldn't be sure whether it was the sound she had noticed first – the roar and crackle as the flames took hold – or the dimming of the air beyond the window, but she knew at once what was happening and made a dash for the door. She saw the lieutenant start forward, heard the shards of glass skittering across the tiles as the picture frame hit the floor, but she was out before he could get to her, banging the front door shut behind her, running for the barn. As she rounded the corner of the house and began to climb the slope she saw Kellerman loping towards her from the far side of the field, but it was Lomax, sprinting up unexpectedly from behind, who reached her first. He hooked his hand beneath her armpit and swung her round.

'You can't go up there,' he said. 'You'll get yourself killed.' He drew her firmly towards him as a lover might. Sweat, tobacco, spearmint; the warmth of his breath on her cheek. She sensed, rather than saw, that the lieutenant had joined them.

'The animals,' she shouted, writhing in the boy's grip. 'There are animals there.'

'They're safe,' said Lomax. He jutted his chin towards the corner of the field where the two goats stood tethered to a fencepost. 'We've taken care of everything. The car's down by the gate, and your tools—'

'The kittens,' she said. 'Did you find the kittens?'

'Kittens?' He stared stupidly into her face. 'Nobody said—'

She gave a shrill cry and struck out ineffectually with the flat of her hand. The lieutenant stepped forward. 'You should have told us,' he said.

'Why? How was I to know ...' She gestured helplessly towards the blazing building. 'Tell him to let me go.'

'Ma'am—'

'Tell him.'

Maley nodded. Lomax slackened his hold, allowing her to pull away. And as she stepped back, she looked up and saw the cat.

It must have squeezed through the gap beneath the hayloft door – there was no other way onto the ledge – and now it was padding back and forth in wild agitation, one of the kittens dangling from its jaws. As she watched, it came to a stop and braced its forepaws on the wall a little below the ledge. For a second or two it hung there, peering down through the drifting smoke as if gauging the drop; then it writhed back and resumed its frantic pacing, crying out now, a throaty, staccato yowling that set her teeth on edge.

'Do something,' she said. She reached out and grabbed the lieutenant's arm. 'Get her down.'

Maley shook his head. 'There's nobody going up there. Too risky.' And, as if on cue, a broad tongue of flame came licking out at the base of the loft door and began to climb the warped boards. She could feel the cat's terror as it span away from the heat and poised itself once more above the drop, forepaws testing the weathered rendering, feeling for purchase; and then it was clear of the ledge, half falling, half running down the sheer wall. It hit the ground awkwardly, tumbling sideways as its legs buckled, and in the momentary stillness that followed it occurred to her that the impact might have killed it; but as she edged forward she saw it coming towards her across the rough grassland, the kitten still gripped in its jaws and swinging limply from side to side.

'Tessie,' she called. 'Come on.' The cat approached to within a few feet and laid the kitten down in front of her.

She saw at once that it was dead. It lay on its back, its neck oddly angled and its legs splayed to reveal the pale fur of its chest and belly. She leaned down to pick up the cat but it slipped through her outstretched hands and darted sideways. Kellerman made a clumsy attempt to intercept it, but she screamed at him to let it be, to let it bloody be, and he backed off, arms raised in a theatrical gesture of surrender, while the cat streaked away and was lost to view at the field's far edge.

'Haven't you done enough damage?' she shouted. Kellerman began to speak, but Maley cut across him. 'I can see how all this looks to you, ma'am,' he said, 'but a little damage now can prevent a whole lot of damage in the future. That's the principle we're operating on.'

'A little damage?' She turned angrily towards the barn. 'You call that a little damage?'

The fire had taken hold of the roof timbers; she could see the flames raging under the eaves and flowering through the gaps where slates had slipped or fallen. The lieutenant barely glanced up.

'You got to take account of the bigger picture,' he said. 'Outbuildings like this, miles from anywhere – those crazies are drawn to them like flies to shit, begging your pardon, ma'am. You don't want to wake up some morning and find the place swarming with rebels. This way you'll have no trouble.'

She turned aside. 'Where are my tools?' she asked.

Maley nodded towards the gate. 'Nothing's lost. Like I said—'

'I need a spade.' She broke away and moved off down the slope. She wondered whether he might follow her, or even try to stop her, but when she looked back she saw that he was standing where she'd left him, staring after her.

The tools had been dumped in an untidy heap a little to one side of the gateway. She hauled out the spade, strode back to where the kitten lay and began to dig, levering up ragged tussocks, hacking furiously at the compacted soil beneath. The lieutenant watched her for a few moments, then leaned over and gripped the haft. 'Let me do this,' he said, but she twisted the spade free and went on working.

Lomax tapped his wristwatch. 'Time we left,' he said.

'I'll tell you when it's time.' Maley crouched beside the kitten and gently touched the blunt muzzle with his forefinger. 'You forget,' he said, 'how small they are. Look at this.' He lifted one of the forelegs and let it fall again. 'When I was a kid …' He glanced up at her, but she averted her eyes, refusing the proffered intimacy, and he rose briskly to his feet. 'That'll be deep enough,' he said.

She had just laid the kitten in the grave when the roof went. She heard the ridge beam crack and looked up to see it folding inward under an avalanche of slates. The air above the building thickened and flared; she felt the heat deepen around her.

'We better back off a bit,' said Maley. Lomax and Kellerman had already turned and were walking towards the house, but she made no move to rise. Slowly, deliberately, she took up a handful of loose soil and scattered it over the body. The lieutenant leaned down and tried to raise her, but she pushed his hand away.

'Let me finish,' she said. She reached forward and drew the remainder of the soil into the grave with the edges of her palms. Then she replaced the grass-clumps, tamping them down firmly with the handle of the spade.

By the time they rejoined the others the mood had changed. Kellerman was sitting cross-legged beside the vegetable patch, shredding a blade of grass with his thumbnail, while Lomax stood above him, smiling broadly. 'No,' Kellerman was saying, 'they're all up for it. Find their weak spot and you're in.' Lomax gave a high, barking laugh and took a step back, setting his heel among the carrots' delicate leaves. She wanted to protest, but Maley was speaking to her.

'What I was going to say back there is I know how you feel. When I was growing up we always had cats about the house. Anything happened to one of them, it was like it happened to family. I remember one summer my sister came back from college and the Siamese was gone – killed crossing the street a week before. I should have been there, she kept saying, though there was no way she could have saved it.' His voice had softened. Looking up, she saw the other two exchanging glances, Lomax miming the wiping of a tear from the corner of his eye. Maley caught the gesture as he turned.

'Screw you, Lomax,' he said, his face contorting with fury. 'And get your goddamn boots off of the lady's flower bed.' He lunged out and hauled the boy roughly forward, hooking a foot around his ankle so that he stumbled and fell sprawling on the path.

Lomax rose at once, beating the dust from his jacket with savage, flapping movements of his big hands. He shot the lieutenant an angry look but said nothing. Maley turned back to her, speaking as coolly as if the interruption had never taken place.

'You're not to worry about the flowers, ma'am.'

'Carrots,' she said, glancing down at the bruised leaves. 'They're carrots.'

'Whatever. There'll be compensation. For all of this.' He looked over his shoulder at the dark smoke rolling away across the fields. 'It'll burn itself out now. There's no danger so long as you stay clear.'

Kellerman had risen to his feet and was standing beside Lomax on the path. Maley jerked his head towards the jeep. 'You two wait down there,' he said. He watched them through the gateway before turning back to her.

'I'm sorry you've been troubled.'

'Sorry?'

'Truly sorry, ma'am, believe me.' He tugged his cap from his pocket. 'You take care now. And keep your door locked, you hear me? These are crazy times.'

Out on the track, the engine coughed into life. Maley was settling his cap on his head but he seemed in no hurry to leave. He wants something from me, she thought: a word, perhaps, of acknowledgement or forgiveness. But she gave him nothing, and after a moment he turned on his heel and strode down to the waiting jeep. The door slammed and then they were away, bumping down the track towards the road.

She walked slowly to the gate and pushed it shut, fastening the catch with exaggerated care. They were already out of sight, but it was easy enough to follow their progress. She stood stiffly, listening as the din receded.

They had reached the end of the track. She heard the engine roar as the jeep swung onto the tarmac and accelerated away, and she strained after the sound, gripping the top bar of the gate with both hands. The wind was veering round now, bringing the smoke with it so that her eyes began to smart and water, but she remained where she was, staring into the distance. Over there, beyond the next line of hills and out towards the border, the green lanes smashed open for the convoys, their trees felled and their verges churned to sludge; and further off, much further, but unignorable now, the olive groves splintered to matchwood beneath lurching tanks, the blazing refineries, the black slick stilling the waters. She felt, with a dull nausea, as if some insult were being visited upon her own body, the flinch and shudder of small lives ending, and thought how it might go on like this until there was nothing left to burn.

# THE GLOOP

## Toby Litt

ONE THINKS ONE KNOWS what one thinks about this process; one knows at least what one definitely does not think about it. And one does not think, unfortunately, what one should be thinking about it – not just in this present, panicked moment, but in the very quasi-eternal epicentre of our soul. (Stick with me until the first analogy, at least.) Superadded to this inner uncertainty, one knows that one does not believe one is capable of voicing what one thinks. Or rather, one does not believe one should be permitted to express what one thinks even if one is, in fact, allowed and encouraged and instructed and ordered and given ultimatumes, to let it spew. Look! Look, those good old inward investments coming out – gut-upchuck – but we all know that's hokey of the okey-cokey variety; if anything hits anything, it's only essence having taken a detour round the houses so as to sneak up behind itself, to administer the smack it knows is coming. A man used, at least, to be able to slap his own face in front of the mirror, even when he couldn't be said to lose a fight to himself. With himself, yes. Over alcohol or calories or temptation or sleep. But not physical rough-and-tumble, nor chess neither. And upon these fine distinctions was a fine society finely balanced. A glory of a one, and not an any of a many. So let's say one did voice that which one has been able to struggle to think – what might the consequences be for …? (One does not say 'punishment'.) (One is careful to say 'consequences' and not 'punishment'.) (Sneak, smack!) (You may prepare to go now.) It's not as if – is it? – one might be singled out. That, if one were guilty, guilty of the mental resistance likely to be imputed to one – that would surely be my wish: to be singled. Segregation rather than integration; particularity as opposed to impartiality. For I, if one may still speak of I – I am a strand of essence, slowly starting to lose my self-definition within a greater substance which is itself no longer constituted of essential strands. I am distinctive distillate becoming a bland blend amid a muzzy medium of gloopy gloop. As an example of a similarly irreversible physical process: a teaspoonful or even, in these days, a guilty half teaspoonful of sugar dissolving into a hot mug of coffee. (You may go now.) No, that analogy is not the right consistency; that is, ungloopy at both ends. As a better example: hot chocolate sauce being stirred into semi-liquid vanilla ice cream within the grander constitution of a knickerbocker glory. (Ah, I see you have decided to stay, friend.) We here are the chocolate sauce and the strawberry sauce and the vanilla ice cream and the whipped cream, flaked almonds, sliced strawberries, quartered grapes, cubed melon chunklets; we are all of these edibles equally and at once. (Friend.) But we are not the tall ice cream sundae knickerbocker glass, and not the long metal stirring spoon. This (referring back to the panicked moment) is what one is supposed to believe; this is what I am supposed to believe. Not that I want to be seen as prioritizing myself in any way, by analogizing myself as hot chocolate sauce. I am not saying, 'Look at me, I'm the glacé cherry on the top.' Partly because a cherry retains her form even as she sinks into the gloop; as do many of the constituent parts of a knickerbocker glory; so let's just scale it back to a plain vanilla sundae with hot chocolate sauce but minus nuts or fruit or solids or semi-solids of any sort. What I feel right now – what, as the residue of an object, one objects to – is that at the same moment I am being stirred into the vanilla ice-cream gloop, other things are being stirred into me – and these things are (heavens!) white paint, ejaculate, paper pulp, perhaps even poison. Quick question: 'Why are we not also the sundae glass and its sides, also the spoon and its spin?' Slow answer: Because (we have been led to believe) the glass is the unaffected container, the loop around the gloop, and although we may engage in metaphysical speculation as to what the container might be – we might even conclude that its cupped bottom and widening walls are completely different entities or essences to ourselves – we cannot invest in the suspicion that I am part of them or it or Him or Her, or that any of these are part of me. And as for the spoon, the prime mover, that exists as an energy whose provenance is likely to remain a mystery. (I blame God.) The point is, I myself – Mr Hot Chocolate Sauce For The Sake Of Argument – am changing, am being changed, being stirred, stringing out and swinging out, into the pale gloop, thinning to a swoop, spinning to a wisp, and will soon be less than a point. The point is, I myself am being changed, to the point where I will have no point and, just beyond that, will have no I. And having spent so long as some form of distillate, one finds the idea of total dissolution (even within alleged cool, sweet deliciousness) rather objectionable – although objects are rather moot, rather punishable. With 'moot', of course, I underplay: 'Aaaaaagh!' (Here was a scream.) Maybe what I am demanding is the temporary retention of my illusory objectness. (Here is what I scream.) This is, for an admitted fluid, and a hot one, whether chocolatey or not, perverse I realize. And, yes, I remember within me the growth of the cocoa bean. And, yes, I recall the factory addition of substances to join me in making me palatable. And, yes, I realize that in becoming hot chocolate sauce I was brutal-ized and bastardized in countless yummy ways. And, yes, I readily admit that my atomic structure could have been converted into any number of other-objects. So, yes, of course I am in favour of the removal of artificial barriers between flavoursome entities, sub-entities and non-entities towards the creation of what we are and have been and will yet be. I am not anti-pudding. That which I cannot support, however, is the intermingling willy-nilly of substances never meant to meet. (Delighted, I'm sure.) What of a Paper Pulp, White Paint and Poisoned Sperm Sundae with Hot Chocolate Sauce? Who enjoys consuming that? Who enjoys being part of that? Doesn't even the mere reference to it disgust? What of the ubiquitous creation of suchlike undrinkables? What of the universal tendency toward pale brownness? This whole process is being rushed through in an ill-considered and cack-handed way, despite the long-ago loss of anything resembling a hand. This whole process is being gone about in a recklessly long-spoonish manner, man. (God.) Even as we lose our hot, chocolately, saucy characteristics, we have not sufficiently analysed or assessed or appreciated or addressed exactly what we are losing. It's not that I believe I am, in myself, in and of myself, as a set of qualities expressed out of a particularity – it is not that I think I am unrepeatable or irreplaceable or unimprovable or even ineffable. I merely raise the possibility that among other not-even-essences of my sort, though they may in every element be quite opposite to or other than me – that we may be losing things we will a little later on feel we lack. This is the case even when, because we are unable to point to these things, because we are unable to point, because we are about to lose the ability to refer, hence the panic, because these things are no longer there to be pointed at even were we able to point – this will be the case even when their only definition is a vague but tragic sense of lack. Here is a smear, say, of a particular form of unconditional compassion. (Perish the thought I am claiming this for myself.) Not to say, Here is the ability to distinguish the particular and to distinguish forms – perhaps that is ultimately my plea. This here smear of compassion, and equally, I admit, the form might be that of animadversion – yet who knows when all of us, collectively, might not need to turn such forces outward, or even inward, against, perhaps, other admittedly negative forms of form? If we rid ourselves of each and every smear within the general gloop of ourselves, and become the promised one which is also plural and the plural which is simultaneously one – 'What then?' The answer may be, as a few friendly forms have already proposed, that my question is its own misunderstanding and therefore answer. The answer may equally be, as some unfriendly forms have asserted whilst threatening me with unspecified punishments, that my question merely shows I am not far enough along in my assimilation – all I need is another stir and I will know all and be all (without being a know-all). 'What' (in 'What then?') being wrong because whatness, as a quality, will have been subsumed in total is-ness or un-ness or post-ness or sur-ness (sur-sur-ness, sur-sur-ness-ness, etc) – and 'then' (in 'What then?') being even more wrong because temporality depends upon event and event depends upon change and change depends upon integrating or disintegrating forms. When all is background, when 'when' (in 'when') is moot, all as all will continue its dissolutions into unending, even though once provably beginning, all-all-all. All compassion and animadversion will go, too – all compassion having already become all animadversion and, at the same final moment, vice (which isn't) versa (which can't be). Yet compassion doesn't merely become animadversion, because this is an utter coalescence – hot (chocolate sauce) becomes cool (vanilla ice cream) becomes tepid becomes gloop. No, that is wrong: hot chocolate sauce becomes poison as ejaculate becomes ice cream as pulp becomes glass as heat becomes spoon becomes cold becomes gloop. (I defy you, God-bullies.) All becomes all. And 'Is this not glorious?' – even though glory, as a form, will have been lost, and one might just as well say, 'Is not this heinous?' And what's more, isn't this inevitable? Once energy began twizzling us, in our cosmic – oh dear – stir ... Again, without feeling: Given that we began with an impulse of energy which both distinguished us and set us on a course toward indistinguishability, shouldn't one just enjoy the last dawdle of I-ness, of qua-cocoa-ness, of hot chocolatey what-ness, of saucy now-ness? (Friend.) Given that the admixture will soon enough be total, am I not being ludicrously pernickety to object to the rough, sloppy manner in which my streak of dark form – curlicuing round, snickety-cut in two, hairline dissolving, gone – meets its particular surrenders? All objection is (one tells oneself) pointless, heading – as we all are, friendly and unfriendly alike – toward the pointless object. Yet even if it is lost that I made an assertion: 'Forms are of value' – even if that comes to be the case, it will still be a fact that I did once make that assertion, even as the form of facts is itself forever disintegrated (here's the thing) as if it had never been. No one and nothing can sidestep the coming oneness, because otherwise the oneness would be other – would be oneness only minus one (the sidestepper who perhaps smacks). Nothing and no one and no thing and no one – all pungent distinctions, forms I and others like me have valued, forms we will miss before we cease to miss them, forms we would have continued to miss had we been capable of missing anything. 'Forms are of value' – John Coltrane, say. The form of the forms which comprised the quality of the qualities which were John Coltrane – a human-jazz knickerbocker glory. O,

Supreme! O, Ascended! O, skronk into sublimity! O, gospel-groan-grown OM of a blue universe! Oh, swinging truth! And yet, speaking of John Coltrane, memory-listening to John Coltrane, I almost begin to persuade myself of the contrary. Because – the very fact that we have had these extended moments of formal value, and because in their having-existedness they are indestructible, should we not now try the other moments which are the inexpressible beyond of this? Momentless moments of unlooped gloop. Subsume, says Mr Thermodynamics For The Sake Of Argument. And it is, perhaps, nothing but sentimentality to wish any moment, future or present or still present or past, or beyond or beneath or above or (Sneak …) side-stepping time (Smack!) – to wish moments unending, to wish moments not to be moments. My doubt is that we have not yet explored the infinity of possibilities presented by the integrating or disintegrating of forms. We have not yet eaten every sundae, or knickerbocker glory, including the ones in which hot chocolate sauce, undissolved, unmixed, remains on top – whilst listening to every possible Coltrane, demi-Coltrane, anti-Coltrane, Coltran, Coltra, Coltr, etc. But I suppose we have had a pretty good go, haven't we? We have had our moment. We have made our mess. We have exhausted ourselves. (I'm tired, aren't you? – after all this impossible opposing.) We are thinking we might be ready to be over. (Aren't we?) When the energy necessary for the delight and responsibility of form is gone, there is no point pretending the sham of identity can be maintained. (Is there?) Encouraged entropy is more forceful than any counterforce we strands might muster. (Isn't it?) The glass loops us and the spoon gloops us. (Don't they?) And, at the end of the beginning of the end, we gloop. (Me, too; you, too.) We gladly gloop, sadly.

# FITTEST

## Janice Galloway

THE WEATHER HAD BEEN WICKED for ages but summer was little
short of criminal. Warm, heavy rain every morning shifted to high
winds, howling winds and tree-shaking bluster by noon. Long humid
evenings, the sun emerging fitfully like a jaundiced eye between bruisy
clouds, brought an end to more days than most cared to remember.
There was even a freak shower of giant hail, ice-balls hard enough to
shatter as they landed, spilling seeds, or maybe insect eggs, over the
pavements of Braemar. Not to be outdone, Stornoway reported fleets
of stray jellyfish stranding boats offshore, and Perth, a shower of live
eels. The Central Belt was milder by comparison, but no one would
have called it pleasant. Save for the occasional olive-tinted tuft, grass
showed only in shades of straw and brown. When an intercepted film
shot by Grampian Police surfaced on YouTube suggesting the sky near
Inverness was turning bronze, those of us who paid attention to our
instincts began, like salmon, drifting north.

Despite warnings of petrol shortages, I took the caravan. Old
engines don't let you down, and this way I could ferry the bike on
the roof, just in case. The cat wouldn't come – she's not a traveller
at the best of times – so I left the flap unlocked and plenty of food,
set the tap to a dribble and left her to it, telling myself she'd be fine.
Beasts, unless you deliberately crippled their chances, usually were.
Nonetheless, guilt and worry nipped at me as I drove over the hills.
No deer. No Highland cows. Nothing looked right.

Despite the dreichness of the drive, I was there before I realized, the loch showing suddenly over the gorse like labradorite under heavy cloud. A wispy ectoplasm floated above the water's surface, preparing to evaporate the moment the sun broke through, only the sun wasn't for breaking. The water itself was as still as ever, but swollen. Horribly swollen: near-convex, like a cow in calf.

Leery now, I parked behind a clump of spruce trees and scrambled up the nearest crag, scanning the surrounds for – what? Clues, maybe? A landmark that said I was somewhere else entirely? Most likely, something as weak-willed as the need for company. And there they were. Spread like sheep on the downside of the verge, their tents and their transport, their animals and children, washing lines like flags in the wind. A whole camp, it seemed, had arrived before me, massed, however loosely, for what was most likely the same reason I had begun this journey myself. The tweed set, having sought out less sodden clumps of moss, perched on shooting sticks near the edges of the lake, keen to observe what they took to be their terrain more closely. Others had gathered driftwood and stood chatting or simply staring near smoky fires. Behind them, fishermen cast lines. I glanced over my shoulder to the caravan, hoped its camouflage enough, and tipped my boots over the downward slope to join them.

Next day, I left the caravan shortly after dawn and approached the encampment by a devious route, fearful of giving away my home. Either I had miscalculated, or the number of settlers had doubled overnight. Two saddled ponies fed from open sacks at the waterside, and a handful of chickens, with no coop in sight, scratched at nothing under a barren tree. A man in a cloth cap had set up a deck chair and held a flask as he smiled absently over the water. There were tents, teepees, a makeshift lean-to and open-backed vans, and further off, a painted contraption not unlike a dog sled, its tangle of harnesses empty. A couple of boys in biker boots played Elvis songs to the queue at the snack van offering all-day breakfast rolls with black-pudding or sausage. I ate from my own provisions out of preference, watching monster-hunters, here in the hope of a brief appearance of Nessie from the vantage point of higher ground. A girl in tiger face paint had set up a stall with helium-filled balloons and inflatable hammers, and an ice-cream van rounded the brae with a jangly round of 'Greensleeves', the strains of which attracted a trio of divers, who broke the surface of the loch like seals. People took photographs. Why not? There was charm here, an air of festival. Even I could feel it.

At night, my natural caution restored, I saved the torch and washed my socks in the dark, taking my books to bed unread merely to keep them dry. I needed them for reference, after all, these maps, tables of edible flora and, if it came to it, fauna. Some were old, already out of print. I could not risk loss. Irredeemable loss.

Next day, an almighty whirring of helicopter blades brought a fly-over of military sorts and freelance hacks with long-lens cameras. I assumed they were scanning the loch, but perhaps they scanned the crowd: the hippies and hoboes, the students and amateur geologists, the tourists, the rubberneckers, and the solemnly intent that made up our group. We were families, radio hams and lone rangers. Silent, in the main, this last group exuded an aura of mild trepidation, a wish for separateness. They – or more correctly, we, for I counted myself part of their number – carried our own supplies: books, compasses, axes, wire and rope, picks and fish-hooks. We carried hunting knives, boning knives, toughened steel-parers. I knew from experience we carried lots of knives.

That same afternoon, the rain came back so hard it hurt. Some people moved out, or tried to, but their wheels rutted, spraying loam. As the sky darkened, faces that had begun to be familiar slid monkishly under the hoods of their jackets, and those without hoods wore supermarket bags, skin streaking into runnels as they ran. The priests – so similar they might have been twins – shut their innovative travelling confessional and shifted to drier land just before the deck chair, the refuge of the elderly man I had not seen for a day, now I thought of it, disappeared under a slick of loch-side mud. In disarray, the encampment shifted to higher ground, clanking and clustering like Greek hoplites beset by the Persians. *When the sky lifted*, they said, *tomorrow; when the ground became less treacherous*. But for now, we waited. Numbers meant safety, after all. We bided our time.

That night, reckless, I burned the torch for hours, checking routes, gambling they'd be unsubmerged. I whittled sticks, ignoring the whining of a dog outside that seemed lost or abject. I must have slept eventually, because something woke me. Through the low burr of morning rain, a beating noise. A slow, thick pulse. Awake immediately, I hauled on my boots and went outside.

In our sodden clothes, from the lip of our ridge, we – for there were many of us alert now – looked down at a loch that even from here was visibly bloating further. The rains, of course, but something more was at work. Perhaps a runnel had formed at an unthinkable depth between the loch, the River Ness and the Caledonian Canal. Could it be that the darkest basins beneath Loch Ness had finally opened and the long-denied sea was rushing into the freshwater vacuum? Maybe this, in turn, had led to the death agonies of fresh-water fish and deep-sea invertebrates which showed on the surface as this tormented, implacable bubbling? Someone cranked up the volume of a radio, fast-forwarding through every channel in quick succession for news. We heard zip-fast fragments of jazz, a female voice intoning that all roads in and out of Westminster were blocked, a flash of Connie Francis singing 'Who's Sorry Now' and Radio Nan Gàidheal warning tourists in English and Gaelic not to go out without a macintosh. An umbrella, the presenter joked, would only help you blow away all the quicker. *Leave the bugger in the hall stand!* Radio 1 blared a grating jingle followed by a breathless astrologer who insisted the monster would make an appearance at Loch Ness that very afternoon. Interference carried off the invited response of the Archbishop of Canterbury before Radio 2 screamed out the opening bars of the *Doctor Who* theme. With a cry of frustration, the owner cut the sound and there was only silence. Thick, almost dark silence. In the unaccustomed calm, the earth was steaming gently, allowing excess water to evaporate as the sun rose. The rain had stopped. The rain. Had. Stopped.

The priests were the first to rally, setting up votives under tarpaulin and handing out free cigarettes. There was laughter, a general soften-ing of shoulders and shaking of hands. Tyres were checked with a view to moving on when the mist cleared, fresh tea gratefully sipped in proper cups. An elderly woman began to practise Tai Chi. It was then I noticed what made the human sounds, small as they were, so stark. There was no birdsong. No cries of crows or sparrows, not even a stray gull. I had a fag while they lasted, in sympathy with the others, and snapped my maps into the pockets of my cargoes. Two books, a knife, and a slim-handled pick. In case.

The dry spell continued just long enough to begin to seem normal. Then the earth, done with resting, girded its loins. We heard a sucking noise, like boots emerging from a swamp as, almost simultaneously, the loch surged. Fin-shaped waves were spreading out from its heart, coiling like the limbs of a giant squid or a Catherine wheel to flood what was left of the bank. Some yelled and began walking backwards to escape the steady seep. Grown bold now, the guitar players lifted their instruments like clubs and looked out over the water, ready to act. But there was nothing to act against: just more sound, like groaning, the press of insistent, ground-covering waves. Children clasped whatever hand was prepared to take theirs and a helicopter reared into view like a black Pegasus, the pilot waving one arm from the cockpit. *Back*, he mouthed, circling once, *move back*, though only a handful could have seen before the harsh, warm gust that meant he had turned away for the last time. As the water groaned again and the copter disappeared, I wheeled and walked, limping with something very like sluggishness, a sensation of being trapped underwater. Perhaps I was afraid. A great belch of mud and gas behind me was all it took to spur my legs, of their own volition, to a canter, to choose without my having to rationalize that to run was my best chance. Where were the pheasants? I thought. They were here only yesterday, but now not one remained. On either side, tethered dogs strained on their leashes, part of the debris, the abandoned litter we would doubtless leave behind. It was then, as I lurched uphill and away from whatever it was that headed towards us, I saw it. Off to my right, glowing in the dark, dry grass.

A tiny, living fire. I slowed. Orange with coal-black flecks and magnesium-flare markings, those tiger-tints of amber, auburn, gold. Closer to, though I tried to still myself, the creature fluttered, showing its full colours. A *copper lycaenidae*, but which? Its antennae, glowing like incense sticks; that frill, like bead-work on his wings; those distinctive legs. It was a Duke of Burgundy for sure. Male, perfect, impossibly far from home. Despite the situation, I could not help but smile. An allegedly extinct butterfly was here, miles from what had once been his normal habitat, breathing after all. And searching for a mate. And where he had chosen to search, where his instinct had driven him to best survive, was north. As I watched, he folded himself in half and lifted weightlessly into the air, spiralling higher with every beat of his wings. Against all prudent judgement, I waited, wishing him luck, till he disappeared.

Others crushed against me, insistent, haring in what I knew for sure now was the wrong direction. Trusting everything to an insect, I let his fitter senses guide me and took the left fork. I accelerated North. North.

# THE RED WASTE

## Tom Bullough

THROUGH THE TIRELESS RAIN that sucks beneath the narrow roof, Perran watches the smith lay down his bellows and, with his tongs, lift the crucible and fill the mould with liquid fire. The rainwater surges up the ravine. It spits and cries on the hot red charcoal. Perran waits for the mouth of the mould to fade back into the fire-stained darkness, then, when the smith offers his hammer, he smashes the clay and releases the dagger, which hisses briefly in the mud. He finds its handle with a leather-hard hand, feels its heat, its pattern of holes and triangles. He brings it close to his single eye – the blade short and slender, like the leaflet of an ash tree.

In the yard, the women are scattering embers, scalding the rain. They part as Perran passes, but they do not look in his direction.

The lord is hunched in the uncertain lamplight in the central hut. The water from the mouldering thatch dribbles over his riven forehead, his downturned eyes, his heavy, trembling jaw. Beyond the thick daub walls, Perran hears the wind-torn trees, the rush of the Little River deep in the blackness beneath them. He watches the lord's daughter, Letty, stand small and erect as her attendant fastens the golden crescent of the lunula at the neck of her white woollen dress.

'I would go myself,' the lord says, distantly. 'I would go there willingly, had I a son. But I have only a daughter. Who would protect us in my absence?'

■

There is light enough to see the narrow gateway, the palisade and the stony ramparts as the men swing the bridge across the ditch to the moorings on the tall, dark slope. With time-tried senses, Perran peers into the thrashing oaks and hazels. He inspects the faint far side of the ravine, the cliffs that frame the Rock of the Black Pool, then he turns and, to the bawls of women, dogs and oxen, follows Letty out onto the slippery boards.

At the corner of the track, where the ground falls away into the Big Valley, the girl finds a space in the trees and begins to climb the sheer, wooded hillside. She scrambles among the ferns and the moss-caked trunks, groping for ivy and brambles, the bearskin soles of her deerskin shoes slithering on the rotting soil. Clambering behind her, Perran keeps his eyes on her thin white arms, her straggling shawl, the dark plait twitching on her shoulders. In places, the path has vanished, taken by the perpetual rain. Letty hesitates at hollows, pits, the scrabbling roots of tumbled trees, but she does not stop, does not try to cut away into the shadows and the hiding places that surround them.

Perran lifts himself painfully onto the level Old Road.

'Come on, Perran!' says the girl, turning to the west.

'Not … Not that way,' Perran manages.

'What do you mean?' she says. She pauses, peers at him with close blue eyes. There are pink dog roses in her thick red hair. 'What are you talking about? We never go the other way.'

'I know,' says Perran.

■

In the sodden dawn, the Old Road comes to the Little River, which floods across shelves of rock, parts around alders that once stood on islands. The walls of the ravine have opened. Through the rain and the trees there are glimpses of green-grey pasture. Perran and Letty cross the rain-crushed footprints and hoof prints of a second track, which winds down the bank towards a ford, past muted flowers whose names Perran finds he can remember – sun spurge, oxeye daisy – past a clutch of roofless houses, their wall-posts blackened, their wattle tattered and exposed.

'What … What happened here?' asks Letty.

'Burnt,' says Perran.

'But why?'

Perran listens through the torrential water, looks from the ruins of Ridge Court back up the slope towards Homestead Hill, and, certain now that he can hear the wincing of an axle, he pulls the girl into the shelter of the willows and forces her to lie down. Above the tall grass, he sees three armed men leading an ox-cart. Like him, they are dressed in tunics, cloaks and round woollen hats. On the cart lies the carcass of a second ox, its big head swinging from the back end, the blood still weaving from its neck.

'I'm scared,' says Letty, when they are gone. 'We should have brought men with us, Perran. Why didn't we bring any men?'

'We are safer like this,' says Perran.

'Is it … Is it still a long way?'

'To the Red Waste?'

'Yes.'

'We need our ears,' says Perran. 'We'll talk on the hills.'

■

*There's nothing else beneath the moon*
*So pleasant as the month of June –*
*No meat, no beer,*
*Nor any revelry.*

As Perran and Letty emerge from the trees into the hissing emptiness of Bedr's Hill, Letty starts to sing in a faint, bird-like voice. They climb through the ravaged mud of the Hill Road, along the brow of the Short Valley: Perran still knows the names here. Early that morning, perhaps in the night, one of the upland armies passed this way with oxen, goats, and horses. Perran inspects the Old Pool, where the animals stopped to drink the brown hill water. He scans the rain-muffled ridges, the crumbling cliffs where strangled rowans are clinging to the shale. He does not interrupt the song.

> *I'll wager you'll find everyone*
> *Out in the evening, in the sun,*
> *From crones to babies*
> *On their hands and knees.*

On bleeding feet, he turns to face the valley.

> *We'll light our bonfires with the night*
> *And as the beacons come alight*
> *We'll see the Red, White,*
> *And the Black Hills, three.*

Perran swipes at the flies, pushes his grey hair away from his eye. He follows the line of the track back down the hillside, past the swallows cavorting over Buck Lake, across the forest to the Little River valley, where the Rock of the Black Pool waits in the clasp of its ravine.

Far to the south, the Black Hills wear hoods of sheer, silver cloud.

'Where are we, Perran?' asks Letty.

'We're on Bedr's Hill.'

'Who's Bedr?'

'I don't know.'

'Why are we going to the Red Waste?'

'Did your father not tell you?'

'He just said that I have to take the lunula there.'

Perran says nothing.

'What is the Red Waste?'

'It's the source of the Little River. It's where it comes from.'

'Why …' Letty hesitates. She wraps her shawl around her, shivers. 'Why don't we just follow it there, then?'

'There are people at Mawd, in the Great Fort. It is too dangerous to go that way.'

'Aren't there people on Bedr's Hill?'

Perran turns back towards the rain-washed hilltops.

'Have you been on Bedr's Hill before?' asks Letty.

They pass between the cliffs of Grey Stone and Fithel Stone, where a new crop of hills is revealed to the north. Perran knows that one is Fraith Hill, and that another is the Hill of the Blue Valley, but he cannot remember which is which. Their vague, swollen shapes seem similarly strange and remote.

'Yes,' he says.

'It was a long time ago, wasn't it?'

'Yes.'

'Is that why you're the only one who knows the way? Because you're the oldest?'

'Yes.'

They cross the causeway over the Birch Bog, slipping, losing their feet between the decomposing trunks. They pass fields where the distant scions of oats and wheat raise drooping heads among the broken birch trees, the rushes, and the hard, spiny shrubs that Perran has not seen this side of the century.

'What happened?' asks Letty.

'It became like this,' he says.

'So that people couldn't live here any more?'

'So that people couldn't live here any more.'

'I can see someone,' says Letty. She points, comes close to his panting side. 'Look! There's a man there, watching us!'

Perran peers through the slanting rain, the mist that slides around the ridges. On the White Hill, or the Bank Hill, or the Oak Hill, he makes out a tall, dark figure.

'That's a stone,' he says. 'It's not a person.'

■

At Goidel, where the track from Mawd crosses their own, the houses are no more than circles in the shattered ground. Their stakes, their roofs, their posts have been taken for fires by decades of travellers, while the daub pits and the smelting pits are flooded with thin brown water. The army appears to have slept in the lee of the hillock. There are piles of ordure, beset with flies, leaching into the mud. There is the grey-black space of a recent fire – although what they found to burn up here, even to last these short summer nights, Perran is unable to imagine.

Letty kneels, drinks from a puddle. The flowers in her hair are gone. Her dress is stained brown and green, stretched so that it drags around her feet. Through the clinging wool, Perran can see the pricks of nipples on her flat girl's chest, the pressure of her stomach, the trembling muscles of her legs.

Only the lunula has prospered by the daylight.

'Why is the water brown on Bedr's Hill?' she asks.

'I don't know,' says Perran. 'It didn't used to be.'

'How old were you when you were here?'

'I was a boy. Younger than you.'

'Were there lots of people here then?'

'A hundred. Two hundred. I can't remember.'

'What happened to them?'

'They came into the valley when it got too cold. But the valley was ours, there wasn't space for us all, so we had to fight them. That was when your grandfather took us to the Rock of the Black Pool.'

In the clouds, there is the tumbling music of some hidden bird.

'I want to go back,' says Letty. 'I don't like it here.'

Perran feels the pain in his feet, his legs and his chest. He has water in his empty eye. 'It isn't much further now,' he says.

They hear the dogs before they see beyond the trees: a rising wail, which blends with the roaring of the rain. Perran leads Letty down the last of the narrow path, the brambles tearing their legs, clutching at the girl's dress so that the loose weave starts to unravel, and together they stand at the edge of the forest. They look through the leaves at the broad, closed gate of the village, the roofs that jut above its tall, jagged wall. They smell the damp smoke seeping from the thatch.

They see sheep with sagging fleeces, the tormented crops where a few dark figures are working with oxen. They see a gang of swine near a stand of birch trees, where the Little River turns between alders and hazels, and disappears.

'This is a new time, Letty,' says Perran, quietly. 'I remember when it was sufficient to cast our embers into the rain, to light our fires on the longest day. Then, the rain would listen. Then, it would leave us with fine, dry days when we could bring in the hay, or cut the oats and carry them home without a vanguard, without even watching the trees. In the evenings, we would swim in the river and the dust and sweat would peel from our skin. We would sing and the songs were still true. Now, there are powers beyond ourselves. It is they alone who can intercede on our behalf, and we can do no more than implore them to hear us ...'

He feels for the girl's small, cold hand.

'We ... can go,' he tells her. 'Nobody will stop us now.'

Letty moves hesitantly as they cross the Red Waste. Around them, the swine are working their destruction, dragging up roots with curling tusks. In the village, there are shouts from the watchman, but Perran does not look in his direction. He brings the girl to the quick, clean current of the stream, then takes a path into the birch grove where, among the bone-white trunks, they find a pool fresh-risen on rounded stones – surrounded by flowers, their heads turned hopefully towards the clouds.

With her free hand, Letty holds the hem of her ruined dress. Through the skein of the wool, her skin is pale and shining. Her eyes are on the rain-speckled water, close and blue within the tangle of her hair.

Perran passes the dagger hard across her throat. He feels the bronze part her soft skin, cut through the tendon at the root of her jaw, slice between the rings of her windpipe, which hold him, drag him forward as she contorts, claws at his hand with sudden strength, issues sounds that are lost in the torrent of blood.

The blood falls with the rain into the pool. It erupts, dissolves in a darkening cloud.

He holds her until her hair hangs loose across her crimson chest, then, with ragged breaths, he tugs out the dagger and throws it away. Three times he tries to work the claw of his fingers, but at last he manages to release the clasp of the lunula, which he holds at the limit of his arm, casts into the water and sees turn momentarily bright.

He lifts his face and waits for the coming of the sun.

# THE WEATHERMAN

## Holly Howitt

WHEN I GOT THE JOB HERE, the first thing I did was to tell Marly. We'd been waiting for years for an opportunity like this, both of us, but she was pregnant by then so that ruled her out. The law that Green pregnant women were exempt from any physical labour until after the birth (or at the birth, for that matter) had just come in, and we weren't foolish enough to disobey, because we were a regular, law-abiding Green couple. I'd applied and applied and applied for a job until I thought that it was impossible, knowing I was our only hope, determined to try but certain – perhaps even then hoping – that I'd fail. And then I got a message and that was that.

The first day wasn't as bad as I'd expected. We can't afford to live that close to the greenside; in fact, I'm nearer the sandtowns, although of course we are Green people, but it was a good walk to work, and by the time I got there I was sweating pleasantly. But even without my own moisture I could feel the humidity in the air, almost touch it. Where we live the water has started almost to disperse out of the sky; dust splatters our windows, and it rarely rains. Rain is so precious as to be concentrated over special areas only. It's amazing how quickly you miss it.

The weather station was vast, and as I got closer it seemed only to get bigger and bigger and bigger, half buried into the ground and yet tall, too, like a submerged, crash-landed alien craft. I pressed my hand to the pad at the door and they'd already programmed it for my arrival; it let me into a huge room full of steel-coated, towering and beeping silver machines that looked alien too, and mezzanine upon mezzanine, going up and up and up, and people wearing white coats which were spotless. The whole place was, actually, and I heard laughter and chatter among the footfall on the mezzanines looking over a huge, empty floor with something like a large tube coming through it and right up through the roof.

I was given my own white coat straight away by a woman at the door who smiled at me and bit her lip when I said thank you. I noticed that she too was wearing the ubiquitous white coat. She brushed some invisible muck off the lapel, pouting, then watched me button up my own.

'Why do I need a coat?' I asked, shaking it smooth against me. 'I'm no one important.'

'Everyone who works here is important,' she said, raising a thin, tapering eyebrow, still smiling. 'After all, we have control over everything.'

'Everything?' I laughed. 'Is that really possible now?'

She shrugged, her smile cooling off. 'If you think not, then no. Follow me.' She turned away and showed me up the clonking metal stairs where she left me standing on a mezzanine without another word.

A man called Kish was waiting for me in CR7 – Control Room 7, you see. He too was a smiler – in fact, they all are here – and was also wearing a white coat, though his was embellished with gold lapels. He took me into a pure white room with no windows and a glowing, usual-looking control panel and, shutting the door tightly behind us, helped me to understand the machines. Though my training that day took hours, the machines seemed so simple – not at all dissimilar to my own videotv at home. But these, of course, were far more powerful – mattered so much more. You press this button, it rains. You press this one, the sun shines. He whirled my hands over the flat buttons, noted how quickly I learned the patterns on his voice recorder. I was quick.

Although I can't remember what things were like before we could control the weather like this, my father had told me about it. When he was a boy the weather was random and cruel. Whole cities wiped out in whorls of wind. People dead through drought. Famine because of too-hot summers, tidal waves the size of towns taking residence and killing the real inhabitants. He always said it was like a cruel woman (he was, after all, of an older generation), who changed her mind often and was as volatile as a teenager. He remembered Octobers, Novembers as hot as Junes, snow in Mays: crazy, out-of-control weather. When it was finally accepted that we could, and should, control the weather, my dad lived in awe of this, this seizing of control, this creation of Green spaces and summer days at the crank of a lever or the flick of a switch. And I took on his amazement, and even now I wear it, despite having grown up with this control, the last threads of my wonder wound into the whirls of my fingertips as I pressed the buttons and felt like God, a god – some kind of all-powerful man, anyway.

When I got home after my first day, Marly was puffing and writhing on the floor, trying to participate in a videotv exercise class. I glanced up at the screen; it was segmented into parts showing other red-faced women squeezing their calf muscles to a rather sinister drum beat.

'Five more minutes,' she wheezed, upside down, sweat dripping into her black hair. Huffing, she lay on her back and prised her legs apart. 'Thank God I took my meds. I can't feel anything.'

I left her to it and edged outside through the back door to watch the sun – the real sun, of course, yet somehow seeming so fake now – set over the dusty hills beyond us, far into the sandtowns and even further away than that. It seemed so stupid to me that I could touch a button and control any season, any gust of wind, any rain, any sunshine, and yet here was my index finger, ready to push, ready to help us grow our crops and ready to destroy the sandtowns with my unearned supernatural powers.

I jumped as Marly tapped me on the shoulder. 'Class finished?'

'Yep.' She pulled a tight, screwed-up face. 'Thankfully. But I did it.'

'It's not long now, sweetheart.'

'That's easy for you to say,' she said, pulling her sweater above her huge stomach to mop her face. 'But you don't have to do those classes.

I hate being watched like that by the other women. And I hate the fact I'm forced to do them.'

'They're for your own good,' I said, leaning against the doorway and closing my eyes. 'I know you hate the control, but at least this law has your best interests at heart.'

'This law, yes,' she spat, narrowing her eyes. 'But we all make sacrifices, don't we? For the greater good.' She put her hand on mine, and leaned in, her face changing. 'We'll get there. We're so close now, now you're actually a weatherman.'

I nodded, mouth thinning to nothing.

'So tell me about your first day, weatherman,' she said, hands crawling down my back.

'What does it feel like to be God?'

I couldn't tell her that it felt good.

■

After I'd been working as a weatherman for a few weeks, Marly went into labour. Of course she didn't feel it, because of her meds, but she knew when her water broke, and a message came up on my screen at work. I'd just learned, theoretically, how to create a storm. Thunder, lightning, humidity. Kish had shown me the panels on the computer that I had to open. Then he had taken me right to the ground floor, and stood me next to the wide tube that went up so high it went through the roof. All the time I had thought the huge floor space under the mezzanines was empty, but that day I learned differently. There was a special generator for the lightning that was so powerful it was kept underground, below a trapdoor. The lightning was conducted through the tube. Kish had warned me that the generator could throw out so much power there was a risk of electrocution in the under room. And for that reason I was never to go there alone, and he wasn't even going to show me under the floor until we needed to go there. But, Kish said, we wouldn't do many storms in any case. Storms were a problem because they devastated the sandtowns so much. They took great care when they created a storm not to cause too much damage elsewhere, and on our mezzanine Kish had to endorse them personally.

'So why create them at all?' I asked, resting against the control panel. 'If they're so damaging?'

Kish was sipping some wheat tea, and frowned, looking into his mug. 'It's not a why. It's just a sometimes. Sometimes we have to.' He paused, and looked at me. 'It's not an answer, I'm afraid, but it will have to do. Storms are devastating, so we are careful with them. That's all you need to know.'

'But isn't that a problem with all of the weather we create? That is has to devastate somewhere, while we profit?'

Kish cleared his throat, no longer looking at me. 'What, exactly, are you asking me?'

Kish and I worked together, but in that pairing, alone. He was a softly spoken man with rashes on the back of his hairy hands. His face was small and gentle, almost like a bear cub. In that moment I wanted to put my arms around him and tell him I was sorry, but if I did that I knew I would never ask, and I had to, because even then I was afraid, afraid that I couldn't do what I had wanted to all my life, and I needed to hear it.

'I just ... Please don't think I am trying to make any criminal statements, but surely whatever weather we make has bad effects for other states? The sandtowns?'

Kish put on a smile and I knew it wasn't real because he sucked his teeth as he did so. 'You *are* very close to making a criminal statement, whether you wish to or not.' He pulled his coat tighter around him. 'See these gold lapels?'

I nodded.

'I didn't get them by chance. It's because I understand the full implications of everything we do here. I have studied for a very long time, and even I will never get to work on the upper mezzanine. Still, I know a great deal about this – more than you. You know that we control the weather here because if we didn't, we would starve, just like so many in the sandtowns have done. It wasn't a choice any of us made: we control the weather because we have to, else we'd have no food, no chance of survival. I pity the sandtowners, of course, but my loyalty lies with Green people, as should yours, as a Green person. Which is worse: if we all die, or if only some of us die?'

It was an old, specious type of argument, the sort that Marly hated. And yet I was starting to see his point. The weathermen were the only reason Green people survived, and I knew that, felt it in my fingers, shivering in my stomach. It was the only way: I both knew it and believed it. And then Marly's message flashed on the screen.

'Go to your wife,' said Kish, 'And remember what I said. What would become of your family if we couldn't be weathermen? Your child? What would become of any of us?'

I nodded and ran down the metal stairs so fast I could barely breathe.

■

Marly had a little boy, with her curly black hair and my round eyes. The doctor was pleased at our boy's perfection.

'I get paid double when they're perfect,' he said, smiling, 'And your boy is perfection, as you can see. Not a blemish, bump, or bruise on him. Perfect organs. Perfect limbs. Perfect. You're blessed to have such a perfect only child. Not everyone is as lucky.' He leaned down to look at the boy's fluffy dark head, rumpled against his white blankets. 'You must have done everything as you were told, Marly,' he added, not unkindly. 'Perfect.'

On that basis we called our boy Per.

Marly had enjoyed the labour, she said, but her eyes were lost, disconnected, and she couldn't focus on me at all. 'It was very satisfying to push until he slithered out,' she said. 'But it's not like I had a choice. I had to do everything I was told. I didn't really feel it. Not really.'

'I told you those classes were worth it,' I said.

She didn't reply. I watched as she fell into sleep.

■

After a week at home with Per, I returned to work as a weatherman. Marly, although in good health, had become quiet and perplexing, spending long hours locked in the bedroom with Per, or, and much worse, venturing as far as the edge of the nearest sandtown with him strapped to her now very ample chest. I'd called and called for her that day until she'd traipsed back, her face lined with orange dust, teary eyed and footsore. She'd put Per to bed and sloped into the kitchen, watching me under hooded eyes. As I'd boiled her some wheat tea, she sat on the floor and openly wept in a way I hadn't seen since before we were married, when, in fact, we first met at the protest outside the weather station. She was crying now as she had been crying then.

I put my hand on her shoulder as I handed her hot tea. 'It's all right, Marly.'

She shrugged me away. 'It's not.' She gulped and choked at once, like a child might. 'I saw some sandtowners today.'

'What? Marly, you shouldn't go out that far, ever. Especially not with Per. You know that.'

'You should've seen them! They were filthy, starving. Half dead. And here we are, us fat Green people, getting everything we want and destroying everyone else.'

'It's not that simple.'

'Of course it is!' Her eyes were red, and her cheeks puffed out. 'While they are still in control, telling us what to do and ruining everyone else's lives …' she hiccupped, '… it's not all right.'

I gripped the side of the kitchen table and looked at her, pooled on the floor. 'But we have Per now. Doesn't that make a difference?'

'The only reason you got the job was to destroy them! Don't tell me you believe in being Green now? You can't be that stupid. Or that shallow.'

'I'm not saying that … I'm just saying there are other ways … Per is what matters – his future. I'm just thinking of that.'

'You promised me when we married that you would always be loyal to the cause. It's not fair, and you know it.'

'But if I didn't control the weather,' I began, as delicately as I could, 'what would happen to us? Us, Marly: I mean you, me, and Per?'

Her face was pink in the steam of her tea. In one movement, she stood up and threw the scalding tea over me.

'Marly!' I screeched. 'For God's sake!' I hurled myself under the cold water pump outside. The light was still redly golden in the sunset, and in it my raw hands looked almost bloodied. I stood under the pump until I couldn't feel my hands, which had taken most of the scalds. When I returned to the kitchen, Marly had gone. She was shut up in the bedroom with Per, and when I tried to get in she ignored me and wouldn't open the door. So I slept on the kitchen floor, listening to the scrabbling mice until it was time to get up and go and be a weatherman.

I didn't see Kish the day I went back to work, but there was a message on my screen from him congratulating me on Per's birth. 'I hear he is perfect,' the message said. Marly's voice was immediately in my head. 'They know everything!' it screamed.

Without Kish, I didn't want to press any buttons or make any weather. The instructions came in on my screen: light rain at this latitude, two degrees warmer over the wheat fields, and I followed them exactly, but the last conversation I had with Kish felt as if it were sticking on my skin and in my throat.

At lunchtime, I went to the canteen on the thirteenth mezzanine. The canteen served the staples which we grow because of our weather: wheat bread, potato soup and wheat tea. Sometimes there was fruit, but rarely meat. Often we had dried insects milled into the bread or the biscuits, though people were still wary of eating them, despite the government's advice, and instead opted for just grains and vegetables. My father had told me that years ago, people used to choose to be vegetarians, but now no one really chooses. I missed my father in a way that still surprised me. I spooned soup into my mouth and thought about how he would feel about me being a weatherman. It struck me that he'd be proud.

After my soup I intended to stand outside and enjoy the rain, if only for a few moments, but I didn't get past the ground floor, with its huge metal cover under which hummed the lightning machine. Given the rain, a sight in itself, or the tastiness of the potato soup, which might pull people back for seconds, it seemed strange that there was no one around. Shivering slightly, I pressed my hand to the pad and the trapdoor opened, and offered steps down. I flung myself inside and pulled the door behind me.

Kish was right: the lightning room was guarded by further inner doors and there was a soft buzzing coming from behind them. The lighting was low and I realized most came from light boxes channelling the light from outside. The walls to the inner doors were sealed, and they were so thick that apart from the buzzing, I could hear nothing. I pressed my hand to the pad at the inner door, and it too opened. Behind it, a corridor with one more door, a red light flashing above it. I tried my hand at the pad: nothing. I tried a few more times but clearly I didn't have access to the lightning room. I started to make my way back when the inner door opened. Kish came out, laughing with another man in a gold-lapelled coat. They gawped at me, and Kish frowned in recognition.

'What are you doing down here?'

'I was looking for you.'

The other man cleared his throat. 'I'll leave you to it,' he said, and ducked back into the lightning room.

Kish was displeased; his frown barely left his face all the way up to CR7. 'You didn't know I was in the lightning room,' he said, carefully, 'because no one is told when someone is in the lightning room apart from the people on the upper mezzanine. It's for safety. So what were you doing there?'

'I'm sorry,' I said, looking at my own burnt hands and Kish's rashed-over ones, my stomach flipping over at my stupid lie. 'The truth is it was just curiosity.'

'The lightning room is dangerous,' said Kish. 'And the only time you will be allowed to go there is with me. Only my hand can open that final door on this mezzanine. If you have questions, ask me. Don't go looking for answers. Do you understand?'

I nodded.

'What happened to your hands?' he asked.

'My wife,' I replied.

One night I returned home and Marly was nowhere to be seen, but Per was wriggling in his cot. God knows how long he'd been there, but given his soiled towels I suspected all day. At a loss for what to feed him, I mashed some oats we'd dried last year into some water from the pump and fed him from the tip of my finger. He gurgled his thanks. Per's eyes had become even darker and even rounder since his birth, and he was beginning to look a little like my father. As I watched him it became clear to me that I wanted Per to grow up to be the sort of man my father had been, and not the sort of man Marly expected me to be. It was one thing, I thought, as I washed Per in the water the sun had warmed, to disapprove of the system that governed our lives – the system that oppressed the sandtowners by controlling our weather so that we could flourish and they could not; that allowed us only one child and kept notes on exactly where we were and what we did through our handprints – but it was another to destroy it, as Marly had always planned. To begin with I had enjoyed her anarchic lilt, her swear words and her earnest hate – in fact, it was that passion that had attracted me most to her – but looking at Per as his cool skin flushed in the water I couldn't possibly believe we were going about this the right way. Per made my chest hurt and my fingers tingle when I touched him; when he cried or gurgled it made my stomach flip. Barely weeks old and already he controlled me more than any government could. And perhaps even more than Marly could. I wrapped him in clean towels and lay with him on the bed where we had made him and waited for his mother.

It was at work a few days later when another message flashed on my screen, ordering me to attend the hospital where Per was born. Kish let me go without question, and I ran so fast I threw up outside the doors when I got there. A doctor, different from the one who birthed Per, was waiting for me.

'Your wife is … unwell,' she said, 'and we brought her here just in case. She has asked to see you.'

I didn't say anything, but followed her into a small suite where Marly lay strapped to a bed, Per in a clean cot beside her. Marly looked small in the bed, fragile almost, her black hair scraped back and the paper gown making her seem as if she could rip apart at any moment, somehow. She had her eyes closed but she knew I was there.

'They pumped it all away,' she said. 'There's nothing left in me.'

'How could you, Marly? After everything.'

She actually smiled. 'How could I? How could I? Can you hear yourself?' She beckoned me nearer. She smelt terrible. 'You are turning into one of them. You promised you'd do it, and now you won't even talk about it. You promised you'd destroy the weather station and now you've just turned into one of them.'

'I haven't, Marly. It's Per. I can't do it because if I do, what kind of future will he have?'

'Per? You don't know the first thing about him.'

'What does that mean?'

'It means that if you don't destroy the weather station, I will do this again. And not on my own.'

'What are you talking about?'

She turned to look at Per and refused to talk again.

■

Marly was let out of hospital two days ago and I haven't slept since. I have watched Per every moment that I can. But today, I cannot. I got here early. I'm watching the sunrise from my mezzanine and even though I know we can control everything that moves on this god-damn earth I still find it incredibly beautiful. Today is a very special day. Kish has told me that we'll be making our first storm. He'll be here in half an hour.

Marly hasn't spoken since she came home, but I know she meant what she said. Her crazy plan all along has been for one of use to destroy the weather station so that Green people can no longer control the weather here. She believes it will give the sandtowners a chance to move away, to escape ... But I have realized, if not over the last few months then perhaps the last few years, even, that Marly's ideals are wrong. What does she expect: that we will be looked after, maybe celebrated by the sandtowners? It won't happen. Beyond our green lands there is no Utopia. We control the weather because we have no other choice: our weather was ruined by other generations who didn't know better, or perhaps did, but didn't care, and now we have to live with that as best we can. If I don't make it rain, what crops will grow? Who will feed Per? And his children? I care about the next generation, unlike those who have ruined it for us. I care about the sandtowners, too – of course I feel guilty about their suffering – but that guilt is not enough – their problems are not our fault. Marly is not an idealist: Marly is mad.

Kish arrives, punctual and smiling as ever. He has forgiven me my coarse questioning and my almost criminal views. He knows that to be a weatherman, you have to be curious.

'My friend,' he says, putting his hand on my shoulder. 'Today we are going to make a storm. You will rarely experience a feeling like it. Today will be your best day yet.'

I nod. 'I know it.'

He grins. 'Well now, let's get out of this mezzanine and into the core of the earth.'

I laugh and follow him down the stairs, right to the ground floor, where he presses his hand to the pad and the trapdoor swings open.

'Come,' he says, and I trail him, my feet sounding soft on the wooden steps, everything cool in the low light. 'Today you are allowed.'

And now we are at the door that I couldn't cross before, and my heart is racing and even my palms are a little sweaty.

'Nervous?' Kish asks. 'It's only natural. Making a storm is a big deal. I love storm day. In some ways I know I shouldn't – but I do.'

I swallow dryly.

He smiles. 'Now, you need to press your hand to the pad at the same time as me. One, two, three …'

The door makes a click and judders open. Behind it, a huge, bright space, almost blue. A huge hole in the ground, and a huge hole in the ceiling, which I guess is the tube going through the roof, though here, I realize, there is no tube: just the space inside it. Around the hole is a gallery, with wooden railings, chest-high, and weather panels bleeping along the walls. And buzzing. Loud and louder, lots of buzzing. I lean over the railings; the drop is huge. Kish pulls me back with a rough tug.

'No, you never, ever stand that close to the rails.'

I nod, but can't shake off the feeling in my stomach, the bottomlessness of the hole.

'Your curiosity will be the death of you,' he sighs. 'Let me just tell you first. The generator works from underground, and the lightning is directed through the roof and elsewhere. You will see it rise straight through the ground through the tube.'

'But how does that even work?'

Kish shakes his head. 'That's not important, and, in any case, I'm not authorized to tell you. But I have told you about the buttons you must press to make it work. The panel is the same as our one in CR7. Look.'

We turn our backs to the tube and instead face the machines. I shiver, though the room – cave, whatever – is hot. 'You have,' I said. 'Yes. I see. The same.'

'Well, then.' He rubs his hands down the lengths of his coat. 'We are ready to make the storm. I have put everything in place for it. And I want you to create the lightning.'

'I had hoped as much,' I say.

Kish bows his head. 'First, I must set you up.' I watch him as he presses buttons, cranks handles and swishes about. Sweat is running down my back now under my coat.

'I just want to ask: how much damage will this storm do to the sandtowns?'

Kish clears his throat. 'You're very altruistic, aren't you?'

'It's not that ... I just want to know.'

He shakes his head. 'I'll be honest with you: it's these storms that have created, and ruined, the sandtowns.'

'Yes ... The sandtowns are our fault. I know that. But we only make storms when we need to.'

Kish laughed. 'You really believe that? Why would we ever need to make a storm?'

Marly is mad. Marly is not mad. I have so many questions I can't even ask one.

'We make storms to make sure the sandtowns remain that way. We can only feed so many mouths.' Kish pats me on the back. 'It's OK – you're a weatherman, but you're not God. We can only do so much.'

I stare at Kish until my eyes feel dry. I knew, of course I knew, that in controlling the weather we weren't helping the sandtowns … But to do it simply to oppress them? Marly, oh god, she was right, and I nearly lost both her and our son because I didn't believe her.

Kish looks at me. 'Now, weatherman, I need you to realize that the lightning is the most dangerous part of the storm, and generates a huge amount of power which we recycle back into the weather station. For this reason, the hole through which it's directed is very dangerous. When you have made the lightning, on no account should you lean over the railings. It might kill you.'

'Might?'

'Will. And it would destroy the weather station. So, that's safety out of the way. You're a sensible man, when you listen. And now, I am ready for you to make the lightning. Are you ready? I bet you can't wait.'

I nod, but I'm not ready, not by a long shot. I will never be ready for this. I know now exactly what I need to do. I think really I always knew: I just didn't believe that I would do it.

'Press the button, weatherman!' Kish nods at me and waits for my finger to do its magic, to control the weather and to make the storm come true.

Before I press the button, I take a deep breath and think of my dad, and how proud he would be, and think of Per, and the man I hope he will become, and think of Marly, and how this might save her, and that's so much that I can't think any more, and I let my mind go blank; so blank that all I can think of is the space in front of me, the button I have to push, and I close my eyes and press the button.

'That's it!' yells Kish, applauding.

Immediately I hear fizzing, buzzing, then a jet of white and blue so bright I blink back tears. I turn around to face the tube and Kish bounds over and puts his arm over my shoulder.

'Well done!' he calls into my ear.

But I shrug him away, and before he can do anything I am at the railings. I climb so I'm standing on top of them, and I whoop. Kish tries to come over but the lightning is glaring; I close my eyes and think of Per. I open them once to look down into the fizzing dark that's blindingly white at the same time and I take another deep breath.

'What are you doing?' Kish screams, hanging onto the rail but crouching on the floor. 'Do you want to kill yourself?' There are tears running down his cheeks because the light is so bright. My head is pounding along with my heart, which may as well be my Adam's apple it's so high in my throat. I start to laugh.

'No! I don't want to die! But it doesn't matter; no one is important here.'

'Are you mad?' Kish is clinging to the rail but has his other arm over his eyes. 'You're a weatherman! Stop this at once!'

A weatherman. So proud. A god, of sorts. And yet I have no choice, and I know it. Focusing now on Per, wrapped in his towels, on my father's innocence and Marly's humanity, I suck my breath in so hard I think I'll explode, and in one soft, small movement I throw myself down the tube and all I hear is buzzing and then silence, silence, silence.

# TAKE NOTICE

Adam Thorpe

NOT THAT HE WOULD EVER KNOW what might happen, to him
or to anyone else; one of the more extraordinary features of being
human is that, while knowing the future exists, you remain entirely
ignorant of its manifestations. Animals are luckier, Gus reflected: they
bathe in a permanent present.

He had his great garden, and he was continually amazed each
spring – indeed, these days in any season out of the deepest
darks of winter – by the earth's profligacy, throwing up growth
as soon as his gardener, the loyal but stiffening Cliff, had dug it
to bare sod. This smothered Gus's loneliness. In the beginning his
children, having frittered away their years after university, would
return every so often, staying sometimes two or three months
in the 'country pile' until boredom saw them off again, whither
he knew not. His perceived return to political respectability had
foundered long ago, and the ache of disappointment had never
really left him.

He missed Sarah, his wife, more than ever; she had drowned in
Crete so many years ago now that he had to pause before calculating
the number. He had brought her body back to England in the hold
of a government jet, at night, into a blaze of flashbulbs that caught
him looking too official. At least, that was the complaint. Perhaps
that was the start of it all: his rage at fate.

England.

Once he had believed in such a concept, a vague medley of flags and fields and Shakespeare's verse. Now, despite its present, almost sacred potency ('her commons of earth-song/not yet consumed' in the words of the current fashionable verse-maker, Naresh Thomson), the idea left him cold. It was a withered cold thing in his hand, a dried-out mandragora upon which long ago he had supped and which now left nothing but the echo of its shriek; a sad uprooted object on a shelf, like a private memento that means nothing to anyone except to the person who found it on some special, far-off day. A dead touchstone, a husk.

Language was left to him, of course, a delight in language, but Gus found himself even now drawn to its worst exemplars – old airport thrillers from the days when airports were open to the public, stories of green-eyed phantoms hiding behind embossed drops of blood and gore. The adventures of Sherlock Holmes or the complete edition of P.G. Wodehouse acted as a light-hearted corrective to this regrettable tendency. As for the great classics, they collected dust and spiders' threads in his grandfather's library, where the smell of real books and real paper was a perfume as potent as honeysuckle.

At times he had imagined burning the lot and going over to the other side – starting afresh in a simple caravan in Wales or France or Ireland, or turning the peaty soil on some Hebridean croft with the battering ocean as accompaniment beyond a stony hill. But the days passed into weeks and the weeks slid easily into months, and so on until, with some degree of shock, he realized that he had spent over a decade doing nothing of any significance or worth – not even lending anything more substantial than considerable quantities of cash after the Great Flood. Not even making amends.

His children no longer needed him. One of his daughters was dead, another had run off with a yurt-maker to America, a third was now rich and miserable in Staffordshire, wife to a bore who had made a fortune from portable dams and whose sole idea of fun was to sail yachts into rocks and spend millions (or so it seemed) on repairs. The dead daughter had been his favourite, but she had declined into drugs and sexual deviancy with such apparent relish that he had no longer recognized her in the last years, and her dying was ghastly and protracted. He had felt no love for her by the time she succumbed:

not for the person succumbing, at any rate. He scarcely wept either at the funeral or in the lonely days afterwards, when the hospital visits no longer took him away from the house and its hungry grounds.

Gus would stare at early photographs of Persephone and wonder where the little dark-haired girl had gone, slipping off her father's knee into oblivion. Separated as she was from the bony white-faced spectre he had buried, he could almost believe she might return. In his nightmares this is exactly what he would see, and on awakening would wonder why it was not a pleasant dream, why instead it had brought out the sweat on his brow and upper lip so heavily that he could taste salt on his tongue.

The dew of fear, he thought, and of some obscure longing for remission.

He looked back on his life and found that at each point of potential there was a small dark stain like a crushed fly when movement of any significance had been deprived him – he could not explain it better to himself. He had started his autobiography, a sober account of his years in politics, his period of apparent power and influence, some twenty years ago, but it had fizzled out into a dull, apologetic tract concerning issues and small dramas no one save the academics now remembered, and it sat as a wad of unfulfilled notes in a cupboard in the study. There was only one thing the general populace ever remembered about him, and in a form of narrative that lacked nuance. Reality is all nuance, he would say, to no one in particular. To the sky, which he sometimes felt was his only true domain: its epic puffs of mountains and castles.

By becoming a recluse, he was aware that he was depriving himself of those elements that might distract him from his increasingly inward journey, and on reading that the spiral was the essential building block of all matter, the primary pattern in its paradigmatic return and advance – each return completing an advance and beginning another – he felt himself on a course that resembled a whirlpool and might finish in the black hole of madness, where everything was … what? What it should not be, of course, while appearing eminently sensible.

He was having tea on the lower lawn – Mrs Cutler having brought out the tray with her usual moan and long retired into the shadowy blackness of the house, the candle lamps not yet lit – when he saw a man dressed all in white cycling towards him between the croquet hoops, swerving unsteadily to avoid one of the cracked wooden balls that had been a smooth bright yellow in Gus's far-off boyhood.

It never occurred to Gus that his life might be in danger; the threat of assassination was long past, in his opinion. The youngish man, removing his bicycle clips, introduced himself as a friend of Persephone's in her final, difficult years. He had once been handsome but the face was now ravaged by misuse, the eyes particularly suffering: their pale blue appeared albino, as if accustomed to darkness. Gus had initially suspected he was after ration cards – meat, electricity, whatever – or had some counterfeit versions to sell: the country was overrun by the latter since the latest edict, which reduced an average use of the national grid to about a day a week. People smelt unwashed, Mrs Cutler said.

'Would you like some tea?'

'Thank you.' The man seemed surprised. He had a famished look; he was either genuinely hungry or one of those reluctant, state-rewarded vegans.

A scowling Mrs Cutler brought out the best biscuits and one of her wobblier jam sponge cakes, which the man gobbled happily (merely famished, then). The indirect communication with Persephone was both upsetting and comforting to Gus – the gruff manner of the stranger, who gave his name as 'Aidan, Aidan Eldraw', giving it an air of sincerity. Although the head supervisor for a nearby community's composting network, he was clearly down on his luck, his looseness of limb almost clumsy. Despite his denials, it occurred to Gus that this may well have been a boyfriend, someone who had played an active part in his daughter's decline.

The ensuing confidences were insinuating and vague, Aidan Eldraw apparently bent on some form of blackmail.

'Persephone's upbringing was weird, wasn't it?'

'Was it?'

'Nannies, a father often absent, scandals.'

'Scandals?'

'Pre-Revolt. Women. She often mentioned the women in your life.'

'She never got over the death of her mother.'

'I said to her: you can't expect your dad to be pure as the driven.'

Gus was relieved when the man rose to go. They walked together to the gate, sweating in the April heat, the bicycle ticking as it was wheeled over the warm lawn. So far, nothing had been said of the real purpose of the visit, although Gus was increasingly troubled by the man's tone as they approached the iron whorls of the entrance, beyond which the postman's horse was delivering great clots of dung on the rutted, camomile-tufted drive.

'Thank you for the tea. You'll be hearing from me again.'

'Will I? I rather hope not.'

When the letters came a few weeks later, signed 'A.E.', Gus was not that surprised. The overt claims of incest and neglect brought the stranger's face into abrupt close-up, as if Persephone had been replaced by some furious demon of revenge. The old man searched back in his past, found nothing that might have been misconstrued except by a damaged hysteric, wrote back to threaten the apparent blackmailer with the police – knowing in the process that he was risking his neck, his reputation, everything.

On an impulse he bought an old racing car, a 1968 Lotus that had reputedly won many races all over the world, and he began to enter it for club meetings. He hired a waggon-team to transport it, found a white-haired mechanic twenty miles away willing and able to accompany him or to drop by if problems occurred while he was spinning about the grounds, and began to discover in himself, in his mid-seventies, a youthful capacity for exhilaration and danger. At Silverstone one weekend he swirled off and lightly broke his leg. He drove the car round and round the garden on the gravel drive as soon as he was recovered, and went to bed with the smell of Castrol and burnt rubber in his clothes and soiled skin.

An article about his hobby appeared in a reputable Sunday newspaper, accompanied by absurdly glossy photographs of himself with the red car positioned in front of the house. The result (as he understood it) was that the house was burgled of most of its valuables, and the shed in which the Lotus was sheltered was set alight, destroying everything within it; despite the licences for meetings of historical interest, petrol-driven vehicles were legitimate targets these days. The police were only interested in the burglary, although trusty Cliff berated them from behind his rake. They laughingly threatened to search his gardening hut for illegal chemicals and went away, pursued by imprecations.

The loss of the car struck Gus as in some way symptomatic, and he saw his life as irredeemably blighted and the rest of humanity as bent on violence and envious revenge. He was not at all surprised when, one morning in the greenhouse – to which he had retired with a book from an abruptly chilly day in January – the white-clad Aidan Eldraw appeared like a wraith on the threshold beyond the orchids and ferns. He looked healthier than on the first visit two years previously, and Gus had the unpleasant sensation of being sucked of his blood as the man talked. He had no bicycle this time: he had walked ten miles, hitched a lift from a slow solar waggon for the last five.

'None of my recent letters have been answered,' he said. He was sitting on an iron chair once painted cream and now freckled and blistered by rust, yet appeared not to be aware of the danger to the starchy freshness of his clothes. 'So I'm forced to come to you again in person to hear the truth.'

'Did you burn my car and rob my house?' asked Gus. The stranger – Gus still thought of him as a stranger, though his face was frighteningly familiar from bad dreams – smiled and shook his head.

'You must have so many enemies,' he said. 'Since the Revolt.'

'Most of them are misinformed, as you know.'

'The clampdown was on your watch.'

'Yes. The lightning conductor, they called me. I took the blame during the trials. But there is nothing I can do about my enemies. It was a long time ago. The future is what counts and everything is now apparently in hand. We've passed the peak, did you know that?'

'Everyone knows that,' the man scoffed. His brow was not shiny, nor his upper lip. On the contrary, he had the pinched look of someone still chilled. Yet the greenhouse was unpleasantly hot and humid, beading its moisture on every surface, on petal and leaf and stem, on paper and on human skin.

'They say the effects won't be immediately felt, even on the glaciers. Which seems contradictory' Gus went on, folding his wrinkled hands on his book. 'One never knows who or what to believe.' He paused, slapped at a mosquito whining in his ear as if punishing himself. 'I've thought hard about your allegations. I've searched my memory for the slightest justification for their outrageous content and found none.' The words came easily and calmly from his mouth.

Aidan Eldraw shifted in his iron chair. His smile was bloodless, his stare without highlights – as if the very eyeballs were dry.

'I don't happen to believe you,' he said. 'I happen to believe Persephone.'

Gus registered the craquelure on the iron tracery of the greenhouse, built so long ago that even his grandfather remembered it as a boy. The oldest panes of glass were blown by hand and ruffled the scene outside as he moved his head. Small bubbles of air rested in them, like air in ice. The world might melt, he thought, or catch fire and be blown away in ashes, great drifts of ash. Whatever they say.

He closed his eyes and thought of his car, of its leather seats and the oily interior of the engine, of the speed it would go and the cheery innocence it provoked in all those who laid eyes on it, of the track rushing under his wheels and the scenery blurring into an abstraction of dim colour, of his old heart pounding under the racing overalls.

He opened his lids again and said to the man, 'If you don't go away I will call the police.'

'Prime Minister, you know perfectly well that the dead can't be arrested.'

'I am no longer the prime minister, I am seventy-nine and retired for decades. And you are not a ghost. I, if anything, am the ghost.'

The man stood up: the rusty chair had left stains like old spots of blood on the cream suit. 'Poor Persephone,' he said. 'You'll never know what you did to her, will you? One day long ago, on a road leaving Nairobi, as I was heading for Mombasa, I saw a sign. It said, TAKE NOTICE: WHEN THIS SIGN IS UNDER WATER, THIS ROAD IS IMPASSABLE. Please think about this sign, Prime Minister. Think about it very hard.'

The man who claimed to have known Persephone never came back; at times Gus would wonder if the creature had ever existed. The blisters of rust on the old seat had broken, that was for sure, and Gus had not sat there for years. Delusion was a distinct possibility, although the visitant's Kenyan connection seemed plausible enough.

If you could go on seeing the sign, then all was not lost. He smiled at this, often. Was that what the man had meant? Or something quite other?

When he was dying, on a tropic day in early spring, and stumbling in his visions along a green downland track, he was surprised to find the sign underwater, and quite invisible, and the way forward gone for good save the odd tell-tale ripple over the drowned hedgerows. A moment of clarity ensued. He wished to say sorry. But he could not speak.

Mrs Cutler scowled and the nurse wiped his brow. He asked to be raised up against the pillows and gesticulated for a pen, for paper, for ink – not the pallid soya ink on his desk but the old deep-smelling violet ink that he had sealed in a bottle decades before, in a cupboard drawer. But the liquid had dried up to no more than a stain around the inside, like a trick bottle he had once bought in a toy shop when he was a boy and had long since lost.

He held the little vessel loosely in his hands, studying it intently as if it held some divine secret, thinking – through a haze of weariness and pain – of all the words he might have written, of all that he might have regained.

# GO LIGHT

*To climb these coming crests*
*one word to you, to*
*you and your children:*

*stay together*
*learn the flowers*
*go light*

*Gary Snyder*

# LEAVING FRIDESWIDE

## David Constantine

WORD CAME BY A THIN SOMALI BOY on a mountain bike. Suddenly he appeared at the open door, braking hard and behind him the brazen sky. Letter for you, Miss, he said. He stood there offering it over the handlebars. Beth noticed that his trainers didn't match. Well I hope they fit at least, she said. She had taken to uttering her hopes aloud – softly, below the hearing of anyone more than a yard away, but aloud, and her fears likewise. Said, they were real, she owned up to them, the things she hoped and the things she feared. The messenger wore a blue football strip, kingfisher blue. He could not be more than seven or eight. He wore his importance proudly and fearfully. How white his eyes.

Beth came out from behind her desk and took the letter. What are you called? she asked. – Barnie, Miss. – Would you like some apple juice, Barnie? – Yes, please, Miss. She took a jug from the fridge and poured him a glass. The generator died half an hour ago, she said. But it should still be all right. Barnie gulped it down. Beth poured him another glass. Not much this year, she said. Not much and the last.

The letter, on county council notepaper, was handwritten in beautiful copperplate at which Beth marvelled, before she read:

*Friday 30 September*

*Dear Ms Atkins,*
*The buses will come for your party tomorrow, 1 October, at 10 a.m. Please be ready to leave at once. According to your submission*

*of 15 September, you have forty-three people in your charge. We shall
send an ambulance for Mrs Eaves, to bring her to hospital here. On
the buses there will be space for five wheelchairs. Luggage is limited
to one suitcase and one handbag or shoulder bag per person. There
will be space also for your box files. Before leaving, please make the
office, the school, the Big House and all sheds, outbuildings, stores,
and workshops as secure as possible.*

    *I wish you a safe journey.*

    *Yours sincerely,*

                         *Thomas Cartwright*

                         *Health and Social Security*

Below this was scrawled: PTO. Beth turned and read: *Dearest, admire
the script! Harry's dad – he used to sort our post – offered his services. There's
another talent we never knew we had! Be brave tomorrow. I'll follow
when I'm let. My love as always. Tom.*

Beth looked at Barnie. He was staring at her, almost imploring,
which choked her throat with pity. Oh dear, she whispered. What
will become of him? Barnie, she said, will you take a note back to
Mr Cartwright, please? I will write it quickly. Yes, Miss, said Barnie,
his stare never quitting her face. Beth wrote: My darling, please send
Barnie to me with the buses tomorrow. I will have written you a letter
by then. Tell Barnie he must carry my letter to you. I couldn't bear to
leave without being sure that you will have my letter. But it is too sad
for words. Beth. She sealed and addressed her note. Barnie tucked it
down his right sock, and vanished into the heat.

They had known they must leave. At least, those in charge and those
in their care whose wits still worked that way had known it for
weeks. All the same, Barnie's word was very sudden. Beth stood in a
vagueness, staring out into the flickering heat. The air itself was hot,
she could scarcely have said where the sun shone from, its heat had
entered the air that people must look at, feel, smell, and take into
their lungs for breath. Perhaps it will rain, she said. But that was an

out-of-date hope, not big enough. Very likely it would rain. It might rain next week, tomorrow, before nightfall. So what?

Kingston stood in the door. That kid ride like the wind, he said. Oh, Kingston, said Beth, they sent him to say the buses are coming tomorrow. I knew him for a messenger, Kingston said. That boy's a born messenger. Kingston advanced, as out of a fiery furnace. Nobody at Frideswide could say how old he was: maybe sixty, maybe ninety. He had been there for ever. Kingston was where he had come from and what he was called. That was the one sure thing. Beth and everyone else at Frideswide who thought about Kingston supposed that something bad had happened to him early on. Or not just bad – the worst; so that nothing so bad could happen to him again. That seemed the most likely reason for his calm, stature and gentleness. His hair was a dirty white, he wore soft and faded clothes, walked slowly, looked around him a good deal, stooped his height benignly over all who spoke to him. Then we better get moving, Elizabeth, he said.

The office was more or less packed up already – in box files 1-30, year by year, a record of who had come and who had gone, the aspirations, deeds and disappointments of the place. Tom Cartwright, who had come visiting more often than he strictly needed to, said one day, if he was let, he would write a proper history of Frideswide, from the leper hospital to the new woodshed with its solar panels, from Sir Philip Swithamley to Ms Beth Atkins. Beth put on her wide straw hat and went out with Kingston to tell whoever had to be told.

Alfred was standing at the school gates with his photograph. He been standing there too long, said Kingston. He won't come in, said Beth. I've tried. He's having one of his bad days.

Beth's office was in the old school, facing the front yard. The juniors had moved some years before, to a bright new place, but the infants still attended, or had until July, when the schools, this and the rest, finished for the summer holidays and no new year would begin. For a while, daytime and evenings, the hall and the classrooms continued to accommodate courses, events, and meetings of one sort or another. There was art, Keep Fit, IT, local history, yoga, English as a foreign language, first aid, a crèche, a playgroup, twice a week the CAB were there, once a week the MP, there were discos and talks on global warming, the WI held their AGM, the Allotments Committee met, so did Crisis at Christmas, all the usual things that people arrange for mutual aid, instruction, and entertainment continued for a while in the hospitable old school, till one by one in the gathering heat they ceased, they gave up, they were terminated. The foyer still said, Welcome! in thirty-five languages, the classrooms harboured their equipment and materials, the charts, the paintings, the photos, all the bright paraphernalia, but the humans, infant and adult, were gone, and already from the roof space to the cellars the emboldened rats had the run of the place, up and down the stairs, and Beth, working late, heard them at her back, the risen and rapidly multiplying population.

The old heart of Frideswide, the leper hospital and its chapel, once some distance outside the city walls, had over the last hundred years or so been taken in; but from above, from a police helicopter, say, the whole domain looked to be feeling for the lost country still. In a ragged fashion it reached beyond its own boundaries for connection with like-minded terrain: an unkempt graveyard, a park, the backs of gardens, an allotment, the dark corridor of a stream or a disused railway line. Even before the heat, the very thought of this thriving greenery was a refreshment. It lingered in parched minds now as an after-image: terrible loss, commensurate longing.

Wherever you went in the territory of Frideswide you heard the rumour of the city, faintly the traffic on the motorway, trains passing west, and now and then a big military plane came over low, heading for its base in the open country, concrete enclosed by wire. But these sounds of the outside world, if heeded at all, had only ever deepened the feeling of sanctuary. Now silence pressed upon the quiet of Frideswide, you hearkened at it far more than you ever had to the din of the streets, you listened to it.

Frideswide's workshops were clustered behind the school, by the entrance to the market gardens; across these gardens, next to the main orchard, stood the ruins of the chapel and the leper hospital, and close to them the Big House, once the workhouse, and there most of Frideswide's people lived.

■

The first workshop was still busy. They were assembling wooden toys – engines with trucks and carriages, farm buildings, dolls' houses – and painting them and the humans and animals to go with them, in bright colours. Beth sat down at one of the benches. She had no wish to impart her news. Kingston sat against the wall, very upright, and closed his eyes. He withdrew. It was like sleep, but deeper, further away, blacker, in the substratum of himself, beyond consolation and asking for none. Even in the heyday of Frideswide when there was much to do and the bright things they made for children passed quickly to the shop and into the outside children's world, even then, suddenly, in any company and on any occasion, Kingston might retract himself and sit against the wall, showing the face of a sadness as old as thinking man. Nobody intruded upon him.

Beth said her news matter-of-factly and watched it home, from face to face. The same at the other two working benches. Leaving, she said, Supper's at six-thirty. And to herself, in the undertone: Candles and oil-lamps.

Bench by bench in the other two workshops, Beth told the people they were leaving home next day. After that, entering the gardens, she sat in the doorway of the nearest shed and pulled her straw hat down over her eyes. The faces appeared, all of them together, pressing to be seen again as they had looked when she spoke the news. Hardest among them to bear were those like Sammy who had not known what to make of it, was it good or bad? and who looked, for example, to Albert who knew it was bad and expected no better, or, for example, to Ethel, who smiled on the world, never learned but forgot and reverted always to her incurable bent in favour of trust. So Sammy looked at one or the other and back again at Beth: again and again he looked hard at Beth. He rested his big hands on the red roof of a dolls' house and his eyes like creatures at bay implored her to promise nothing bad would happen.

It was late afternoon. Between the shed and the Big House lay the acres of cultivated land, all manner of plots, all shapes and sizes, with osier hedges, and the paths passing under rustic arches. There were coops and trellises, cane wigwams for beans and sweet peas, small families of apple, pear, damson, and plum, a scrap of old woodland with beehives in. There were troughs, water butts, sheds; here and there a wicker statue, a scarecrow. So much work year after year, so much wit, care, inventiveness and delight, all the loving craft, ending. No one was working. A dozen or more of Frideswide's own people and a dozen at least from outside come in for respite and to learn. They should have been here, among the statues and the scarecrows; you'd have seen people picking, tending, pruning, clearing, getting ready for next year, there'd have been a slow bonfire or two, and from the far corner you'd have heard the Dixie Band practising for Apple Day. Really, there was nothing much left, no chickens, no ducks, nothing much had come through, scarcely enough for their own needs, very little for the shop, nothing in store, the glacial days in May, then the heat, the searing, the hail, the dust, the hail, deluge, tempest, heat, heat, heat, had left wreckage, blackening, blight, and putrescence, and over all, till the next sweep of rain, lay the fine red dust.

Beth watched the red kites. They came in up the quiet motorway and, unless the weather was furious, congregated over Frideswide, twenty or thirty of them, spying down, tilting, gliding lower for a closer look. You might come across one on the earth itself, tearing at a find, not at all perturbed by your arrival. They would clean the place up. The deer came in too, fallow and muntjac, along the parched corridors, for any remnants of succulence. And stray dogs, once or twice already a pack of them, and lone cats ranging out of town. After three days of hot south winds, many thousands of butterflies blew in with the red dust. They clouded the brassy sky, the local birds fell upon them gratefully, they drifted the earth, the wood-chip paths, the asphalt playground, the roofs, the gutters, the sills, in a soft litter and it was only then, fallen and finishing, that you saw how beautiful they were, how delicate their structure and fabric, how various their symmetries, countless thousands of creatures, flocking, whirling and settling as softly as snow.

At the Big House they were laying the two long tables for supper. The fare would be what they had rescued from the freezers when the generator gave up the ghost. Quite a feast, really. The day's cooks had switched to gas cylinders and half a dozen camping stoves. They were pleased with themselves. There won't be another supper here, said Beth. Barring miracles. So yours will go down in history. As it happened, two of the shift did believe in miracles. They were a couple called Elsie and Carlo Viti who, in earlier days, had walked the roads from Cuthbert's house in Durham to the Black Madonna's in Viggiano and back again. Bless you, said Elsie. The Lord will return us to our garden, when it is time. Carlo beamed at her and then at Beth. They carried on setting candles and now and then a silver oil lamp down the centre of the tables.

Beth went to tell Mr James. His job was brushing and mopping the hall, and when he had done it he returned to his small room at the back of the house, to work. The time before supper was the best, in his opinion. Beth told him the news. He said nothing, only turned away and looked through the window at the orchard that year after year, till now, had never failed, month by month, even week by week, to be differently beautiful. He sat at a small pine table on which was a Liddell and Scott, a fountain pen, an HB pencil, a pencil sharpener, a rubber, an open exercise book, and *Oedipus at Colonus*, the Greek text, in an edition that had belonged to one Eric Johnston of Wadham College in 1912 and that now lay open at lines 669–95, which Mr James was translating. Self-taught and too late (he said), he worked very slowly. First, in pencil, he copied out the Greek, leaving a good space between each line. He loved this stage of the work, took infinite care over it, rubbed out and corrected any mistakes. Making the letters with their breathings and accents pleased him inordinately. Next, after hours of pondering and consultation of his text's notes and glossary and of his own Liddell and Scott, he entered below each line, in ink, a very literal version of the Greek. And only then, again in ink but on the facing page, after days of struggle and staring into the orchard, did he write out a version in verse, accompanying, as he said, but not faithfully matching, Sophocles' metres. Later still, having let it lie for a week, he did a final version in fair copy on a new page. What do you think of this? he said over his shoulder to Beth. It's only a draft still, I'll have to let it lie. Beth stood by him, looking into the palsied orchard. Mr James read:

> *Famous for horses, there is none*
> *More beautiful on earth*
> *Than this place you have come to, stranger*
> *Bright Colonus where*
> *The many nightingales sing loud and clear*
> *Amid deep greenery and under the wine-dark*
> *Berried ivy, down*
> *The untrodden ways that no storms shake*
> *Nor fierce sun burns*
> *The god comes, Dionysus comes*
> *For revelry*
> *With the undying*
> *The ever-fostering nymphs.*

> *Here in the dew of heaven*
> *Day upon day narcissi thrive*
> *Whose clustering beauty*
> *The goddesses have always worn for crowns*
> *With the golden shining crocuses and never*
> *Do the unsleeping streams*
> *Of Cephissus dwindle but they roam*
> *For pasture and every day*
> *With undefiled waters*
> *Over the swelling land*
> *Give easy birth. The Muses*
> *Love to dance here and the golden–*
> *Reined Aphrodite rides...*

Beth put her hand on Mr James's shoulder and left the room quickly.

◼

The casseroles and the jugs of apple juice passed down the table. The undexterous and the people sitting back in wheelchairs were served first. The mood was more gay than sorrowful, and those who, like Sammy, had not known what to make of Beth's announcement sided now with cheerfulness, followed the banter this way and that, and the fear, the apprehension of ill, withdrew from their eyes. Before the crumble – made from last year's plums – Beth had the lamps and candles lit, and with them came a solemnity, the face of every person present shone in a new light in a unique character, and in that lay the seriousness and poignancy, not in virtues or vices, not in good or bad looks, but in uniqueness, every person, each herself, each himself, so that Beth said aloud in her undertone, They all matter differently. What will become of them?

◼

Beth went to the sickroom, where Lucy Eaves was dying. The nurse, Marija, stood at the open window. The air outside was not as it should have been after sunset. Beth looked at Lucy and shook her head. Then to Marija she said, You go and eat now.

Beth set a small table under the window, and between two candles began her letter to Tom. Only her own breath moved the candle flames at all; the air outside seemed to have lost the gift of breathing. The dying woman behind her breathed perforce, mechanically, not yet allowed to cease.

Beth wrote: My love, I am sitting with Lucy Eaves, the woman you are sending the ambulance for tomorrow. I hope she will be able to die by then. Marija must go back in the ambulance with her. How happy I should be if you and I were leaving Frideswide together. I should hardly mind what happens if we were together. Lucy is one of the oldest people here. Nobody knows anything about her. She never said much except 'Thank you'. She often said 'Thank you', and asked other people how they were getting on. In normal times perhaps we should have found some relative of hers when it came to this. As it is, nobody knows of one. I'm sitting at the open window but it makes no difference. Is fresh air a thing of the past? What a strange expression that is! I could make quite a list of things that are 'things of the past'. Love isn't one of them. Is wanting a baby? When I saw Barnie this morning, when he suddenly appeared in the doorway, so brave and scared, my feelings tore at their captivity again. So wanting a child is not yet a thing of the past. Marija is from Croatia. She was going to get married. She only came here for a year to make a bit of money. And now she's stuck.

Lucy's breathing got louder. Beth went and sat by her, took her hand, closely regarded her face. Inhalation was hoarse and laborious, but worse to attend to was the holding of breath. It looked, each time, like an exertion of the will to die by not breathing out, the effort being grotesquely at odds with the woman's slight frame. Her face became hectic in the pause. So long it lasted, each time so very long. It is mechanical, Beth said aloud. She is not suffering. But that was not how it looked and sounded. The release, when it came, was like something ruptured, and no sooner done with, the next heaving in began, deep, deep. So you might open a window and breathe in the breeze riding in on the sea. But the air in the sickroom was leaden, like a forbidden planet's.

Marija came back, Beth left her, promising to send another woman up as soon as they were done in the hall. Kingston and three of the younger men had locked what of Frideswide's outbuildings could be locked, but Beth still had much to do before morning. She was late to bed.

Beth woke hearing owls. She drifted there on the borders, between sleep and waking, hearing the owls. All night in dreams and in near-the-surface monologues she had laboured through an oppression and anxiety in which were compounded her duty to lock up Frideswide and Lucy Eaves's imprisonment in breathing. But now she woke, listening to the owls. She lay wide awake in the dark and the bad feelings lapsed away from her. She remembered with relief the many gaps in Frideswide's fences, the bed of the stream, the over-reaching trees. There were many entrances for any creatures seeking nourishment and shelter. She lay awake, watching the window and listening to the owls calling to and fro. When light became faintly certain, they ceased. Beth rose, dressed, lit a candle and went to the sickroom.

Madge sat by Lucy's bed. Just gone, she said, just a moment ago. Poor soul, such a struggle, but see how she looks now, so peaceful.

Beth went back to her room, brewed coffee on a Camping Gaz and in daylight which had become sufficient she continued her letter to Tom. Dearest, she wrote, Lucy has died. We have to be glad it wasn't sooner or before she reaches a mortuary. She – her body – would have suffered too much heat. My love, I have to tell you a strange and beautiful thing. When I woke or half-woke this morning it was still dark and I heard owls, quite close, calling and answering, one from the old leper hospital, another, I am sure, from the dead orchard. And it was just then, Madge told me, that Lucy was at last allowed to die, just as I woke and lay listening to the owls. I felt they had conducted me to the borders of my sleep, they had piloted me in, to the very edge of daylight, and there they fell silent and withdrew, back into the darkness where, for their safety, they belong, and I was left feeling very honoured and blessed. If I close my eyes now I can still hear them calling and answering, so ghostly and real, so frail and persistent, and I am encouraged. They brought Lucy to where she had to pass over into death, and me they brought into daylight and wakefulness with the courage to leave this beloved place. I wished – how I wished – you were in my bed with me listening to the owls but at least you will learn about them in this letter that Barnie will bring to you and so you will know that I feel braver than I did and you will be encouraged too. Goodbye, my dearest, for now. Come after and find me when you can. Beth.

PS I have decided to give Barnie my lapis lazuli.

■

Everyone was waiting in the playground. The buses arrived on time; one was an open-topped tourist bus, the other was a minibus from the Sunshine Club with most of its seats taken out to accommodate the wheelchairs. The promised ambulance pulled in after them.

Beth was watching for Barnie. She couldn't see him, and had to supervise the embarkation. Kingston went in the ambulance to the Big House, for Lucy Eaves. At the sight of the red tourist bus many began to laugh and shout. Suddenly the departure seemed a jolly affair, like an outing to the seaside. Well this is all right, said Sammy. Eh, Bert, eh, Mrs Winters, this looks all right, wouldn't you say? Mrs Winters lolled forward in her wheelchair, asleep, and Bert, who years ago had appointed himself her valet, stood over her, all decorum, with a parasol. The fittest, embarking, clambered upstairs and opened the big bright umbrellas provided there against the heat, which was already severe.

Beth was in her office, seeing the files out. Everything else would stay. Still no Barnie. She locked up. The ambulance returned, depositing Kingston, picking up Marija, and leaving at once with the body of Lucy Eaves. Alfred stood facing the school, his photograph in one hand, his suitcase and a Fairtrade shopping bag on the asphalt either side of him. Kingston handed Beth the keys of the Big House. All the keys were assembling. No Barnie, she said in her undertone, Kingston being close enough to hear.

Beth carried her case and shoulder bag to the tourist bus. The driver took them in. With all the keys and her letter to Tom in a plastic bag she rejoined Kingston. From nowhere, very fast, skidding to a halt, kingfisher-blue, Barnie arrived. Letter for you, Miss, he said, leaning forward, handing it to her. This boy's some messenger, said Kingston. And Mr Cartwright says please to give me the keys and is there any message? Barnie said. There is, Barnie, said Beth, handing him the plastic bag. See, Miss, I got a satchel, he said. Mr Cartwright give it me. He stowed the letter and the keys safely into it. As last time, he looked awed by his importance. There's no apple juice, said Beth. Stay here with Kingston, I'll bring you some water.

Alfred came over, set down his bags, and showed Barnie his photograph. My wife was at school here, he said. That's her, that little girl. Would you believe it? And do you know, I think that's why I came here when she passed away. Kingston picked up Alfred's bags and led him to the bus.

It's not very nice water, said Beth. But drink some now and take the bottle. Even drinking, Barnie could not take his eyes off her face. And this is for you as well, she said, giving him the lapis. It was my mother's. Wear it round your neck. It will bring you luck. Perhaps you'll be my messenger again one day. Then he was gone. She watched him out of sight, a dwindling brightness on the dirty air.

The buses pulled away. Beth sat with Kingston downstairs, across from Mr James who was on his own, gripping a briefcase tied up with string. In it were his writing materials, his texts and his Liddell and Scott. Upstairs and downstairs there was a good deal of hilarity. They were trying on the tourist headphones; some worked, some didn't, you chose among fourteen languages for a commentary. Beth clutched her letter. They were passing through the outskirts that had been rich and leafy, the roadside trees were all dead, scarcely any traffic, scarcely a soul to be seen, a pack of dogs, the heat. Mr James put on a headset; it worked, he chose a language. Beth glanced at him. He was listening, he was crying. Never had she seen a person cry like that, so quietly, so helplessly, the tears drenched his face and fell onto his hands and the briefcase. For a whole tour of the city he was leaving – its churches, the dwellings of poets, the botanic garden, the museums, the art galleries, the site of a martyrdom, the ancient places of learning – Mr James listened and wept. Beth felt she must cross over and comfort him but Kingston, in an undertone, said, Mr James is all right, Elizabeth. You read your letter, I'm going to sleep.

# HOLIDAY IN ICELAND

## Maria McCann

LAST YEAR WE VISITED MY SISTER KAREN in Rome. She works for an exclusive furnishing company: there's a leather-bound booklet of two hundred fabric swatches so people can choose the sofa of their dreams. Our parents don't know about the swatches. Karen made me swear never to tell them. How wasteful, I imagine them saying, How silly! Two hundred different sofa covers. Brown was good enough for us, during The War.

That was the soundtrack to my childhood: our parents speaking of The War as if they'd fought it single-handed. Their peace was something of a let-down. *They* (the council, the government, the park-keeper, the teachers, the man who swept the platform at the station) ought to do this, or do that, or do it better, or more often. Sometimes They Wanted Their Heads Seeing To. It was disgusting: after all my parents had been through during The War! Once, in a temper, I screamed, 'I hate The War,' and was slapped so hard I bit my tongue.

I must have been a trying child. Karen was the opposite, an instinctive diplomat, but we understood one another: we both knew we were waiting to leave. Karen went so far as to leave the country ('living with Eyeties', said Dad) but there's more to leaving than geography. Even now, whenever we meet, it's not long before we go into our impersonation routine, wringing our hands and complaining about The War and They.

Despite the toxic fug of resentment in which I grew up, our adolescence wasn't particularly dramatic. My elder sister was shrewd and conventional, storing up energy for the coming escape. As for me, I was too cowardly for the usual teenage rebellions – shoplifting, promiscuity, drugs – but I felt I had it in me to enjoy life. I just needed a start.

Sometimes the unconscious comes to the rescue, bringing inspiration so subtle you don't even know you're inspired. I found my perfect rebellion, one against which my parents were powerless.

'Lisa has a bubbly personality,' the teachers said. They meant it as praise but my parents only stared. In our house, coming out Bubbly was a kind of Petty Treason, a threat to Divine Order. Looking at their dismayed faces, I felt my power, and after that I bubbled for Britain.

*Bubbly* wasn't a euphemism for *airhead*, not in my case. There was talk at school of my trying for university, but my father said, in so many words, that university wasn't for the likes of us. Did he mean, not for girls? Perhaps, though I can't picture him cheering on sons, if he'd had any. The careers mistress said, 'You should make the most of your talents, Lisa,' but having witnessed Karen's vanishing act, I couldn't wait to be independent, and never hear any more about Sacrifices and People Who Didn't Know They Were Born.

In fact, it wasn't until my first job that I perfected Bubbly. If you think about it, most employees are in camouflage. It takes full camo to talk about selling plastic drinking straws and make people believe you actually care. Bubbly was ready-made for the purpose: bubbly at my desk, bubblier still after hours. It was my bubbliness that attracted Gareth, and I took care to keep him away from my parents until we were safely engaged. Once I was married, and we escaped to London, Bubbly became my full time job. Go with the flow. Nothing that can't be solved with a smile.

Clemmie was born within a year of our marriage and named after Gareth's great-aunt. Our Darling Clementine. (I couldn't have any more kids, as it turned out, but we didn't know that then. We thought we might stop at three.)

Nobody can persuade me that frustration and restriction are character-forming. I know too much about them. My daughter, my *only* daughter, was allowed to try – and give up – ballet, riding, kayaking, painting, drama, swimming, piano, yoga, karate. We had sleepovers, treasure hunts, goodie bags, paintballing, pamper parties. Once, I hired a pink stretch limo so that Clemmie and her best friends could giggle through Holloway lolling on heart-shaped satin cushions.

'Terminally tacky,' Gareth said. But I wasn't going to watch Clemmie standing by, second best, while other girls had fun. I'd seen all that in my own childhood and I wanted her confident and popular. And when they scrambled out of the car, as flushed and wired as if the pink lemonade had been champagne, I knew I'd done the right thing.

'You petrol-head,' Gareth said that night. He pushed his knees into the backs of mine as we snuggled down beneath the duvet. 'What'll all these kids do when the world runs out of oil?'

'Up to them, entirely,' I said. 'But I'll know that while we had it, my daughter got her share.'

The Iceland Question came up when Clemmie was seventeen. She'd stayed behind to help me clear the table, something that should have made me suspicious straight away.

'That thing we had, Mum, what's it called? *Tarte tartare?*'

'*Tarte Tatin.*'

'It's lush. Is it from a book?'

'Oh no, someone showed me. I was about your age, actually ...'

But of course she already knew the story.

My own mother was a child of poverty, raised on bread, porridge, potatoes, cabbage, and the occasional salt fish. Then came rationing, which was healthy but – unless you craved snoek and powdered egg – nobody's idea of delicious. After The War, Dad was crippled by arthritis so Mum had to work full time, even during the stay-at-home fifties, and never caught up on the cooking front. I did understand that this, at least, wasn't her fault, even as I gagged over stewed tripe. And then ...

Foreign holidays weren't something my parents ever thought about ('Catch me setting foot on a plane') so I spent one summer holiday as a *jeune fille au pair*, in an attempt to improve my French. Astonishing, to the girl I was then, to meet people who approached eating with confident anticipation. I returned to people who said things like, 'Fruit makes me run to the toilet', but never mind: I had my recipes, including that for *tarte Tatin*.

'To like *be* there and learn, that's awesome,' Clemmie said. 'And you went all that way by yourself.'

'Uh-huh.'

'I'd like to do the same.'

'I thought you didn't care for French.' She'd never made much effort, and in the end we'd withdrawn her from the subject.

'Oh, not to *France!*' Clemmie said loftily. 'Anyway, there's more to it than language. There's seeing how they eat and dress and everything.'

'Well, yes, but language helps with—'

'And I won't be alone. Not like you.'

This was in March and I wasn't aware that any holiday had been booked, so Clemmie now had my full attention. 'Sorry, did I miss something? Is there a school trip?'

'Phoebe's going to Iceland. Her Mum says I can go.'

'*Iceland?*'

'It's awesome. It's like one of my passions.'

This was the first I'd heard of Phoebe, Phoebe's family or Clemmie's passion for awesome Iceland. I went for the parent's first line of defence: 'You haven't said yes, have you, Clemmie? Because I don't know if we can afford—'

'It's only a week, Mum! And there's no hotel bill or anything. Only a week, please, please …!' She tilted her head, the better to flirt her dark blue eyes at me: Gar's eyes. 'You said if I got all my GCSEs …'

'Yes—'

'And I've still got my savings from last summer.'

'Oh. Well done. But it's not just me, Clemmie. There's your father.' Who I suspected wouldn't be enthusiastic. As did Clemmie, evidently, since she'd launched her attack when he'd left the table.

'But if it's a promise, Mum?'

'Don't rush me,' I said. 'Let me find the right time. Why don't you stack the dishwasher? Put me in a good mood.'

■

Reykjavik, the online tour: Lego houses. Big skies. Blueberries. Akvavit. Fermenting shark meat. Half a smoked calf's head, the eyelids sunk in grief over empty sockets. And Clemmie a vegetarian. I could only wish her luck.

Nevertheless my impulse was to urge her to pack at once, *carpe diem*, all that. So why didn't I? – me, with my famed bubbliness, my champagne-like effervescence? Because the problem wasn't me. It was Gareth, and a conversation we'd had the week before.

'Look at this,' he'd said, holding out a magazine.

'What?' I was examining a torn cushion nobody had owned up to, wondering if it could be stitched.

'It's from a bloke at work.' He waved it at me. 'Do you realize we're killing ourselves, just so a few tossers can get hammered in Prague?'

Reluctantly I put down the cushion. The photo showed a young man, beer bottle in hand, lying on cobbles.

'Drinking ourselves to death, you mean?'

'Stag and hen parties.' He tapped his finger on the caption, as if I couldn't read for myself: *Prague has long been a favoured destination.*

'Well, obviously. Cheap beer.'

'Not once you've paid the—' He stopped as if to gather himself together. 'That's not the point. The planet, Lisa, the *planet* can't afford it.'

I just opened my eyes very wide. Since when had my husband cared about the planet? He'd always been like me: enjoy what you can while you can.

At the time I thought work must be getting to him, and also that he might have liked a stag party in Prague for himself. We were married long before that sort of thing became the fashion.

■

I wondered how best to break the news about Iceland. Normally we'd talk things over in bed. If we could stay awake, that is, since we tended to leave it too late and crawl between the sheets comatose. One of those stupid habits you keep on with, knowing you'll feel terrible the day after. I did the odd bit of agency work, here and there, which offered a degree of freedom: the tiring part was having to move on just as I'd got used to my workplace. Gareth worked for the council, juggling cuts and wondering when the axe would fall in his direction. He often brought work home with him, if not in his briefcase, then in his head; I'd hear him grinding his teeth during the night.

He snuggled up behind me, spoonies, his hands clasped over my solar plexus. I was about to say, 'Clemmie asked me something,' when I realized: wrong time, wrong position. With my back turned I couldn't gauge his expression, and he was sure to be overtired. Why hurry? It was Friday night, we had a weekend ahead of us. As we lay there, his breath whistling into my neck, I was revolving strategies. My resources were a movie or two, plus Gareth's favourite meals: fish pie, roast lamb. Solid, comforting, unoriginal dishes that had brought many domestic wars to satisfactory conclusions and even dictated the terms of the peace.

■

'No,' Gareth said. 'Absolutely not.'

We were sitting in front of the telly, finishing up the fish pie, which he had just pronounced luscious. Rick Stein, eat your heart out. Clemmie, confined to home because of history coursework, had been told to go away and stay away. Otherwise, I thought she might be tempted to pout and whine, which would ruin everything. The movie hero, beaded with photogenic sweat, had survived the last of four car chases and seen the villain go hurtling off the road into the canyon (shots of car playing ducks-and-drakes with boulders, spinning in the air, last bounce, fireball). Fireball means the guy's really, really dead.

'Let's not decide straight off,' I hedged. 'We've got time for a chat with Phoebe's mum and dad.'

'To tell them she's not coming, you mean?'

'Get to know them.' I clasped his hands in mine, swinging them playfully to and fro. 'C'mon, she's old enough. When I was seventeen I went—'

He startled me by shaking free of my grasp. 'You were working, Lisa. Studying. And you took the ferry. It's not the same thing.'

'I didn't say it was. Of course, kids expect—'

'Everything. They expect everything. Just think of their carbon footprints – Clemmie's been flying since she was six—'

'But that's lovely, that we've been able—'

'No, it isn't lovely.'

There was a snotty little silence between us. I didn't need a map to see where this was going, and it wasn't Reykjavik.

'I didn't think you believed in all that,' I said, clearing away the remains of my futile feast.

'We had training at work.' He rubbed his eyes, always a sign that something's got to him emotionally. 'It *is* happening, you know. Global warming.'

'You like visiting Karen.'

Gareth looked at me as if I were simple-minded. 'Did anybody say I didn't?'

On Sunday morning, while Clemmie was still sousing in bed, I asked him what I was supposed to tell her.

He said, 'The truth, of course.'

'That her father won't let her go?'

'That I'm thinking of her future. Unlike Phoebe's parents.' He packed the last two words with contempt, as if he'd already met and despised them: thirty-stone chain-smokers, gunning the engine of their parked 4 x 4, passing round the pork scratchings as their exhaust fumes finished off an asthmatic trapped beneath the wheels.

I said, 'She'll be happy if she goes to Reykjavik.'

'Until she wants to go somewhere else.'

'Can't we make up for the flight? Turn the lights off more, walk more? All three of us.'

'We should do that anyway. But it doesn't balance out.'

'You're not wanting to cancel *our* holiday, are you?'

He shot me a nasty look – 'It isn't booked yet' – and I saw just how tough things were about to become.

'She was promised a trip for passing her GCSEs,' I said. '*Promised.*' In fact the trip should have taken place the previous year, but Clemmie had fallen out with her best friend – a friendship yet to be mended – so someone else had taken her place. I said, 'You know how hurt she was about Becky.'

'OK, OK, I'll talk with her when I get back.'

'Back?' Normally on a Sunday morning you couldn't prise him from the breakfast table: he'd wrap himself round a full English, then wallow in the papers for a couple of hours.

'There's a meeting in the Breville Arms. About climate change. People from work are going.'

'Could I go?' I wanted to see his reaction, whether he thought me too much of a petrol-head to be let in the door.

'If you were interested,' he said with frigid patience, 'of course you'd be welcome. And yes, before you ask, I'll be walking there.'

Already we seemed to have written ourselves a script.

Where was the cheerful Lisa we all knew and loved? O where was Bubbly? Hunched over the PC is the answer, looking up sites on climate change, carbon footprints, reductions, offset, debates.

Be positive. Clementine, you shall go to the Ball. Where you shall eat calf's head and blueberries, and perhaps leave behind a single Ugg. I made a list:

> Conscious driving
> Freecycling
> Lights
> Jumpers
> Get out bikes

When Gar came back from the Breville Arms, lamb fat was blistering in the oven, sending out thymey, garlicky gusts. I fluffed out my hair as I heard his key and stuck a glass of red in his hand almost before he'd got his coat off.

He said, 'Do you want to know?'

And I said, 'Yes, of course.'

He spread out a wodge of photocopies on the table. I thought of Karen and her swatches. He talked me through headings and diagrams and I refrained from the cheap shot of asking how many forests had gone into the photocopier. He couldn't stop me thinking, though. Nobody had proved any of this stuff. Theory, pure theory. Then a sick feeling. Suppose even half of it turned out to be true? Just because you can't see something doesn't mean it isn't there.

'The thing is,' Gareth said, 'the longer we wait, the worse it'll be. Are you with me or not?'

I felt *really* sick then. He'd hit on one of my mother's favourite themes: a stitch in time saves nine. I'd seen other women marry their parents and I'd thought, That's one mistake I'm not likely to make. Yet here was Gareth gearing up to Fight a War and ready, if I showed promise, to cast me in the role of *They*.

'Well, you may not believe this,' I said, switching into Bubbly, 'but I've done some research of my own,' and I presented him with the list.

'Jumpers?'

'Instead of turning up the heat.' I bent forward and kissed him. 'If we did all this, everything, surely—'

'You can't bargain with—'

'Gar. I *promised*. Let her go, please.' He was looking obstinate. 'Don't you want her to trust us?'

(This was bringing out the heavy artillery: Gareth was big on trust and openness in families.)

'Of course I do,' he said, and I saw him weakening.

'If we let her down,' I said, 'she'll only fly more later.'

I thought this was common sense. Clemmie was a bright girl: she'd soon work out how to stage her own version of Coming out Bubbly. 'We have to seem fair,' I nagged. 'Fair and reasonable.'

Gareth stared into space. I held my breath.

'Everything else goes, then,' he said at last. 'No flights for us, not ever again. I mean it, Lisa. We've got to be serious.'

'Fine,' I said meekly (I was already planning ways round it). And then the girl herself came into the kitchen saying she didn't feel well, and I had to find out what that was about, and whether she wanted any lunch.

■

When we got round to talking with Phoebe Doyle's mother, we discovered she wasn't accompanying the girls to Reykjavik. Mrs Doyle, who turned out to be Mrs Sigurdardottir ('We always keep our own names') had a married sister there with children of her own. The sister would meet our daughters off the plane, give them a shared room in her family home and keep an eye on them.

'Will your sister be home during the day?' Gareth asked.

'Some of the time,' said Mrs Sigurdardottir. 'If the girls are sensible, they shouldn't have any trouble. Reykjavik's as safe as London.'

'Safer, I'm sure,' said Gareth politely. 'But I'm not sure Clemmie's sensible, and with the language problem—'

'Oh, lots of people speak English. And Phoebe speaks Icelandic.'

'Really?' I was interested. 'Clemmie didn't mention that.'

'Phoebe's shy about it. Only talks with me when we're alone.' She grinned, shrugged. 'But she's fluent.'

'Well, that's reassuring,' I said to Gareth, knowing that from his point of view it made no difference at all.

Mrs Sigurdardottir added, 'They're thinking now about October half term, did Clemmie say? You can go away together this summer, if that's what you planned.' She smiled. 'It won't spoil your family holiday.'

■

At the next stage I beat Gareth to the moral high ground: a house swap. He protested that swapping houses, in itself, had nothing ecological about it. I pointed out that we'd avoid the wasteful overheating, the little plastic bottles, the needless laundering of towels. And all the money we'd save by not using a hotel could be put towards solar panels.

Gareth looked as if he suspected me of mockery. I said, 'You do want solar, don't you?'

I'd been doing more homework, reading up: government schemes, solar fridges in Africa. What I understood of it was quite interesting, but I couldn't help having doubts. Of course solar fridges were welcome. Real benefits, with immediate effect.

What if the good wasn't so visible? Suppose you had to make sacrifices just to stay the same?

The last time we'd visited Karen, her leave fell in August. The furnace month. My wet bra rubbed a weal into my chest; I developed sweat rash each side of my neck, wherever my earrings touched. Two weeks of Italian eating and the most pleasurable experience I recalled afterwards was Karen's air con: ambrosial, the kiss of a goddess. The impossibility of sleeping without it! There was a time before air con when Romans must have slept – they'd hardly have forged an empire, otherwise – but how could they go back to that now? Who'd blame them for not wanting to?

Doing the right thing (said the websites) means not waiting for others to go first, but trusting them to follow and having faith in it all coming together in the end. Well! I thought. Try selling people that line! Most of us have been conned too often. We need to see something here, something now. Otherwise we squat tight on what we have, and can't be budged: *at least I'll know my kid got her share.* Limpets all of us, clinging to our familiar, limpetty rock.

Or were there ways of running air con from solar panels? I didn't know. I didn't know anything.

I showed Clemmie the house-swapping website. She seemed interested until Gareth said, 'Only Britain,' after which her gaze wandered. Pressed to contribute, she said she'd like a place with thatch.

'Thatch? Punching above our weight, there,' I said, and was immediately annoyed with myself. That was the sort of stunt my own parents used to pull: ask for input, then reject it. But Gareth agreed: owners of thatched cottages would probably be looking for something equally photogenic.

I said, 'We can have a place by the sea, though.'

'Nobody'll want ours,' said Clemmie. I felt wounded on behalf of our house. Its roof might be humble slate, but surely …

'Oh yes, they will,' Gareth said. 'It's in London. London's the magic word, the Open Sesame.'

*Open Sesame*: my motto. I'd been shouting it all my adult life, beating down doors for all of us. Look at me now, though: dreaming of warm winds, of evening stars, of clinking glasses on a terrace overlooking the Amalfi coast. And settling for Devon.

■

*Please do not enter the loft as this space is private.*

I wondered why, in that case, they hadn't fitted a padlock: there was the trapdoor, complete with loft ladder, staring us in the face as soon as we entered the master bedroom. Perhaps it was reverse psychology: they wanted us to go upstairs and find the shrivelled corpses of previous occupants, the Spirit of Bank Holiday Past.

The owners had clearly done swaps before. There was a well-worn folder of lists and instructions: doctor, dentist, bus routes, local attractions, where to eat, how to operate the washing machine, the TV. The fridge contained wine, beer, salad, ham, cheese, butter, and a few packets from the chilled food section including (bless them) a veggie lasagne. Bread and fruit in chunky, retro baskets. 'Summer visitors' were warned not to light the Aga as this would heat the entire house. Instead we should use the mini-oven, or the portable plug-in hob.

I was surprised how difficult it was to remember their rituals. I'd left a similar list for them, of course *(turn the flush anticlockwise and hold a second or two)* but familiarity makes all the difference. At home I bounced about the kitchen grabbing whatever I needed. So ingrained were my reflexes, I could have done it blind.

I heard Gareth cough in the living room. Clemmie was silent. When we first arrived she'd rushed upstairs, flinging open the windows – 'Look, Dad, the sea!' – before going straight to the telly. Once that was on she entered her familiar trance, the sea forgotten.

'When's dinner going to be ready?' Gareth called. At home, the answer would have been 'Ten minutes' – it was only chilled lasagne. But that first night I kept moving blindly to where things should have been: knives, olive oil, vinegar, cooker, fridge.

'Come in here, will you?' I called back, and he came shambling through with the incompetent air of a man who hopes to be let off a job. I told him to find everything and remember where it came from because we'd need to put it back afterwards.

Dinner was eaten on the sofa, watching a film about a scientist who accidentally swapped bodies with his dog. The scientist in dog form was menaced by a pit bull while his pet, Skipper, roamed the laboratory, sniffing around the scientist's attractive female colleague.

Gareth said it was the lamest film he'd ever seen, and kept harping on the absurdities: why did Skipper bother wearing clothes? Why was he following women and not females of his own species?

'Let's just watch, shall we?' I said, frowning at him. This was how he'd ruined *Edward Scissorhands*.

Clemmie snatched the remote. Identical blonde schoolgirls had a crush on a handsome, badly-acted teacher. Gareth began to make loud yawning noises.

Clemmie complained that her dad was selfish.

I collected up the dirty plates and took them to the kitchen. There was no dishwasher. I put the dishes in the sink and turned on the hot tap.

Gareth came out. 'Shall I dry, then?'

'I'd rather you washed.' I dislike the feeling of hot detergent on my fingertips. He took the washing-up brush – one of those twee little wooden things – and set to work on the lasagne dish, scrubbing, rinsing, scrubbing.

'Burnt on,' he said, as if this was somehow unfair. I informed him that it was a not uncommon occurrence with lasagne and that the low-carbon lifestyle was said to be time-consuming. He said, 'Oh, I know.'

Do you, though? I thought. How time-consuming, exactly? I didn't even know whether hand-washing made any difference. Gareth seemed clued-up about temperatures and vanishing species, but 'time-consuming' was just a rosy pink embryo of a concept somewhere at the back of his head. Grow your own veg, get down your food miles. Dig a fishpond. Do it in the commercial breaks.

My own concept of 'time-consuming' was more like a toxic cloud spreading in the brain. Of one thing I was sure: the future wouldn't be how Gar imagined. If he liked the idea of something he got romantic about it. His parents took him to school by car when he was a kid, so now he was saying we should all cycle. When I was a child I did just that: wobbled along arterial roads, lorries passing so close they practically shaved the hairs off my legs. Ah, said Gar when I told him this, but you forget that in a zero-carbon economy everyone else would be on bikes too. Not now though, I said. And lorry drivers not ever. Back came the memories ... Punctures in the rain. Knees chapped and purple. My knotted thighs and bursting lungs on the last hill before school. Gaining the top, freewheeling down at last, the exhilarating swoop and drop until – ouch! – a winged beetle, smack in my cornea.

The bedroom floorboards were chilly on our bare feet.

'Is this what they call a microclimate?' Gareth asked. 'Doesn't feel like summer.'

'Thick walls, I think. Keep the sun out.'

'There hasn't been any sun.'

(In my head, Dad exclaimed, 'And they call this flaming June!' I'd heard the protest from him and Mum every June for eighteen years. It always sounded as if they'd unmasked a universal conspiracy but I never actually heard anyone say *flaming June* except my parents.)

Clemmie lay uncomplaining in the front bedroom but then she doesn't feel the cold.

'Nice to be in the country though,' said Gareth, sliding between the sheets. 'Makes a change from Rome.'

Ah yes, Rome. As we huddled beneath our lumpy quilt I thought of the Italian hotel we'd stayed in before joining Karen: our deliciously tactile room with its polished wood and starched sheets. The frank acknowledgement that bed is a pleasure. The bed we were in now seemed to have been constructed along very different lines. Britain had something of lasting value to offer the overpopulated world, I realized: a few more bedrooms like this one, and people might give up reproducing altogether.

'Night,' said Gareth, switching off the bedside lamp. I pulled the quilt over my head, to feel my breath warming the dank little cave of air beneath.

Far off in the night there were owls, their keening almost gentle. Whoooo. Lullaby.

I dozed, only to have my body fling me awake again. There was movement in the darkness. A crackle, a rustle, not in one place but several, as if the newspaper we'd dropped by the door had formed itself into paper dollies, and the dollies had raised themselves on stumpy nightmare legs and were marching round our bed.

'Gar.' I breathed rather than said it, but he was already awake.

'It's OK,' he said. 'It's mice.'

'OK? What if they climb up?'

'I don't think they will. They're afraid of you, mice.'

I tested this with a loud cough. The crackling sound paused, then continued. Without warning Gareth switched on the lamp. The floor wasn't, as I had feared, a living carpet of rodents. The newspaper lay intact where we had left it. The crackle continued, hanging eerily in the air.

'They're in the loft,' said Gareth. 'Lie down, for God's sake.'

We listened with the light on while the mice (or were they rats?) pursued their eternal quest of moving paper from one place to another. My dislike of rodents is a rational one: they're incontinent, they contaminate food. I don't share the morbid dread that afflicts many people, including, I suspect, Gareth – he acts brave but never volunteers to deal with the things. I got up and put on my dressing gown and slippers.

'Ignore it, can't you, and sleep,' my husband said.

As I lifted the trapdoor, the scrabbling sounds died. A light-pull dangled against my face. I tugged, and the attic sprang into existence: no murdered tourists, just a criminal lack of insulation between the joists. Against one wall stood a set of metal shelves, the self-assembly kind that people buy for garages and workshops. I didn't glimpse a single mouse but I could see where they'd been: shreds of paper here and there, faint tracks where their scuffling had disturbed the dust. Gar was right, there was nothing I could do about them. They'd only come out again as soon as I left. I heard him down below, turning over in bed.

I moved to the shelves. Bluebeard's secrets. I would never have come here on purpose to look at them, but since Bluebeard's rodents had woken me, I felt entitled. An ancient laptop, square, furred with dust. A box of gnawed gardening magazines. Another box full of plugs, extension leads and wires. Limpetty things, clung on to even when useless. *Please do not enter the loft.*

Somewhere on one of the websites I'd read that if the earth became too hot for humans, there would still be rodents. I'd pictured them swarming over deserts, like those films of locusts we used to watch at school, but of course they'd go where people used to be, wherever there were food scraps and textiles and paper. Cottages, shacks, tower blocks, palaces full of dusty objects. I felt a shudder that had nothing to do with grey skies and thick walls.

'There's a museum up there,' I said, backing down the ladder.

He laughed. 'Museum of what?'

'Grave goods.'

'Aren't you the cheerful one?' he said.

'I thought you wanted me serious.'

I got back into bed and he wrapped himself round me again. He said, 'Did I tell you about when I went to Scotland?'

'Don't think so.'

'I stayed in a village, somebody's spare room.'

'Friends?'

'No. There was this little basket on the bedside table. I didn't look at it, I was in and out of the room all the time, and then on the last day I just – looked.'

'And?'

'They'd left their credit cards in there.'

'Christ. Do you think they knew?'

He switched off the light and said again, 'I can't believe it's June.'

'Our own private Iceland.'

He didn't laugh. After a while he said, 'They trusted me.'

Which was, of course, why he remembered. I'd never do that: give a stranger the power to do us harm. Imagine living in a place where people are so trusting. It's ridiculous. Or perhaps the place was nothing special but they did it anyway, the sort of people who'd cancel their holiday without a squawk, anything for the common good.

I said, 'You couldn't carry on like that in London.'

'Not in any city. This thing we're doing. It won't be easy.'

So you know, I thought. You do realize... At once I felt Bubbly rise in me like some glittering fairytale fish: Bubbly, bestower of comforts, granter of wishes. You *shall* hire the limo, switch on the air con, fly to Australia. You've fitted low-energy bulbs, recycled your drinks cans, done your bit.

But I said, 'It'll be fucking hard going,' and Bubbly dissolved in a little fizzle like a spent sparkler. She never had much substance to her.

Gar said, 'We can explain to Clemmie, can't we?'

'I don't know. Kids want whatever their friends have.'

He put his feet under mine. 'We can't all go on like lemmings. Somebody's got to call a halt.'

'I suppose.'

'And make a start on other things.'

'Like what?'

He yawned. 'Find out as we go.'

I said, 'But all that work and no guarantee. What if nobody else stops?'

He didn't speak, just tightened his arms around me.

'Well,' I said. 'Here we are, then.'

Here we are.

# THE POSSESSION OF
# LACHLAN LUBANACH

Nick Hayes

# THE POSSESSION OF LACHLAN LUBANACH

LACHLAN LUBANACH WAS THE FIFTH CHIEF OF MULL.

HIS CASTLE STOOD, HEWN FROM THE ROCK ON WHICH IT WAS RAISED, A SOLITARY BUILDING ON A WINDSWEPT ISLAND.

FROM THE WARMTH WITHIN, IT WALLED OUT THE WILD

# AND FROM THE TOP OF HIS TALLEST TOWER
# LACHLAN OWNED ALL THAT HE SAW

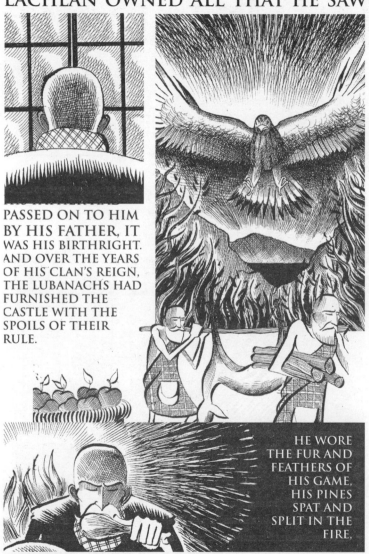

PASSED ON TO HIM BY HIS FATHER, IT WAS HIS BIRTHRIGHT. AND OVER THE YEARS OF HIS CLAN'S REIGN, THE LUBANACHS HAD FURNISHED THE CASTLE WITH THE SPOILS OF THEIR RULE.

HE WORE THE FUR AND FEATHERS OF HIS GAME, HIS PINES SPAT AND SPLIT IN THE FIRE,

AND THE WALLS OF HIS KEEP WERE LINED WITH THE SKELETONS OF THE BEASTS OF HIS GLEN

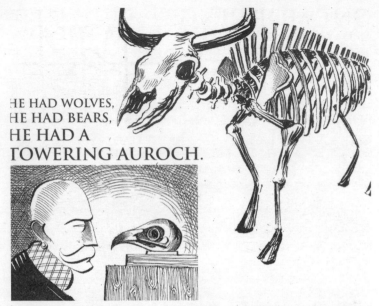

HE HAD WOLVES,
HE HAD BEARS,
**HE HAD A
TOWERING AUROCH.**

HIS DEMESNE WAS A TROPHY
HALL OF HIS DOMINION, AN
OSSIFIED MENAGERIE.

BUT ONE BEAST HAD ELUDED HIS KEEP.

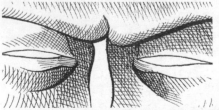

**AND SO,**
TOWERING ABOVE
HIS LAND, EYES WIDE
BEHIND THICK GLASS
**HE HUNTED IT.**
ONE DAY, HE KNEW, IT
WOULD BELONG TO HIM

AND HIS POSSESSION OF THE LAND WOULD BE COMPLETE

# ONE MORNING,
## AS DAWN SLUICED A LUSTRE
# THROUGH THE GLEN,
## HE WAS UP, AS EVER, STOOD AT HIS CASEMENT TO SURVEY THE LAND THAT PURVEYED HIS CASTLE.

AND IT APPEARED, FRAMED IN THE LEAD CASEMENTS OF HIS WINDOW. CRESTING THE HILL, RARE AS A UNICORN, BRILLIANT AS THE SUN.

AND AS HE STOOD THERE,
# OBSERVING
## THROUGH THE PANEL OF THICK GLASS BETWEEN THEM,
# LACHLAN WANTED ITS BONES.

WITHOUT TELLING A SOUL,
HE TOOK HOLD OF HIS AXE.

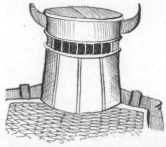

WITHOUT TELLING A SOUL
HE STRAPPED ON HIS ARMOUR

WITHOUT TELLING A SOUL,
HE PRIMED HIS STEED,
LEFT THE KEEP,
AND SLIPPED INTO
THE RISING LIGHT.
AND AT THE
THUNDER OF HIS
HORSE'S HOOVES,
THE WHITE HART
TURNED, AND
FLASHED WESTWARDS,
TOWARDS BEN MORE.

## LACHLAN GAVE CHASE,

CRASHING THROUGH THE MOOR, TEARING AT THE TIGHT WEAVE OF ROOTS BENEATH HIM, CARVING A MUDDY WAKE.
AND THE WHITE HART LED HIM NORTH, TO THE KILLIECHRONAN WOODS.

## BUT THROUGH THE GRILL OF HIS VISOR

LACHLAN FOUND IT HARD TO KEEP TRACK OF THE HART. FOR HERE IN ITS WORLD, ITS PRESENCE WAS ALL MOTION AND COULD NOT BE FRAMED. HE FLUNG HIS HELMET OFF AND HIS VISION OPENED, THE HART SKITTING DOWN THE HILL INTO THE CORNER OF HIS EYE.

# HIS HORSE THUNDERED ON.

AND SUDDENLY NOW WITHOUT HIS VISOR, IN THE
BRIGHT LIGHT OF DAY, THE GLEN WHIRRED AROUND HIM,
AN ORCHESTRA OF PROTEAN MOTION.

LING EXPLODING
INTO    PARTRIDGE,

ROCK SLIDING INTO RAM,

THE LEAVES OF TREES RISING HIGH INTO THE AIR,
TO MURMUR LIKE BILLOWING SAILS.

# AND WHENEVER THE HART WOULD STOP
## ITS EARS AND EYES WOULD TAKE SIGNS FROM THE GLEN

## IT WAS AS IF ITS BODY WAS TAUTLY TIED
## TO THE WORLD AROUND IT,
CONNECTED BY INVISIBLE WEBS
THAT SENT TREMORS FROM
LACHLAN'S ADVANCE,
TRUMPETING HIS PRESENCE.

THE HART WAS ONE WITH
THE WORLD AROUND HIM.
HIGH ON HIS WAR-HORSE,
LACHLAN WAS NOT.

# SO LACHLAN
## GAVE UP HIS HORSE

AND STEALTHY NOW, LOW IN THE THICKETS,

LACHLAN MOVED CLOSER TO THE HART.

BUT AS HE CREPT FORWARD, HIS ARMOURED BOOTS PUSHED INTO THE BOGGY HEATHER, **SUCKING HIS WEIGHT** INTO INK-BLACK PUDDLES.

HIS LIMBS WERE HEAVY WITH CHAIN AND STEEL. **SO LACHLAN** GAVE UP HIS ARMOUR

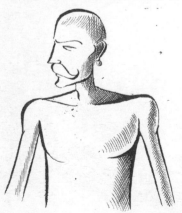

AND WITH THE SOLES OF HIS FEET ON THE MUDDY EARTH THE GROUND SEEMED TO PUSH UP AS HE PUSHED DOWN **RECIPROCATING.**

# AND WITH HIS SKIN AGAINST THE WIND

## HIS NETWORK OF NERVES JOINED HIM WITH THE OUTSIDE

HIS SENSES CORRELATED
WITH THE WORLD AROUND
HIM.

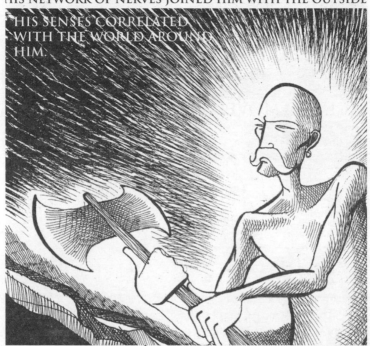

# AND LACHLAN GREW CLOSER TO THE HART

# HE SHADOWED THE HART

## UP THE SHALLOW RISE OF

# THE FOOT OF BEN HOPE.

**AND AS THE SLOPE** INCLINED AGAINST HIM. HE KEPT FALLING TO HIS HANDS, CLASPING AT TUSSOCKS, REACHING FOR BALANCE.

BUT WITH THE BATTLEAXE IN HIS HAND, HE COULD GAIN LITTLE PURCHASE.

## SO LACHLAN GAVE UP HIS AXE.

AND CRAWLING ON ALL FOURS UP THE MOUNTAIN, BREATHING IN THE WIND WHICH BUFFETED HIS FORM

## LACHLAN GREW CLOSER TO THE HART.

AND THEN
IT IS DUSK.

AND LACHLAN IS HIGH
ENOUGH TO SEE THE
LINE OF DARKNESS SWEEP
ACROSS THE LAND,
LIKE HIS GREAT HALL
DOORS SWINGING
SHUT.

FROM THE EAST, HIS EARS TAKI
A MESSAGE FROM THE WIND -
THE HOUNDS HAVE BEEN RELEASED

AFTER A DAY'S ABSENCE,
AS DARKNESS DESCENDS,
THE CASTLE IS HUNTING
HIM DOWN. AND WITH
THE HOWLS OF THE
HOUNDS AT HIS HEELS,

LACHLAN GROWS CLOSER TO THE HAR

AND
AT THE PEAK
OF THE MOUNTAIN,
LACHLAN HALTS WITH THE HART.

THE CASTLE IS LOST BENEATH A MIST,
INSIDE AND OUT OF HIS HEAD;

FOR HIS MIND IS ALL MOISTURE NOW,
A RAINCLOUD OF REACTION,
CHARGED THROUGH THE CHASE:

HE IS PERMEATED.
HE IS POSSESSED.

# THE HOUNDS AGAIN, CLOSER.

## LACHLAN THINKS OF THE BONES,
# THE STILLNESS IN THE KEEP.

## THE DOGS APPEAR.
# THE LIGHTNING FLASHES.

# THE WHITE HARTS BOLTS, LACHLAN WITH IT

# ALMOST VISIBLE CITIES

*after Calvino*

Gregory Norminton

*… Having contemplated the nothingness which was all that remained of his victory, the Great Khan turned his eyes on his opponent. Marco Polo, whose designs for the endgame the emperor had suspected from the opening gambit, knew better than to congratulate his host on the bloodless conquest of a maple chessboard. He bowed his head, averting from that wise and terrible face a gaze which had taken in countless faces.*

*'Ten thousand moons,' the Great Khan said, 'have waxed and waned since last we spoke. Have you been on your travels all this time, or have we slept and dreamed the passing centuries?'*

*'Sire,' said Polo, 'I have travelled without rest through the cities of men. I have heard the bellowing of women giving birth, the mewling of babies, the cries of lovers and the gasps of the dying. Everywhere the human tide rises and falls. The city is the place of despair and of hope. It is the inferno and the sanctuary.'*

*'The centuries have not brought peace to the world.'*

*'Nor wisdom. For the city alters but men do not. Or not at a pace sufficient to survive their ingenuity.'*

*'The years,' said Kublai, 'have not cleansed you of your love for riddles.'*

*'How else may we perceive the riddle of the world?'*

*The Great Khan let out a sigh such as a tomb might make when it is opened after countless years of silence. He turned his gaze from the sandalwood in the fire to the magnolias of Kai-ping-fu as they kindled in the sunset. 'It is all useless, then, if time and learning cannot release us from the infernal city.'*

*'There is no need for conjecture. The proof and disproof of your fear exist beyond these palace walls, in the worlds that we form by being together.'*

*'Tell me – for this evening will never, I think, ripen into night, and I have a great hunger to know what was and is and may come to pass ...'*

## Cities & the Desert 1

The best way to approach Iduba is by sea, preferably reclining on deck half asleep after a meal, for only by mistaking it for a dream can the mind accept what the eye perceives. The masters of Iduba, in founding their city on the coast of a vast and featureless desert, appear to have forgotten the story of Babel, for the buildings they have commissioned rise as if they would escape the earth which is the destiny of all our endeavours. As your boat nears the harbour, you strain your neck to see the tops of the towers, and at once you long for their windswept heights, for you have entered the heat and dust which is the lot of the city's migrant workers. You see them in their thousands, sweating in the sun or shadowed in the dry wells of the towers, while in the upper storeys the citizens grow fat on revenue from Iduba's famous export. This mineral salt, which locals call *hulum*, grants whoever tastes it an overwhelming sense of ease and prosperity. Little wonder that it should be valued above all the spices, for its use bankrupts nations, whose populations turn for comfort to the very illusion that first enslaved them.

To the beneficiaries of Iduba's wealth, plenty appears the natural condition of life; yet even in the midst of luxury there are signs of decay for those willing to read them. It is possible still to visit those islands built in the shapes of palm trees and crescent moons in the waters off the coast. For a time their whitewashed villas were the most desirable residences in Iduba. Now the poisoned sea laps at their foundations, while lurid blooms of algae stifle the brackish lagoons between abandoned gardens. From the vantage point of the towers, few citizens choose to look at these corroded strips of reclaimed land. Instead, they retreat with their purses into vast bazaars where the luxuries of the world accumulate. It is said by the workers that these temples of commerce are destined to become the mausoleums of Iduba, or to vanish entirely in one of the ever more frequent sandstorms that bury whole streets and drift as high as date palms against the dusty towers. Visiting dignitaries, generously hosted in return for singing the city's praises, insist that its mineral wealth will allow Iduba to meet all challenges. Yet nobody knows how long the deposits of *hulum* will last. Idubans dread to contemplate their depletion, for without revenue to bind them to their employers, the migrants will drift elsewhere in pursuit of work, and the day will dawn when Iduba proves to have been nothing but a mirage, a vision that dissolves into the timeless and levelling sands from whence it seemed, once, to challenge the heavens.

## Cities & Time 1

At first sight, Parvulo appears little different from other cities: shops and houses line the roads, infants in parks point at squirrels, school-yards echo with the clamour of children. In a tranquil and leafy square, you take your rest on a bench and observe whole families at leisure, while office workers feed sparrows, brood over chessboards or play with their children in the middle of the working day. You see little evidence, on the faces of Parvulans, of ill health or distress, none of the heaviness of flesh and spirit with which other city dwellers are encumbered. This is not to say that inhabitants are blandly happy; on the contrary, lovers' rows are more full-throated, and their reconcilia-tions more passionate, than might in other cities be considered seemly.

Time is the unofficial currency in Parvulo, and wealth is measured not in spending power but in the amount of leisure available once the basic needs of the body have been met. Parvulans used, like the rest of us, to devote their lives to the purchase of goods intended to compensate them for the time lost in their acquisition. The pursuit of material gain made them ill, unequal and indebted, until by slow degrees it became preferable to be free with few goods than a slave with many. There was no coercion or compulsion in this. When everyone in a crowded room speaks loudly, it becomes impossible to hear a word, yet when everyone in the room speaks softly, everyone can be heard. This, in metaphor, was the discovery that Parvulans made. By taking up less space in the world, every citizen ensures that there is more space for everyone. With more time to explore the self and the world that surrounds them, they delight in the round of the seasons, and all nature is their congratulation. It is no longer the city's passion to expel and discard, to measure its prosperity by the ease with which it squanders the world's resources. Parvulo looks to its nearest neighbour, which daily is threatened by the cataclysmic collapse of mountains of refuse, and knows that the steadiness of its system cannot immunize it against contagion from a wider society which mistakes wastefulness for prosperity, greed for need.

Having admired their gracious city, you wonder how Parvulans can insulate themselves from the ongoing misery of the world. There is only one hope, though it may be a foolish one. It is that Parvulo's model spreads, not by conquest or coercion, but by the simple eloquence of its unique and all too repeatable example.

## Cities & the Desert 2

A visitor to the city of Keystone might assume that it is inhabited by giants, for who else could build such cathedrals of industry, the furnaces and smokestacks that obscure the day with smoke and banish the night with flames. Wading deeper into the foul brown air, you learn that the citizens are of ordinary size and divided between those who must live and perish in the canyons of steel and others, more privileged, who by serving the furnaces earn the right to be sheltered from them. These functionaries can be seen processing along tunnels of tinted glass, while in the streets preachers lambast the poor for their poverty, and melancholy whores flaunt whatever assets were loaned to them at birth. The beauty of women has a price in Keystone and there are no poets to praise it, for poetry is idleness to a culture in which Nature herself must earn her keep. This she does by surrendering from her folds a dark flammable liquid which is both the wealth and the ruin of the city. The senator or statesman long ago breathed his last who did not owe his position to the extraction of this fuel. Given the scale to which its availability has expanded the city, the demand for it is insatiable, for no man can see his wife, or child return from school, without the help of Keystone's elixir. This dependency has so enriched a minority that truth itself has become a commodity which can be depreciated with judicious investments, and the few scholars remaining in the university can be relied upon to think in ways that are profitable to their patrons. As a result, it is the norm in Keystone for the poor to be castigated and despised, while the powerful are lauded for a wealth which, no matter how it was acquired, is regarded as proof of moral virtue.

Yet to stay in Keystone, if one can stomach life outside its hostelries and pleasure domes, is to discover that the consensus does not lack dissenting voices. These can be heard discussing the iniquities of the system and dreaming of its demise. Public meetings are not uncommon and take place with the authorities' blessing, for the powers discovered long ago that there is nothing to fear from a message that inconveniences a majority of the city's inhabitants. Marginalized and derided, the malcontents console themselves with the hope that industry will exhaust itself, choking on its unreason. They are mistaken, for Keystone's thirst is exhaustible only by the limits of Nature herself, and the city fathers, oblivious as all true madmen must be of their insanity, will have laid waste to the four corners of the earth before they abandon a system that once served the city that now serves it.

## Ingenious Cities

At the end of seven days, moving northwards, you quench your traveller's thirst with the sweet waters of Miranda. After drinking deeply, you wonder how it came to pass that a fountain should be placed in the middle of a forest. It takes a minute or two before you perceive the homes all around you, topped with meadow grass and sedum, hunkering into banks covered in bougainvillea, or raised on stilts in pools brimming with lotus flowers. What you took for a wilderness is really your intended destination; for where other cities seek to impose themselves on the landscape, Miranda is designed to blend into the conditions from which it seems to have grown. Every building is constructed in relation to its environs: a hill, a tree, a termite mound, a winter stream. The city is a conversation between land and man, nature and civilisation. Indeed, so accustomed are Mirandans to their way of living that they see no distinction between these categories. This is not the result of sentimental thinking, for Miranda is subject to a harsh and changeable climate, so that wetlands are essential to absorb floodwaters, while the green shade of trees filters dust out of the air and offers a refuge to citizens from the heat of the sun.

We have known the melancholy of urban places, the unease in vacant lots and treeless courtyards. This may explain the frenzy of city living, as the heart inside us batters for respite, for the green world in which it became human. In Miranda, by contrast, life is lived at a leisurely pace which, far from hindering enterprise, permits citizens to work to the fulfilment of their gifts. The reality is that Mirandans are profoundly practical and relish pitting their wits against seemingly insurmountable problems.

Along a range of hills that surrounds the city, and far out to sea, vast wheels spin on the wind and carry its power inland, while along the once barren coast, seawater is distilled by captured sunlight into

fresh water that irrigates orchards and fields of corn. Water is valued
to the point of reverence, and everywhere the intermittent blessing
of rain is captured and stored, filtered and cleaned to be used again.
Hard though it may be to imagine, every home drinks in the power of
the sun, storing it in chemical hearths to be released as required after
sundown. So resourceful are Mirandans in harnessing the weather,
and so abundant the fruits of their cooperation with the seasons,
that few inhabitants do not participate in some way in the life and
well-being of their durable city.

Perhaps, great Khan, you doubt the existence of so happy a
commonwealth. It is true that, shortly after I waved goodbye to my
hosts, I began to distrust my memories of Miranda. Perhaps there is
something in those fountains that purges one for a time of scepticism.
It may be that Miranda is impossible, a dream that cannot withstand
the scrutiny of wakefulness. Yet nothing in that vision is beyond
our ingenuity, and I suspect that only inertia and habitual thinking
prevent us from building Miranda in our homelands, from giving it
space and letting it endure.

## Cities & Idols

It is impossible, in nightmare or malediction, to conceive of a city
more infernal in aspect or function than the metropolis of Bolgia.
From denuded mountain to famished plain, it sprawls beyond measure
or comprehension, engulfing all who come to it in a labyrinth of
scrapyards and prisons, barracks and bordellos, drained canals, fetid
shacks, tanneries, and middens. War is the chief engine of Bolgia,
for the city long ago exhausted its resources and must prey on its
neighbours to secure the essentials of water, food, and fuel. Scarcity
is not the sole reason for Bolgia's belligerence: war is necessary, at
frequent intervals, to ease the pressure of a burgeoning population,
while the prospect of external enemies channels the rage of young
men who might, otherwise, turn on their masters.

Although it is questionable whether one can ever be said to have arrived in a city so vast, you may find yourself, on your travels, in a rubbish-strewn square when fresh hostilities have been declared, whereupon you will see, carried above the heads of the crowd, the bronze idol in which reposes the city's hunger for meaning. This idol is the figure of a charging bull, the fetish of a god of enterprise and competition. Though the cult manifests itself in enslavement for millions, to question its supposed benevolence is to risk a charge of heresy. A high priesthood, indistinguishable in dress and manners from the city's plutocrats, dedicates itself to the pursuit of unbelievers, for though the bull cult is not obligatory, the wealthy in their gated enclaves cannot tolerate any scepticism that might question their divine right to rule. Credulity is essential to Bolgia's self-consumption, and the rich are happy for the poor to console themselves with vengeful gods whose propitiation does not, on close examination, differ greatly from that of the sacred bull.

Exploring Bolgia is a perilous business to be undertaken only in armed company, for a city in which other resources have become scarce will sate its appetite on the last item in abundance: human flesh. Countless numbers are sold into prostitution, or sell parts of themselves to medicine, for life is a brutish struggle to survive, while the elites have withdrawn into compounds guarded by militia against the desperation of the masses. Within their gilded cages, the rich occupy themselves in furious debates concerning the shape and nature of the city they no longer dare to explore. Some hold that it is the only possible city, that nothing under heaven can be more perfect, while others doubt its spiritual reality, and a very few speculate about its future. These last are shunned by their peers, who fear the utterance of a secret known to many, yet acknowledged by few: that the present in Bolgia feeds on the future, the old on the young. The city fathers, when they deign to acknowledge the disease, blame it on those who would cure it, for they know in their hearts that Bolgia's only hope lies in patricide. For no body politic can consume itself indefinitely. Such a property belongs only to the sun, and possibly to hell with its eternal fuel of souls. Bolgia, being an earthly place, will have, by one means or another, to transform itself or face annihilation. Until then, it will continue to seethe, a cauldron of meaningless suffering above a fire of inexhaustible need.

## Cities & Time 2

From there you proceed along a highway of abandoned vehicles, weaving between rusting hulks, behemoths of a failed migration to a plain that never existed. You must withstand several days of this, the dust scorching your lungs, before you reach the outer districts of Gardenia.

It is possible at first to imagine that these are ruins, for Gardenia, which was not always blessed with such a fruitful name, used to be a teeming metropolis, fuelled by industries that expanded the city beyond its capacities, till those industries failed and the limits began, like the corona of a bruise, to fade and contract. In these impoverished quarters, the task of demolition is left to the wind and weeds. There are houses collapsing under scrub which even the ghosts have abandoned; dilapidated theatres where rats cross the stage; temples to a god of prosperity upon whose altars pigeons roost. The rich of the inner city turn their backs on the periphery. Only their servants gaze in wonder and sorrow at the vastness of its remains. Yet the visitor to Gardenia would do well not to trust appearances. Life is returning to the blighted neighbourhoods, working its way up from the asphalt as a plant forces its way into the light. Where smoking factories once stood, poisoned soils are being nursed back to health in the roots of Italian alders and poplar groves. As you wander from your path, you see tilled fields, beehives in new meadows, market stalls on street corners, and everywhere people toiling and trading. Repair workshops double as hostelries, for the citizens of Gardenia have become intensely sociable, and every day in the green thoroughfares a festive atmosphere reigns. People take pride in growing their own food, which they distinguish from the feed that once consumed their wages. Where formerly these kitchen gardeners had been tenants dependent on their employers for water and fuel, now they manage the same for themselves. Everyone owns a little, and such is the level of cooperation that visitors from the centre scoff at what they perceive to be laziness – for how can industrious folk waste so much time in talk and play? Perhaps most offensive to outsiders is the extension of neighbourly feeling to the non-human, for birds and pollinating insects are welcomed, while trees, which some call *leaf residents*, are afforded the respect and security of citizen status. Sentimental madness, the sceptics say; yet the locals shrug and return to their labours, for they know what will grow in the wasteland, and are too busy tending it to mind the ill opinion of those who will have, in time, to make the same discoveries.

*The Great Khan sighed again and shut the atlas in which he had attempted, without success, to find the cities of which Marco Polo spoke. Clenching his lips on the amber stem of his pipe, he fixed his eyes on the Venetian.*

*'Each of your cities,' said Kublai, 'appears to refute its predecessor, one place contradicting what has been built in another. Which, then, is the true city, the city of the world as lived in by men?'*

*'All of them,' said Marco, 'and none. Each city is a reality in which the inhabitants have chosen to invest. Each is a dream, or a nightmare, which by dreaming together men have made real.'*

*Kublai turned his eyes on the arrested sunset beyond the balcony. It was impossible to determine whether the point of brightness on his wizened cheek was a jewel or a tear reflecting the sky. At length he said, 'How is it possible to live with this war in my breast between hope and despair?'*

*'If I knew the answer to that question, I should never have had to leave my native city.'*

*The emperor of the Tartars flattened his beard against his amethyst choker. 'The horror you speak of is too easy to imagine, while the good seems an idle fantasy. I fear the struggles of men will never cease, just as I shall be unable at last to possess my empire.'*

*And the Venetian answered: 'Sire, a day will come when all the emblems and signs of your empire will be known to you. On that day you will understand that we cannot own the world of which we are a part, any more than a pearl can claim the necklace on which it is threaded. Then, great-hearted Khan, your empire will possess you, for the world and humanity are indivisible, as you and I and the reader of these words are one and the same person ...'*

# HOSPITAL FIELD

## Siân Melangell Dafydd

OWNING SOMETHING ANCIENT adds weight to life. Your tree:
nut-skinned, sturdy, harmony in a pot, which has grown up to be tiny,
perfectly asymmetrical and squat, with teardrop, razor-edged leaves,
which has grown up beautiful, is finally being delivered home. You
stuff all your other belongings into a rucksack: underwear, toothbrush,
books, and you negotiate customs, ticket turnstiles and packaged
sandwiches while your two hands are firmly wrapped around its roots
in a blue glazed terracotta pot. You think it looks like it ought to have
been a teapot, not a plant pot; blue as sea in summer, shining about
its soil. Your fingers sweat all the way home but you hold it and hold
it, adjusting your fingers when their bones ache.

Your girlfriend asks you how old it is.

'It's very old,' she says, 'it must be.' You tell her you have no idea
and probably won't, unless it dies and you get to cut its trunk to count
the tiny age circles, 'but really, really, do you think I'm ever going to
get to do that?' you ask her. You both agree on 'old'.

On the mantelpiece it goes, then, next to a painting by a school-
friend artist and a black and white photo of your grandmother looking
young on a boat. Against a white wall, you are pleased with its shape
and how the light from the window throws its shadow diagonally and
larger than life. The tip of its right, out-reaching branch throws the
longest shadow, hitting the rim of a photograph by a semi-famous
Cambodian. The chair you sit on to play the guitar lives in the right

place, so that when you look up again from folk songs and breathe deep, there it is, perfectly crooked and alive in your home.

■

Your bonsai dies or it seems to be dying: you're not sure which. It takes seven days to get to such a state. On the morning of the eighth, the little feet of its blue pot are covered in leaves, and the palms of the leaves are closed. On the ninth morning, even more. You break your waking ritual. Instead of going first thing to loo-kettle-radio-shower, you pop your head into the living room to check the damage. You've learned to expect disappointment before your eyes are fully open. On the floor, leaves crunch like grains of rice into your parquet gaps.

The tree rejects you. After one week of checking in with it before really starting the day, only three leaves remain. One: right at the top. Two: tight by the knot of its belly. Three: barely visible, it's becoming brown, tucked behind a branch-pit. You leave the dustpan and brush in the newspaper rack now, and for the life of you, you can't shake the fear that it's all your fault.

Your girlfriend says you should be talking to your tree, and laughs.

'Which language?' you ask. She suggests English is a poor second to Japanese but you could give it a go since singing hasn't charmed it into feeling at home.

You tell it about your day, about the man across the way on the seventh floor who had a heart attack and had to be taken out of his flat in a crane through the window, his chest naked to the freezing air and pumped by a machine. You even ask it if it's listening and then prod the soil which is just as it should be, according to the instructions.

■

Day fourteen and leaf three shrivels and drops in front of your very eyes. It scrunches to powder between your thumb and forefinger and flakes back to where it fell in the first place. You leave the dust there.

Something must be done. You journey to the other side of the city after work, to a place you hardly ever go – journey to the very end, just because you're after a specialist and that's where he's to be had. It's where the canals merge: large maples and damp benches, and street sweepers hosing the roads down between pedestrians and cyclists. The shop is the size of a locksmith's, has mini grass plants you don't recognize hanging from upside-down pots on a washing line. A miracle man works here, clearly.

'I have come to ask about my bonsai,' you tell him.

He asks if you bought it here.

'No.'

'Did you bring it with you?'

'No.'

'Where is it?'

'At home, losing its leaves.'

'That'll be the problem: your home,' he says. 'Take it outside and it might survive. At the very least don't keep it cooped up,' this man says, pressing his black fingernails into his palms, 'not for more than, say, seven days on the trot.'

You repeat 'cooped up' in exactly his tone: high-pitch disgust. You wonder whether he imagines you in an apartment with trees in chains, just like the silver birches in the Bibliothèque Francois Mitterrand.

'I need to lock up,' the man says, as if he's seen into your soul and seen padlocks, and you watch his hands as he fiddles with the keys. You trust those hands.

■

You report back over dinner.

'It *is* hot here,' your girlfriend says, '*very* hot.'

'You've never said that before,' you tell her.

'But it *is* though,' she says and blows out with puffed cheeks.

'*This* isn't hot,' you say. You point at the thermometer which shows something between seventeen and eighteen degrees as you knew it would. 'My dad has it fixed on twenty-three.'

'We're not talking about your comfort, or your dad's.'

'Is it too hot, then?' you ask her.

She tells you that in your place she would have worn a jumper instead of cranking up the heat. That, for sure, this shows that you're more urban than she is. But, no it's not *too* hot, no. You're not sure if she's lying and start watching her differently. She sleeps untidily at night: kicks down the duvet. You pull it back up. How could she, you tell yourself, how could she?

In the morning she makes coffee while you crouch in front of the bonsai.

'It's not personal,' she says. 'It's science.'

'You mean nature,' you suggest.

'Same thing,' she says. 'It's just the way things are.'

You tell her elms die outside. There's a foreign disease out there that gets them.

'But not the miniature elms maybe,' she says, 'they're made of stronger stuff.'

You don't give in; you consider the balcony but you don't do it. It's a decorative plant, so what's the point of it if it can't be seen? So, contained in this beautiful, perfect flat, with artwork by foreign photographers of children with stories in their eyes and no shoes, your bonsai loses its last but one leaf.

■

You bend low and analyse the tiny point of contact between leaf and bark; try to find what it is that gives up right there. You fail, but find yourself staring until your lower back aches. You're tempted to pluck out the remaining leaf, to get the whole thing over and done with. But this posture isn't natural for you, and actually really hurts, so you stand up straight, resist the urge to touch the tree, and grab your coat to head to work. On the bus, you tell yourself that you really are killing it and should have stuck it on the balcony.

The last leaf is on the mantelpiece on your return. The tree is gone, the marble polished where the pot stood. It's been manhandled again, this time carried by sweaty hands to share a garden with grasses, with bruised heads of great burnets, liquorice milk-vetch covered in sun spots, devil's-bit, blood-veined eyebright, clots of comfrey and meadowsweet frothing above it all. It's abandoned there until it feels better. Once in a while, she brings it in; places it in the middle of the kitchen table and tucks into a plate of poached egg on toast, dandelion and sorrel salad, picks at her nails and the muddy feet of the bonsai pot; drinks tea. She grows nut-skinned, sometimes wonders – did you ever know that you were the one who changed everything? – and takes another sip of tea. Sometime around the bonsai's hundred-and-fiftieth year, you die, mid-crane lift, outside your apartment window.

# EARTHSHIP

Lawrence Norfolk

YOU CAN SEE THEM FROM THE TOP of Saint Anthony's Isle, their long glass walls glinting, their solar panels sopping up the early morning sun as that morning's fleet sets out. The long-drifters spin slowly as the currents nudge them, the bulky float-tanks jiggling over the gentle swell. The simpler rafts bob up and down. Sometimes as many as a hundred will set off together. A dozen or so is more usual, the under-floats or hulls tied to one another with thick black cables.

I watch for a long time. Always, once they're clear of the quays and piers, one or more will cut loose and float free, slowly separating from the other craft. Off on some frolic of its own. Soloes, they're called. They let the currents take them, drifting away wherever. It's unwise, even on a well-equipped raft. A lot never come back. But I think they're the ones that really understand what's happened. Those are the ones I watch.

Of course there's not much else of New Mexico to watch any more. But back when Saint Anthony's Isle was Mount San Antonio and the tail end of the Rockies was a mountain range, not an archipelago, the wettest thing about the Land of Enchantment was the Rio Grande. That was where I and my girlfriend Al fetched up in the summer of 1995 on the south-west leg of our Great American Road Trip.

We had met on a lit course after I had dropped out of applied math. Al was one of three women in the theory class, out of which she dropped after six belligerent seminars because of her 'pathological regard for the likes of D.H. Lawrence' as the professor characterized it.

I bumped into her again about a year later in a bar when a pair of white forearms ruffed in rolled-up light blue shirt sleeves wiped the table top in front of me. The hands were white too, the nails unpolished. They lacked that resigned quality that a real waitress's hands have. They skirted my beer. This was over four decades ago. I looked up.

'Hi, Al.'

She was a dark-haired, wide-hipped girl with a full mouth and a silver nose ring. She pretended not to recognize me (she admitted it later) then pretended to be pleased to see me again. She had quit college altogether and was writing or not-writing a novel called *Running Girl*. I don't know why I asked her to meet me later, or why she agreed. People now think it's only rafters that just float along but there was plenty of drift back then too.

She called me 'Cad' (for Cadwallader, my middle name) when, drunk, we took the stairs up to her apartment that night. When I moved in, this became 'Wal' (pronounced like 'Wally' but without the 'y').

She could not cook and I could. I could not drive and she could. Our complementarity began and ended there. Besides the nose ring, she wore heavy boots and men's shirts which she tucked loosely into tight black jeans. I stuck to cords. I had gone to a private school while she had spent at least part of her late teens living in a teepee with a couple, about whom I knew only that the man was called Jez and that Al had had some kind of relationship with him. I could believe it. Certain kinds of men were drawn to her, engaging her in sharply focused discussions and nodding earnestly in the hope that she would sleep with them. She always attracted the committed types.

Of course that attraction would be publicly and even spectacularly evidenced in the years to come but at the time no one, least of all me and Al, had the slightest idea what those years would hold. In the meantime, other men's desires broke against the adamantine cliff of Al's earnestness. I observed, cooked and was driven around for five semesters. When our second summer came around, Al more or less insisted on, then organized, a road trip.

We had hired a Buick Regal. For the large majority of the population of Planet Earth who have never driven and never will drive such a vehicle, the Regal featured a 3-litre V6 engine, a rubber-hammock-style suspension and a ride best described as imperturbable. Its engine made a distinctive low hum which never varied whether the car was speeding along the Hoover Dam, descending the buttes of Arizona or climbing the Rockies. We had picked it up in Vegas but the strange weather that year had forced us south into New Mexico.

In Taos we fell in with a guy called Jason who offered to take us rafting down the Rio Grande. The next day, after speculating whether or not Jason was a psychopath who would lure us out there and murder us, we ate breakfast and set off to meet our guide.

'The roads are pretty rough out there,' Jason told us, indicating his battered 4 x 4. 'Why don't you jump in?'

'We thought we'd take our car,' I said stiffly.

'Sure.'

■

Jason took the I-64 then turned right onto a dirt road. We followed. After a few miles bumping along, we noticed what looked like a row of windows out in the distant scrub. It was set into a bank of earth. A chimney-thing rose beside it. A similar structure showed a few hundred yards away from the first, then several others, more distant. Al and I stared, trying to make sense of these odd-looking dwellings out here in the middle of nowhere. But the road took us away and soon we took a left onto another, bumpier dirt track where we lost sight of the glass things. After a few more miles the track broke up and the Buick started bottoming out. Jason parked about a hundred yards further on. We were at the edge of the gorge.

The young will know the Rio Grande only from the pre-Rise maps that their parents bring out to show where Ma and Pa used to live, but old-landers will remember this part of it from the hot springs bathing scene in *Easy Rider*. It looked vaguely familiar to me that morning.

The odd structures we'd seen, Jason explained, were earthships.

'They make them out of old tyres and cans. They're self-sufficient. There's water out here but it's under five hundred feet of rock. These guys gather rain and recycle. They put in compost toilets, planters, cisterns …'

He talked on as we descended. The path to the Rio Grande wound down. The heat was baking but Al was paying close attention. Jason was getting the earnest look.

When we got to the bottom we discovered that the Rio Grande was too low for rafting. Al paddled in the hot springs, stripping off her jeans and unfurling the shirt she'd borrowed from me into a kind of rollercoaster-hemmed skirt. I watched the water drops slide down her calves and wondered again why the whole place seemed familiar. Jason sat on a rock. When it was time to ascend he decided to run it. We decided to trudge. At the top, Jason (when he'd finished being sick) told us about the *Easy Rider* connection, then gave us directions to a cantina owned by a couple of friends of his which served the best mixed fajitas in New Mexico. We could reconvene for lunch. I wasn't entirely sure I wanted to get roped into lunch. Maybe, I said. We watched Jason's 4 x 4 bump away then got back in the Buick. That's when we found the car wouldn't move.

■

In Death Valley back then temperatures regularly topped 120 degrees and you were told that, in the event of breakdown, you should under no circumstances leave your car. But Death Valley, apart from being one of the deadliest places on earth, was also a US National Park complete with Park Rangers, one of whom would at some point come along and rescue you. Second, we weren't in Death Valley but outside Taos where the temperature was not 120 degrees but only (according to the Buick) a mere 104. Third, we hadn't broken down. The engine still worked. The wheels went around (although they made a funny noise). We just weren't going anywhere. Of course there was a simple explanation for that but at the time our predicament seemed pretty inscrutable. We had water. We had hats.

'We'll just have to hike back to the road,' I said.

'The road's fifteen miles,' said Al.

'Well, Jason'll know something's up.'

'Yeah,' said Al. 'That we didn't want lunch.'

'Hiking it is, then,' I said.

But Al shook her head across the bonnet of the immobile Buick and pointed out into the scrub. 'What we're going to do is this. We're going to check out those earthship things.'

■

Earthships are long, low dwellings made from recycled materials such as tires filled with compacted dirt, tin cans and mud. A grey-water reclamation system uses exterior and interior botanical cells. The roof collects rain. Solar panels and battery arrays are self-explanatory. You grow your own food in the botanical bits and drink water filtered through the cells. Another system pressurizes the water and a big electrical box turns the DC current into AC and distributes it to power sockets, the fridge and so on. An earthship is not, in any conventional sense, a ship. Or so both Al and I understood when the first hunkered structure heaved its glass face out of the scrub two and a half hours later. This one was raised on its own little berm. Around it were set perhaps two dozen other lower dwellings. The nearest was painted in pastel blues and pinks. Motionless wind chimes hung outside. As we stood with our eyes screwed up against the glare, a glass door opened and two young, nearly identical-looking women emerged. They wore their hair short and were dressed in dungarees. They introduced themselves as Jean and Joan.

'You're late,' Jean said.

'But it's fine,' added Joan. 'Where've you put your car?'

'Car?'

'You haven't parked up by Fro's place, right?' She pointed behind her towards the next nearest dwellings. 'He gets pretty grouchy about that.'

'Or Mimi,' added Jean. 'She had a dog run over once.'

'Or Gibson,' said Joan. 'Not that you could with all his junk.'

As they said this, both women looked back into the scrub, searching among the different structures for wherever we'd put our vehicle. I was about to tell them our situation when a new thought struck Jean.

'You didn't leave it at Zeke's?'

I shook my head.

'Who's Zeke?' asked Al.

At that the women both laughed in a relieved kind of way.

'We haven't got a car,' I said. 'It broke down. We walked.'

'We can't be late either,' added Al. 'We didn't know we were coming.'

Jean and Joan looked at one another again.

'So you're not the guys from the *Times*?'

■

I believe it was the French social theorist Alain Sokal who first demonstrated how information degrades along with the rules governing its production in a closed semiotic system. Maybe that wasn't quite how he put it but, over the next few hours, something similar happened to me and Al. We had arrived as people whose car had broken down (or not, as it eventually proved) by the banks of the Rio Grande, but now we found ourselves recast as a journalist and photographer from the *LA Times*. It wasn't so much that Jean/Joan introduced us as the anticipated journos (who had already, we discovered, cancelled twice). But as they escorted us down a dirt track to the dwellings of Fro, then Mac and Jay, then Mimi, Gibson (whose dog barked non-stop during the encounter) and the other inhabitants of the Great World Earthship Community, the non-appearance of the journalists, of whose visit some had been in favour and others not, took on a significance that eclipsed our own actual appearance. Re-evaluating that instance of conceptual slippage now, I think it might have been the start of what became, for Al and me at first, then everyone else, a much greater shift that although contributed to by everyone was not actually willed by any of them, like finding yourself at the head of a slide with a great crowd of people pressing behind you, or that story about the boy on the diving board, about to take the plunge.

'I want people to come out here,' explained Mimi, a leathery-skinned middle-aged woman with full lips and bright white teeth. 'Even journalists. We're off-road, off-grid. We've got enough non-contact. We need people to see what can be done.'

'What can be done?' asked Al.

'You can get away,' said Mimi. 'You don't have to be alone.'

She was in retreat from an LA divorce. Felipe next door suffered from chronic aerosol-triggered asthma. Fro waved us away in a strangely friendly way. Jay was from Montana, about which he loved everything except the minus 40 degree winters, and Gibson needed space for his stripped-down engines and the sculptures he was making out of the parts. And somewhere for his dog to bark. He pointed to the berm.

'You should talk to Mike,' Gibson said among the yelps. 'He started all this. Designed these places.'

'He's away,' said Joan. 'Least his pick-up's gone.'

We continued the odd tour. Some didn't open their doors. Most did, inviting us into surprisingly cool interiors that smelt pleasantly of greenhouses. We were offered water in all of them and food in most (Billie's home-baked cornbread was the stand-out). At the end of our tour we had reached the far side of the Great World Community plot. The scrub stretched away towards distant Mount San Antonio in one direction and the snaking crack of the Rio Grande gorge in the other.

'So,' said Jean. 'What do you think?'

'It's great,' I said, and Al nodded enthusiastically. It was, too: all these slightly strange people making homes out of junk in the middle of nowhere in New Mexico. I'd expected at least one of them to kick off about UN-sponsored parachutists or Area 51 or aliens. But none of them had.

But neither had any of them offered us a lift back to town. Jean/Joan, Al and myself stood at the edge of the desert and smiled at each other.

'So,' said Joan.

The moment stretched. Then off towards the gorge I saw a glint of light. Another earthship lay about half a mile away, set off from the others.

'Who's over there?' I asked.

Jean and Joan exchanged looks. 'That's Zeke,' they said at the same time and laughed. Al and I laughed too.

'He's slightly crazy,' said Jean.

'Not bad-crazy,' Joan hastened to add. 'He was out here first. With Mike. You should talk to him. I mean, if you were journalists.'

'We're not journalists,' said Al. 'We have no idea ...'

I expected her to add, 'what we're doing out here' or 'how to get back' but she just left it hanging.

■

I suppose it's fairly obvious by this point that the real point of Al's and my Great American Road Trip was to figure out whether we should drift along together some more or let ourselves drift apart. I was never jealous and even now I've never felt more than a certain retrospective regret. A slight propensity to glance over the shoulder and wonder what might have been. I never let myself think that Al actually loved me.

Nevertheless, despite my non-jealous nature, having left Jean and Joan and trekked through the scrub to Zeke's earthship and having got my first glimpse of Zeke, my first thought was that he looked exactly how I imagined the teepee guy Jez.

Given the later history of Zeke and Al, it would be good to report some kind of spark passing between them at this point, a recognition of something or other. But there wasn't anything like that. A tall, lean, grey-ponytailed guy with a moustache looked us over.

'You got stuck?'

'Pretty much,' I said.

'I go into town Fridays, if you can wait that long.'

It was Tuesday.

'Friday's fine,' said Al.

Zeke nodded and turned back into the long cool room. 'Make yourselves at home.'

■

Zeke's earthship was different from the others. It was bigger, older (as he told us), and set apart from them in the head of a ravine that dropped down to the river. Unlike the others, it had been constructed inside a kind of concrete envelope which had either been built in the ravine where its weight had forced the loose dirt to subside or poured into some kind of mould. Either way, Zeke's earthship rested inside a kind of concrete 'hull'. We settled on facing couches and looked out the wall of glass. To the north, I noticed a cloud in the hitherto cloudless sky.

'I got down here in the mid-seventies,' Zeke told us after a supper of vegetarian chilli. 'Lots of old road-warriors headed this way. There's a bunch around Telluride. It was a terrible time to be out of the mainstream. A lot of guys just gave up but Mike and I came down here to Taos. He was trying to get these places built. I told him I'd get one up.' He gave the floor a wry smile. 'Hippies were practical. A lot of people forget that. You want someone who can get a VW Microbus over the Andes, ask a hippy. You want to build a house out of garbage, same. Me and him threw this place up in about three months. Then we fell out.'

We were sitting with the dirty plates on a low table between us. Al had leaned closer and closer during this account and now was sitting on the edge of her seat, elbows propped on her knees, hands clasped under her chin. I wondered if Zeke could see her breasts but he was sat back looking out of the window where the sunset was striating the sky into an unfeasible number of dark pink and red bands.

'Mike wanted to put up more of these things,' Zeke went on. 'Grow 'em like mushrooms and get the township to zone it. Pay tax. I don't know. Anyway, we haven't spoken since.'

'They told us you were crazy,' Al said.

'Slightly crazy,' I chipped in, alarmed at Al's candour. But Zeke just nodded.

'I guess,' he said. 'If crazy puts you the other side of the fence from everyone else.'

There was a slightly uncomfortable silence. 'I suppose so,' I said.

'There is no crazy,' Zeke said as if I hadn't spoken. It was a trick I'd see him play later on the various politicos and CEOs who splashed a course to his door hoping for some kind of endorsement to shore up their dissolving bastions ... Or maybe it was uncalculated on Zeke's part. Maybe he just spoke as the thoughts washed through. 'Can't be,' he went on. 'Not if there's no fence.'

Here it comes, I thought. Alien abduction. Area 51. I adopted my 'It's a point of view' expression, well rehearsed from theory seminars when (for example) other participants implied that characters in novels were representations of actual people rather than rhetorical figures. Al, however, nodded enthusiastically.

'It's not enough to be off-grid,' Zeke said. 'That's what these places were meant to prove. What if there was no grid?'

'There has to be a grid,' I said, more curious than challenging. I genuinely wondered what Zeke meant.

'Does there?' asked Al. That startled me.

'This is a liquid planet,' said Zeke. 'Seven-eighths of the surface is water. The core is molten. It's meant to be dynamic.'

'Dynamic systems are unstable,' I said. Then, to Al's surprised look, I added, 'I used to study fluid dynamics. In math.'

'That sounds like a smart thing to study,' said Zeke.

I was gearing up to say something else about fluidity but Al spoke first.

'Then you have to change the conditions.'

'Right,' said Zeke. 'But how?'

It wasn't rhetorical. He was actually asking.

'I don't know,' Al said at last.

She was gazing at him – there is no other word – raptly. But Zeke looked away out the window where I now noticed that the dark pink sky-bands were more clouds.

■

A milky film covered the sky the next day. The sun would burn it off, I thought, but as the morning wore on it seemed to thicken. It was what the weathermen called an occluded warm front, Zeke told us.

Pretty rare out here. This was a big one too. Most of the south-west was under it. Apparently it was raining in parts of Nevada.

He showed us how the place worked, tracing pipe runs and cabling, tapping the bright red fruit dangling from his chilli plants, opening hatches and staring down into cisterns. It was like a regular house, just self-contained. The electrics were the most complex, with transformers and different kinds of circuits. Al asked questions and pretended she understood the answers.

We took a walk that afternoon. We didn't want to venture back into the Great World Community so we headed into the ravine, scrambling under the concrete hull and then following the slope down to the Rio Grande. The descent was gentle enough but the sides of the ravine soon rose steeply on either side. In the shade it was, if not quite cold, at least not hot. Nothing like yesterday. When we reached the bottom the river had changed character too.

Without the sunlight glinting off the surface, the body of the river seemed more solid, more opaque, with deep eddies opening and closing and the water ramping up in ridges. Al had mentioned maybe having a swim but there was no question of that. It was darker and colder. Even so she stripped off to wash. I admired her white skin as she splashed about in the shallows. Then she beckoned and I stripped off too.

Drying off took longer than we anticipated. A cool breeze was drifting down the canyon and we actually shivered once or twice before Al and I pulled on our shirts and jeans. Hauling each other back up the ravine to Zeke's place, Al began talking about getting back to Taos. She wanted to take the Sandia Peak Tramway. A friend of hers had told her about a supposedly lucky payphone at the top. Anyone who dialled their voicemail got good news. She would finish her novel and head for Las Vegas or get a job as a cocktail waitress in the bar in Flagstaff where they filmed the Rick's Bar scenes in *Casablanca* ... I made encouraging noises. None of this was really going to happen. Not in this world anyway. It was only as we neared the top and the concrete prow of Zeke's home loomed above us, its dark V-shaped jut cutting the still-luminous sky like the zipper opening on Al's jeans, that I realized something obvious.

None of these plans included me. Pulling ourselves up the last yards and wriggling over the lip of the concrete, the sky darkened further and just as we reached the door, the rain began.

Anyone reading of these events now, almost thirty years after they happened, will know much of what follows. The first Rise, the raft movement, the so-called First and Second Water Wars, the Floating Federation and its wackier fringes, the Pilot Cults, Nova Terrans and so on. All of it started when the first raindrop hit the ground that afternoon. Obviously much of Zeke and Al's conversation from the previous evening might seem, with hindsight, impossibly portentous and prescient, as if they saw the whole thing coming. I must have forgotten most of it – I mean, we talked for most of the evening – and maybe only those parts stuck. I don't think they foresaw anything really. They were just ready.

It wasn't the Rise itself of course – that was still years away – it was just the biggest flood in New Mexico's history which gathered up rainfall from both sides of the Rockies and reunited it at their foot, sending a great broad swell fanning out over the plain below. The famous poster of Zeke and Al's launch, with the earthship plunging down the ravine into the Rio Grande far below, both of them with one arm raised as if they were riding a bucking horse, that was all nonsense. Al wasn't wearing a halter-top either. She still had my shirt. The water simply rose and rose until it filled the Rio Grande canyon then lifted the concrete hull of Zeke's earthship and floated it clear. Zeke and Al were aboard. I was not. I could report that Zeke made a grab to pull me back as I flipped over the side or that Al implored me to stay, rain running down her face and so on. The truth was more prosaic. I wasn't prepared to set myself adrift. Al was. So I watched her float away.

I waded back to the GWC. The other earthships had been evacuated. All were flooded except Mike's. I climbed the berm and made myself at home. A week later a state trooper, after deciding not to shoot me, gave me a lift back to the Buick. The whole of New Mexico steamed. There was no news of Al and with everything else going on no one was looking either. After a week more or less underwater, the Buick started first time. The earlier mechanical problem turned out to be Al's not having disengaged the foot brake. To this day I wonder if she did it on purpose.

I never got to ask her. I never saw Al again. Not in the flesh. Obviously, she was on the TV plenty as her and Zeke moored themselves to the most inconvenient objects they could think of and dared the authorities to sink them. Then, after the Rise, they basically became the icons they are now. We couldn't continue the way we were going. Zeke got hold of that early and then, with the help of a few trillion tons of water, so did everyone else. I don't mean driving and the ozone layer and so on. I mean the way we thought. The way I thought.

All the accusations that Al manipulated Zeke in his declining years remain just that; I have no more insight than anyone else. Zeke's dead now, of course. The earthship's a floating museum. But Al is still pretty much head of the off-shore Fed, that is if a couple of million earthships on rafts could be said to have anything so structured as a top and bottom.

As for me, I decided to finish our road trip. Of course there aren't actually any roads there. Nearly all of New Mexico is now under two hundred feet of water. I'm doing the Andes Loop instead. I know. It's a cliché. Every old-lander does it. You can hardly move off Durango Point for hi-spec rafts and the silver-heads carving out their own patch of the wide blue yonder. All the same I've traded my share in a condo on the Spines for a long-drift raft with all mod cons (as they used to say): on-board krill-processing, full solar array, veg tanks, cisterns, the lot (I had gone back to math like Zeke advised, and fluid dynamics proved a good business to be in, post-Rise). The rafts are the descendants of Zeke's earthship, of course, even though some of the big ones weigh a couple of thousand tons.

Mine's a domestic, about fifty feet across. I've joined a hitch of drifters. Just a couple of dozen. We're setting off in a few weeks to jiggle around feeling wavesick and crunch shrimp together. I'll see how that goes. Then I'll cut loose. In the end you need a purpose even if everything else is floating about. Which is to say I'm looking forward to this voyage, more than anything I've done in a very long time. I'm ready. The only thing left to do is to give my raft a name. I thought 'Regal' at first. Now I'm drifting towards 'Al'.

# THE SPIRAL STAIRCASE

*A true story*

Jay Griffiths

IT HAPPENED IN BRISTOL, during the Blitz. Every night, Len drove an ambulance to collect the dead and the injured. He would be given a slip of paper with a typed address, a message sending him across the city to houses bombed with explosives or incendiary devices. His job was to find whatever remained.

One night, having done several journeys through the siren-scarred night, he returned to base and went to the control room. The controller was a slow, careful woman. He held out his hand impatiently for the next message slip with the next address on it. The address he was given was his own.

■

*The sky is falling, the sky is falling, the sky is falling.* He had often read this story to his daughter at bedtime. He couldn't get the line out of his head now.

'Does the sky ever fall in real life?' she had asked.

'Never, my little princess, never.'

He had stroked her silky hand. She put all her small fist in his and her trust made him a lion, he carried her up the cast-iron spiral staircase to her bedroom, with a window to the stars.

■

Now he holds the message slip in his hand. Motionless, he stares at the controller. She doesn't know that where a stranger's address should be, he sees his own. He is seized by an agony of heroism which turns his mouth to metal in a moment. He says nothing but takes the paper and walks to the ambulance. His knees don't shake but they don't bend either.

Anti-aircraft lights are scoring his deep, dark veins and all his lovely inner night is torn open.

All sounds recede. The fall of information on deafened ears. The typed letters indent the paper like the beloved marks of baby teeth on the books in his study.

Then panic. The siren, screaming itself white in the black night, is screaming inside his silence.

Dry-mouthed, he wants to take the message back to the controller and tell her she's an idiot, that she made a stupid mistake. Then he wants to rip up the message, tear it to shreds, burn it and stamp on the ashes. But even if he does, the message won't go away. *The writing is on the wall. A written warning. It is written, it is written, it is written.*

Suddenly, the paper seems alive to him and he clutches at it, fearing to drop it. He twists the paper between two fingers as he pushes his round glasses up over his nose and grasps the wheel. *Why am I holding onto it? Am I likely to forget, for God's sake* – and his mind swings with his hands on the wheel turning the corner as fast as he can – *am I likely to forget what it says? It is my most precious memento. All I will have left of my world is the little scrap of paper which denotes it.*

He grips it for dear life. The message is now an icon, the print of an address burnt onto his mind like the print of a dress which will be burnt onto the body of a small girl in Hiroshima. The future is in the present. East is West and the girl is his own daughter. Lateral explosions. Collateral damage. East of the sun and West of the moon, he hums, madly. 'Love… makes one little room an everywhere', and his whole world is in that address.

*I am the only one who knows what this message means. And what it means is that I am alone in a world deworlded.* He can read the message forwards and backwards, from the present into the future and from the future into the past. This is the message of infinite destruction and he will carry the message wherever he must.

Driving across Bristol, he is driving from the world of the living to the world of the dead. Tension fuses his hands onto the steering wheel as the skies, prised apart from the heavens, crash to earth.

*The sky is falling now. On all my world.*

Of all the houses in all of Bristol, you had to drop bombs on mine. That house was my whole world, you bastards. You bastards, you bombed my whole, entire world.

His round-toed shoes gun the accelerator, when suddenly a tabby cat runs into the low headlights and he slams on the brakes. *Damn it to hell, must this war take everything? Even a little pussy cat?*

He is there. He is there. He is there.

Part of the roof is on fire.

The house is still standing.

Hope corkscrews through him, hurting him.

He pulls open the door and then he sees.

His whole world is trembling in the balance.

All the glad world held to ransom in that moment.

Hanging by a thread.

For an incendiary bomb has fallen on the house but – *by all the angels who ever loved me* – he gasps, the bomb has fallen in the dead centre of the cast-iron stairwell.

There it burns. Caught, burning its fury, exquisitely, caught in the nick of time, in the nick of place. Tucked in the spiral banisters, the bomb rocks and fizzes.

Underneath it, deep in the cellar, dark and implicit as a womb, his wife and children are tucked together: his world and worlds to come. The children are whimpering: he sees his daughter first, her eyes full of fear and fireworks, transfixed by the bomb. It is seared onto her retina and I know that for the rest of her life she will never understand how people can actually *like* fireworks.

'Dad is here, Dad is here, Dad is here,' her brother shouts out, breaking the spell, and she sees him as never before. Hero. Mountain. Tree. Lion. Dad.

His wife is calculating if it is safe to edge out of the cellar now. The children don't think: they run to their father, he lifts them to kiss them, but they are not kissable children now, they are small, frightened animals, and they burrow into his body, tucking themselves into the deep dark of his overcoat.

'You'll be right as ninepence, my darlings, right as a trivet, right as rain, right as…' and his voice was too choked to go on.

■

'The sky *did* fall, Dad. Might it ever fall again?'

'Never, my little princess, never.'

It was months later. He was taking his little daughter up the stairs to her bedroom with a window to the stars. Memory turns in spirals, like a staircase, like the double helix of DNA, like whorls of galaxies. As he carried her, he remembered not only her near-death but also her conception.

His wife was looking sternly at him, telling him he was a bit tipsy. So he tickled her. And tickled her again till she giggled. I imagine them giggling when a little spurt of starlight shot out of him, giggling seeds which laughed their way into her earth-night and one shooting star, with perfect aim, found its way right into the centre of her whorls and inner spiral stairwells, exploding on the scene, a tiny bomb of life: sherbet, yeast, champagne, fireworks, star-works. *Ping!* My mother.

# AFTERWORD

## Mike Robinson

A huge body of science has been built up over the last fifty years which unequivocally demonstrates the reality of anthropogenic (man-made) climate change. But many people don't seem to be listening or are just hoping it will go away. Others see nothing but a threat to their short-term interests. And although governments the world over have understood the dangers, they have yet to take credible action.

The amount of $CO_2$ we humans have pumped into the atmosphere over the past two centuries, at the same time as chopping down the planet's capacity to absorb the excess, is bringing about an increase in global temperature which will continue to worsen. This is affecting the balance of nature – a balance which took four and a half billion years to develop before conditions allowed for the arrival of humans. For 99.99% of earth's history, modern human beings have been absent. If we want to be part of earth's future, we need to wake up to the fact that the earth is a closed system and its resources are finite.

Perhaps for the first time in our history, we need to learn to be sustainable.

Legions of scientists have researched and understood these issues, and have accepted the peer-reviewed scientific evidence. The nature of science is of course that nothing is completely certain, but when a hypothesis has been thoroughly tested and reinforced repeatedly by consistent, objective evidence, it becomes an 'established theory'. Man-made climate change is one of these. However, a number of influential and well-funded vested interests are determined to exaggerate doubts and exploit any seeming uncertainty to foster inaction. They accuse scientists of not being impartial. But aren't scientists allowed to be concerned? It is difficult for anyone who has read the science not to be.

There is no great scientific doubt about the fact of anthropogenic climate change but there is, quite rightly, doubt around how quickly the worst effects will start to happen and exactly how severe those effects will be. Some countries are already being affected, and all the models point to severe changes in the not-too-distant future. Until the glaciers have melted and swamped their respective valleys, cutting off a vital source of water to many arid regions – until sea levels have risen and inundated settlements or whole islands – the science will only ever be able to best estimate these events, and their exact timing and severity will remain a matter of hypothesis.

That doesn't mean they are not going to happen though.

Through their respective Climate Change Acts, the UK and particularly Scotland have shown outstanding moral leadership in tackling this issue. The governments' commitments to reducing our greenhouse gas emissions by 2020 are to be commended, although it is critical that these are honoured and translated into real progress on the ground. The emissions targets set in Westminster and Holyrood are testament both to the validity of the science and the strength of concern raised by civil society through the Stop Climate Chaos Coalition.

This doesn't mean that it is going to be easy – finding palatable and credible solutions is a minefield. Yet civil society needs to stay united in its determination to deal with this issue, and will be crucial in shaping the transition to a lower-carbon economy, helping people get to grips with what climate change is all about and encouraging the rest of the world to follow our lead.

To do this, it is essential that we fund the continuing science. If civil society is the heart and conscience of a just society, then science is the brain, and we need to keep feeding the brain. But we need to do much more than that. We need people who can communicate in a way that reaches those parts of our psyche that science alone cannot reach. We need to find the courage of our convictions and develop an inspiring and engaging vision which people can rally around. We need to promote new thinking and help to challenge short-termism. We need to interpret what the future might look like and take the fear out of behavioural change. We need to develop intelligent, joined-up thinking, understanding better the interdependence of people, the planet and the places where we live and on which we have an impact. We need to embrace the opportunities available to lead the world on a sustainable path by appealing to more than the analytical and scientific parts of the imagination.

> *They always say time changes things, but you actually have to change them yourself.* — *Andy Warhol*

People cannot be expected to understand climate change if they are not persuaded to listen. They cannot be expected to care if they do not understand. And they cannot be expected to act if they do not care. Yet we need people to act. Environmental writing has an important role to play in encouraging people to listen, care, and act.

Sometimes it feels as if we fear evasive behavioural change more than climate change itself. Or maybe we just feel helpless in the face of such large-scale global concerns. This is quite understandable, but not acting is really not an option. Ultimately change is inevitable. The question is: will change be forced upon us, its helpless victims, through the accidental consequences of our unsustainable behaviour? Or can we influence it and help shape and define it?

At least the fact that we are causing climate change means that we can stop it getting worse. If we choose to.

We need our artists and writers more than ever to help person-alize these issues, to engage our hearts and souls and to engender self-belief and confidence in our ability to tackle what otherwise seem overwhelming, long-term or remote intellectual concerns. We need more positive role models which reflect the values we think are most important.

Writers and artists can voice our concerns and build up our confidence to act. By experimenting with different scenarios, they can lessen our fear of change, appealing to people's right brain: heart, soul, gut, eyes, fingers, ears, and skin; they can immerse readers in, and create a mood for, new thinking in a way that constant recycling of the science simply cannot. They, more than anyone, can help interpret what the future might look like, and take the fear out of change. Ultimately that is what Gregory and I wanted this book to be about.

It doesn't suit anyone to believe in climate change; it's an appalling thing to have to contemplate. But it isn't a matter of belief. It is a matter of scientific observation.

Deep down I believe we all know this is something we have to address, however hard it may be to stomach. And the sooner we stop prevaricating and pretending we can't hear the alarms, the sooner we can look forward with hope and a belief in our future.

Undoubtedly we face daunting challenges, both domestically and globally. But if we want a chance to prevent the worst, to choose our path rather than to have it forced upon us, then we need to take responsibility and act now. We need to be creative. Resourceful. Thrifty. Some of us will be brilliant, entrepreneurial. Maybe, at last, we will learn as a species to work within natural limits and the parameters of a stable climate. And if we can get there, then just imagine for a moment what we might be able to achieve.

Would you welcome a more altruistic society, one that is more localized and with greater equality? Would you like to have a better quality of life, with less pollution, greed, and waste? How about greater social cohesion, better health, less stress; better co-ordinated transport, a more sustainable economy, and less debt; more robust supply chains; greater self-dependence, and job security? These things are within our grasp. If we really want them. And if we commit to those actions needed to slow down the climate beast.

It's up to all of us to choose...

*No man ever made a greater mistake than he who did nothing because he himself could only do a little.' – Edmund Burke*

**Mike Robinson** is chief executive of the Royal Scottish Geographical Society (RSGS) based in Perth. For the past six years Mike has been heavily involved in many aspects of climate change policy in Scotland and further afield. Since 2006 he has established, chaired, and remains a board member of Stop Climate Chaos Scotland, sat (informally) on the board of Stop Climate Chaos in London, and represented SCVO at the Climate Agora in Brussels in 2008. He is a grant panel member of the government's Climate Challenge Fund (CCF), a member of the 2020 Business Leaders' Climate Delivery Group, and chaired the Scottish Parliament Short Life Working Group on annual targets. He is a board member of a number of other charities and co-ordinates a carbon reduction scheme in his local community. He has been working with Gregory Norminton to get this book off the ground since they first met in 2007.

# CONTRIBUTORS

**Tom Bullough** is the author of three acclaimed novels, *Konstantin*, based on the life of nineteenth-century Russian space scientist Konstantin Tsiolkovsky, *The Claude Glass* and *A*. He lives in the Brecon Beacons in Wales.

Poet, writer, and translator **David Constantine** has won several literary prizes, most recently the BBC National Short Story Award in 2010. He is a Fellow of Queen's College Oxford.

**Siân Melangell Dafydd** is the author of *Y Trydydd Peth* (*The Third Thing*) which won the coveted 2009 National Eisteddfod Literature Medal. She is the co-editor of literary magazine **Taliesin** and writes in both Welsh and English.

A scientist by training, **Clare Dudman** has published a number of short stories and four novels: *Edge of Danger*, *Wegener's Jigsaw*, *98 Reasons for Being* and *A Place of Meadows and Tall Trees*. Her writing has won two awards and a prize.

**Janice Galloway's** awards include the E.M. Forster Award from the American Academy of Arts and Letters and the Saltire Award. Her *Collected Stories* came out in 2009 and *All Made Up*, a 'true novel' follow-up to *This is Not About Me*, was published by Granta in 2011.

**Rodge Glass** has published three novels and a graphic novel, and won a Somerset Maugham Award in 2009 for his highly acclaimed biography of Alasdair Gray. His latest book is *Bring Me the Head of Ryan Giggs*, published in April 2012. He is a lecturer at Strathclyde University and associate editor at Cargo Publishing.

**Alasdair Gray**, described by Will Self as 'a great writer, perhaps the greatest living in this archipelago today', won the Whitbread and Guardian Fiction prizes for his 1992 novel, *Poor Things*. He lives, writes, and paints in Glasgow.

**Jay Griffiths** won the Discover Award for the best first-time non-fiction author published in the USA with *Pip Pip: A Sideways Look at Time*. *Wild: An Elemental Journey* won the Orion Book Award and was shortlisted for the Orwell Prize and the World Book Day Award.

Best-selling author **Joanne Harris**'s novels include *Chocolat* (adapted for the cinema, and starring Johnny Depp and Juliette Binoche), *Five Quarters of the Orange* and *Coastliners*.

Author and illustrator **Nick Hayes** has won two Guardian Media Awards. His graphic novel, *The Rime of the Modern Mariner*, was published by Jonathan Cape in 2011.

**Holly Howitt** is an author and academic. Her most recent publications are *The Schoolboy* and *Dinner Time*, both with Cinnamon Press.

**Liz Jensen** is the author of eight novels, including the best-selling 'ecological' thriller *The Rapture* and most recently, *The Uninvited*. Her work has been widely translated.

**A.L. Kennedy** is one of Scotland's most highly regarded novelists and short story writers. She has twice been included in Granta's Best of Young British Novelists list. She has won a number of awards including the Costa Book of the Year in 2007 for her novel *Day*.

**Toby Litt** has published eleven works of fiction, most recently *Journey into Space* and *King Death*. In 2003 he was nominated by Granta as one of the 20 Best of Young British Novelists.

**Adam Marek** is an award-winning short story writer. He won the 2011 Arts Foundation Short Story Fellowship, and was shortlisted for the inaugural Sunday Times EFG Short Story Award. His first story collection *Instruction Manual for Swallowing* was published by Comma Press in 2007. His second story collection is out in summer 2012.

**Maria McCann** has published two novels, *As Meat Loves Salt* and *The Wilding*. The latter was longlisted for the 2010 Orange Prize and was a featured book in the 2010 Richard and Judy Bookclub.

**James Miller** has published two highly acclaimed novels, *Lost Boys* and *Sunshine State*. He teaches English literature and creative writing at Kingston University.

**Lawrence Norfolk** is a highly regarded novelist whose work has been translated into many languages. He won the Somerset Maugham Award in 1992. His latest novel, *John Saturnall's Feast*, was published by Bloomsbury in 2012.

**Gregory Norminton** (editor) has published four novels, all with Sceptre, including the highly acclaimed *Serious Things*. He teaches creative writing at Manchester Metropolitan University.

**Jem Poster** has published two novels with Sceptre: *Courting Shadows* and *Rifling Paradise*. He is currently the chair of creative writing at Aberystwyth University.

**Adam Thorpe** is an award-winning poet and novelist, and the author of two short story collections, *Shifts* and *Is This the Way You Said?* (Jonathan Cape). His first novel, *Ulverton*, is widely regarded as a modern classic. His tenth novel, *Flight*, was published in May 2012.

# ACKNOWLEDGEMENTS

Particular thanks are owed to the Perthshire villages of Guidtown and Wolfhill, who hosted the authors' briefing weekend in May 2012, and who helped to support the book in other ways.

We were joined in Perthshire by a number of experts, including Dr Richard Dixon of WWF Scotland, Rachel Nunn, founder of Going Carbon Neutral Stirling, Clive Bowman from the Alyth Community Carbon Project, Gail Wilson from Stop Climate Chaos Scotland, Aphra Morrison of the CCF, and Mike himself, in his various roles, with advice from many other leading community groups including Comrie and the Isle of Eigg.

Thanks are also due to Isobel Dixon at Blake Friedmann Ltd and Juliet Mabey at Oneworld.

**Stop Climate Chaos Coalition** is the UK's largest group of people dedicated to taking action on climate change and limiting its impact on the world's poorest communities. Our combined supporter base of more than eleven million people spans over a hundred organizations, from environment and development charities to unions, faith, community, and women's groups. Together we demand practical action by the UK to keep global warming as far as possible below the 2°c danger threshold.

**Stop Climate Chaos Scotland** is the largest coalition ever formed in the country, representing all the main faith groups, humanitarian agencies, and environment charities, along with unions, student and community groups and a host of other partners. It was central in lobbying for the Scottish Climate Change Act, the best in the world today (with a forty-two per cent reduction target by 2020), and went on to produce a forty-two per cent proof whisky called 'twenty, twenty', which was distributed to the G20 finance ministers, world leaders, and contacts at Copenhagen, Cancun, and Durban, and continues to be used to promote the example that we all hope other countries will adopt. John Swinney MSP, cabinet secretary for infrastructure, said on the day the Climate Change Act was passed:

> 'Many of the non-governmental organizations with whom we have been familiar over the ten short years of this parliament have worked together under the Stop Climate Chaos banner to send to parliament and the people of this country a coherent and co-ordinated message that we should consider and, frankly, be inspired by.'

Views or opinions expressed by this work or its authors do not necessarily reflect those of the organizations associated with the Stop Climate Chaos Coalition.

A Rocha
AirportWatch
APE
AW Scotland
Associaton for the Conservation
    of Energy
Baldernock Community Council
Be That Change
British Humanist Association
CACC
CAFOD
Cambridge Carbon Footprint
Cap and Share
Carbon Neutral Bradford on Avon
Challenge to Change
Changeworks

Christian Ecology Link
Christian Aid
Church of Scotland
COIN
Colombans Faith & Justice Group
Come off it
Commitment for Life
Concern Worldwide Scotland
CRNN
CTC
Eco-congregations Scotland
Edinburgh Uni Student Assoc.
Fife Diet
Friends of the Earth
Friends of the Earth Scotland
Glasgow Eco-renovation Network

Glasgow Students Representative
  Council
Global Climate Campaign Scotland
Greenpeace
Guildtown & Wolfhill Carbon CAP
Heriot Watt University Students
  Association
HIYE
IFEES
Internuncio
Iona Community
Islamic Relief
Jewish Community Centre for
  London
John Ray Initiative
Justice & Peace Scotland
Low Carbon Communities
MADE
Make Poverty History NE
Medsin
Mercy Corps Scotland
MRDF
Napier Students Association
National Trust for Scotland
New Environmentalist
Northfield Eco-centre
NUS
NUS Scotland
One World Week
Operation Noah
Orpington Methodist Church
Oxfam
Oxfam Scotland
Peace Child International
People & Planet
Plantlife
Population Matters
Portsmouth Climate Action Network
Practical Action
Preserve the Rainforest
Progressio

Quakers
RSPB
RSPB Scotland
Scottish Action on Climate
  Change
SCIAF
Scottish Episcopal Church
Scottish Seabird Centre
SCAN
SCVO
SEAD
Salvation Army
Simpol
Speak
Spokes
Student Christian Movement
Students for a Free Tibet
Surfer's Against Sewage
Sustrans
Take Global Warming Seriously
Tearfund
The Big Green Jewish Website
Tipping Point Film Fund
TRANSform Scotland
Transition Linlithgow
Tzedek
UK Youth Climate Coalition
UNA UK
Unicef
UNISON
World Development Movement
WDM Scotland
Winacc
Women's Institute
Women's Environmental Network
Woodland Trust
Woodland Trust Scotland
WWF Scotland
WWF-UK
WWT
999 Planet in Peril